To Conjure a Killer

A Witch Cats of Cambridge Mystery

To Conjure a Killer

A Witch Cats of Cambridge mystery

Clea Simon

Cover and jacket design by Mimi Bark

ISBN 978-1-957957-34-0
eISBN: 978-1-957957-49-4

Library of Congress Control Number: available upon request

First hardcover edition November 2023 by Polis Books
An imprint of Polis Books, LLC
62 Ottowa Road South
Marlboro, NJ 07746
www.PolisBooks.com

For Jon

ALSO BY CLEA SIMON

Available from Polis Books

The Witch Cats of Cambridge Mysteries

A Spell of Murder

An Incantation of Cats

A Cat on the Case

Hold Me Down

One

Eight o'clock and still light. Or light enough, Becca told herself as she pulled the door shut behind her with a jangling of bells and locked it. Being able to close the small Central Square storefront and still feel like she had some sunshine left made all the difference in her mood. Not that the day had been bad. Foot traffic always fell off in June, once the students had graduated or gone off in search of summer jobs and the academics who taught them adjourned to the Cape. Plus, the friendly young woman enjoyed being able to chat with the few customers who came in—and immerse herself in the store's extensive library once they left. But, especially on evenings like this one that tinted the gathering clouds purple and red, Becca found herself wishing for a little more than a book, some good friends, and even her three cats.

Giving the door a good shake to make sure it was latched, Becca looked back into the little storefront and told herself to be grateful. She really loved her job at Charm and Cherish, a kind of New Age botanica stuffed with books and charms. With its brightly painted windows open to the street, the shop was a cheery place to work—certainly better than the warehouse-style maze of cubicles that had housed her last job. Besides, despite the summer slowdown, the shop had had a few visitors on this bright afternoon, and Becca had sold two healing stones to a couple of tourists from Des Moines.

The two women, both wearing khakis and polo shirts and with identical short-cropped hair, had come in the hour before, just as Becca was considering closing early. At first glance, Becca wouldn't have made them for customers. Stuck as it was in the middle of a rapidly gentrifying neighborhood, the little magic shop still tended to attract what Becca thought of as "old Cambridge" types—the latest incarnation of the counterculture's flower children in their mishmash of Indian prints and velvet—or else their neo-goth counterparts in all black. Both gravitated to the silver pentangle medallions the store had recently started stocking, one of which Becca was wearing today. She had reached up to feel the outline of the five-pointed star in its circle, a reminder of life's connectedness—and her own affinity to even these apparently straight-arrow types as they began to browse.

"May I help you?" Becca smiled as she spoke. Not only was it good customer service, but she was picking up warm vibes from these two. They were probably lost—the store was two blocks from the T—but they meant well, she sensed.

"We're good," said the taller and, Becca thought, older of the two women. Browsers, as she expected. But just then her companion, whose own close-cropped brown hair wasn't tinged with gray, lit up, highlighting the spray of freckles across her apple cheeks.

"Look, Linda." Soon the two were exclaiming over the basket of loose gemstones on the counter, polished semiprecious stones and crystals that caught the slanting afternoon light.

"They are pretty, aren't they?" Becca approached, stopping before her shadow might dim the stones' sparkle. Linda, the taller one, was reading the chart Becca had posted by the display, explaining the powers each jewel was supposed to possess as well as its relationship to various body parts and astrological signs. "I'm partial to the tiger eye." She pointed to a brown-and-gold trapezoid, her finger tracing its rounded corner. "Even if it is oddly shaped."

"It's gorgeous. But I like the brighter colors." Linda picked up a translucent pink oval as her companion, who had also quickly glanced at the chart, chose a smooth purple cabochon from the basket. "We'll take both of these."

"Lovely. But that chart is an advisory, you know. We can't give any assurances about their healing powers," Becca felt obliged to explain, even as she wrapped the pretty rose quartz and amethyst in tissue paper.

"I'm in software," Linda had replied with a grin that lit up her plain Midwestern face. "I'll be happy if they don't crash."

"Only if you throw them." Becca couldn't help but return the tall woman's smile. "I'm Becca, by the way."

"Linda. And this is Pam." She was reaching for the package when her companion interrupted.

"Wait, you're Becca? *The* Becca?" Eyes wide, the shorter woman pointed to a flier, one of several Becca had hung months before. "The witch detective?"

"Well, I'm trying." Becca looked down at the counter. "There hasn't been much call for mystical investigations recently."

"Still, good to know." Pam ripped off two of the name and number slips at the bottom of the flier, handing one to Linda. Both women were beaming. "And it's always good to meet another woman of power."

Those crystals and her first sale of the day, a book on moon signs, had been it for Becca's shift. These days more than half the little shop's business was online. And while that kept Becca from worrying too much about Charm and Cherish closing, it was these interactions that made the job worthwhile.

"Are you in town for the conference?" This close to MIT, she picked up on local happenings.

"Yup, we came in early," Linda replied. "A week in Boston at off-peak rates. How could I resist?"

"Well, I'm glad you came by. Enjoy." She handed the woman

her change and her bag and watched as the pair stepped out into what was still a warm late afternoon.

That conference was on her mind as Becca herself emerged some forty minutes later. Software and all its manifestations held no appeal for Becca. She wasn't a Luddite, far from it. She chuckled at the thought. While she considered herself Wiccan and, yes, a witch, on her best days, she well knew the value of technology. She may have left behind her position as a researcher for retail, but if she couldn't search the local historical society's archives online, she might never have found the documents linking her to "wise women," aka witches, from centuries before—a search that had led to her joining a coven and combining her interests in magic and research to set herself up as a witch detective. Without the internet, she realized, she'd have no idea who she was.

But for her, tech had remained a tool, rather than a vocation. At heart, Becca was old school, she decided. As grateful as she was for those online archives, nothing beat the smell of a library. Those last two customers might find enlightenment staring at screens, but Becca felt liberated to be looking up at the darkening sky. No, she corrected herself, exhilarated, as the blue behind city hall deepened to amethyst purple and the clouds above glowed a vibrant rose.

Jeff, her ex, had been a software designer. Among his other failings was his unwillingness to believe in magic. For Becca, that was inconceivable. Not only the magic she worked so hard to summon, but, more vitally, that which manifested in nature, even here, in the heart of the city where she lived.

Which was why it would never have worked, Becca reminded herself as she began the walk home. Even if she'd taken the boyish geek back, as he'd begged at one point—after he'd admitted to cheating. Even if he hadn't scoffed at her new job: "You've got a degree, Becca. Granted, it's in history, but still..." Even if he hadn't made fun of her new interest in witchcraft and her family history, that one basic fact held true. You didn't need to be Wiccan to love the mystery of life. You did, however, have to see that the mystery, the magic, was real.

Which didn't mean that Becca didn't wish for someone special. For a brief while, she'd thought that the one man in their coven, the dashing Trent, was interested. That hadn't panned out, which was probably just as well. Trent and Larissa, the coven's founder, rarely joined the group's regular meetings, though word was they might show for the upcoming summer solstice. That was shaping up to be a big deal. Already, texts were flying. A circle, of course, evoking the spirits of nature on that auspicious day, and a party to follow. Last year, they'd managed to hold it by the river, ready to explain the ceremony as a picnic to any authorities who came by. It wasn't like they were an exclusive group. In fact, thought Becca, the solstice circle might be just the occasion to welcome some new members.

That thought, as well as the beauty of the mild evening, put a spring in her step. But her happy, if vague, daydreams about new friends and maybe even a new romance were interrupted by the screech of car brakes.

"Watch it!" A bicyclist was yelling at a driver, a common enough occurrence in the city. But even as the angry cyclist pedaled off, Becca saw suddenly why the battered Toyota had stopped so suddenly. A kitten, little more than a fluff of fur, was climbing up the far curb, inches away from the Toyota's bumper.

"Oh no!" Becca started off the sidewalk, narrowly avoiding her own collision with a bicycle. "Please don't be hurt."

The Toyota had started up again, leaving Becca two lanes of traffic to dodge. But her hurried prayers—"Dear goddess, save this creature"—must have covered her too, because she made it across the roadway in time to see two green eyes peer up at her from an orange-and-brown face. For a moment, it seemed like the little creature was taking her measure: one black brow appeared arched, as if Becca's frenzied approach had been found wanting.

"What are you doing out here?" Oblivious to the cars still honking behind her, Becca reached for the kitten, only to have it dart off between the legs of a runner and the sky-high pumps of the woman who had stepped aside to make way.

"No!" Pushing aside the runner's companion, Becca ducked behind another woman, nearly upsetting what already seemed a precarious armload of groceries. "I'm sorry," she called over her shoulder. In a perfect world, she'd stop and help that poor person with her bags. But the kitten had ducked between two storefronts, and Becca was in hot pursuit.

"Kitty!" Five steps in, and Becca stopped. The high brick walls on either side of her had blocked off the light, and in the deep shadow she didn't want to risk missing the little creature. "Kitty," she called in her gentlest voice, following with the *pss-pss-psss* noise all cat owners, and their pets, knew well. "Where are you?"

Probably cowering in a corner, Becca thought, though she couldn't quite shake the feeling that this kitten didn't scare. That stare, for example. Even if the raised eyebrow was a trick of her coloring. Like there was a light on in that tiny feline brain.

A light! Becca could have smacked herself. Maybe she was a Luddite, after all. Careful not to make too much noise, she opened the big messenger bag she always carried and found her phone. The flashlight app didn't do much to illuminate the long passage, but at least she could see the black garbage bags dumped there, and could carefully peak behind to ensure that, no, the kitten wasn't hiding behind either of them.

Turning the phone, she scanned the paved surface before her. The kitten had to be here someplace. Only, as she stepped carefully—one of those garbage bags had broken open—the light began to dim. Her phone battery. Maybe she was technologically useless. But maybe it was enough. Up ahead, she caught movement. Something small—the kitten, she hoped—darting behind another lump that lay spread across the alley. Yes, those had been green eyes, cat eyes, that had looked up at her. If only her battery held out.

"Kitten, are you back there?" Clothes, she thought. An old sweatshirt, rather like the one that Jeff had always worn. But huddled in the corner behind it, the tiny tortoiseshell kitten. "There you are!"

Stepping over the lump, she reached down, only to find herself blinded by a bright light that suddenly flooded the alley.

"Stop. Police!" She froze. "Turn around. Hands where we can see them."

Rising slowly, she raised one hand. But with the other, before either of them could react, she grabbed the kitten, shoved it into her open bag, and then turned to face the light.

Two

"Hands!" The command startled Becca into compliance. Dropping the flap of her bag, she raised both hand and stood blinking in the blinding light. "Don't move."

She froze, willing her eyes to stay open even as some rational part of her brain realized this wasn't what the voice intended. She barely breathed as the Cambridge police officer approached, sleek hair pulled back into a bun the only thing visible over the light. Out of the corner of her eye, Becca could see another officer bending over the pile of clothing. When he stood, she could see he was taller than his partner by a head, his dark brows bunched in anger that she couldn't understand. Yes, she'd run across Mass Ave with reckless disregard, but surely that didn't merit this kind of reaction. Could it be the kitten? But these officers didn't look like animal control.

While she racked her brain, she realized the two officers had been conferring.

"Call it in," said the taller one, in what might have been intended as an undertone. To Becca, it felt ominously loud. "Damn shame."

"Looks like we're too late." The officer spoke into a hand-held device. "But send a bus. Yes, we have the suspect."

Suspect? That one word jolted Becca out of her paralysis, and she took a step forward.

"Hold it!" The flashlight had been joined by a gun, and Becca jerked to a stop.

"Please." She needed to explain, to understand. "There's been some horrible mistake. I'm not a suspect. I'm Becca Colwin, and—"

"Woman wants to make a statement." Bun muttered, apparently to her colleague. The light, and the gun, remained focused on Becca.

"There's been some mistake," Becca tried again.

"Are you refusing the right to counsel?"

Becca shook her head. "This is crazy. I don't need a lawyer."

The two officers looked at each other.

"I only came down here because I—" She paused, feeling movement in the bag. That poor creature was probably so confused. Would they take it from her? "I lost something," she finished her sentence. It sounded lame, even to her.

"And not because of him?"

"Him?" She was totally lost, but the male officer nodded to something behind her. The pile of clothes. Becca turned to take a better look at the pile, noting once again the sweatshirt, so like Jeff used to wear. Only now, with the light trained on it, she could see that the sweatshirt hadn't simply been dumped in the alley. It was lying there, part of a sprawled mess that continued into jeans and sneakers. And that extending from the sweatshirt arm was a hand, red with blood and very, very still.

"In retrospect, your reaction was not only normal, it was the best thing you could have done." Several hours later and Becca was sitting in the Cambridge police precinct with her best friend Maddy by her side. Maddy, a big brunette with a heart to match, was wrapping her own coat around her friend's shoulders because, for some reason, Becca couldn't stop shivering.

"I think I blacked out."

"Exactly." Maddy pulled her close, her considerable bulk a welcome source of warmth. "That's what an innocent person would do."

"Innocent?" Becca squeaked as her throat began to close up.

"Yes, innocent." Maddy patted her shoulder in a no-nonsense way. "That's why when they realized you had no knife on you, they took you to the ER, and why they're releasing you on your own recognizance, if they ever get the paperwork done."

"Knife? I don't understand." Becca shook her head, the last few hours a blur. All she knew was that she'd woken up to beeps and flashing lights as someone leaned over her and asked what she was on. "I mean, I don't remember."

Some things were perfectly clear. Like how she'd jumped up when the nurse reached for her bag. "No," she'd yelled, while other hands restrained her. "Don't let the kitten loose."

"Don't what?" The nurse had returned to her task, her frown warming into a smile as she called her colleague over to look. "What a sweetie."

"I found her," Becca had explained, realizing belatedly that the police must have already rummaged through the bag and left the kitten in place. "She was running in the street."

After that, the staff had taken a gentler tone with her. They'd even found a box for the little tortie, with a folded towel for cushioning. Becca reached out now to make sure the box was still by her side.

"What's the last thing you remember?" Reaching for her hand, Maddy brought her friend back to the present.

"I remember chasing the kitten into an alley and the police showed up and I grabbed her. But after that..." Her voice trailed off.

"It's simple. You didn't expect to see a dead body, and you went into shock."

"A body?" The memories were coming back now, faster than Becca would like. Maddy, however, was all business.

"I'm just glad you had them call me," she said, her mouth set in a firm line. "I was not going to let them keep you overnight in some nasty cell when it's clearly all a mistake."

Becca could only shake her head.

"Apparently, the police got a call about a disturbance. Someone in the building next door heard a man and a woman yelling, and then they thought they heard a scream. So when the police showed up and saw you..." She mercifully left the rest unsaid, but Becca found herself cringing anyway.

"I saw the sweatshirt," she whispered. "It made me think of Jeff."

"Well, yeah, that's the other problem," her friend said. "It was."

Three

In an apartment less than a mile away, three cats were growing increasingly frantic.

"Where is she?" Harriet, the oldest and largest of the three, was pacing, a level of activity that was unusual for her and attested to the big marmalade's agitation. *"Why is she so late?"*

"She's...okay, I think." Her youngest sibling, a small calico, sat with her tail curled around her white front toes. Her parti-colored ears—one orange, one black—twitched as if she were listening for something only she could hear. *"But she's...stuck. It's hard to tell what's going on."*

"She's fine." Laurel, the middle sister, stretched her caramel-colored torso, her blue eyes closing with the effort. *"I would have picked up on it if she'd been injured."*

"There are other kinds of hurts." Clara, her baby sister, protested softly. The calico too could "read" their person, even at a distance. Not as clearly as Laurel, perhaps, but with a sensitivity amplified by her strong personal connection to the young woman they lived with. A young woman who should have been home hours ago.

"Exactly!" Harriet had an annoying habit of commenting on

Clara's thoughts. *"We should have had our dinners before the sun set."*

"I'm sure she'll feed us as soon as she shows up." That wasn't Clara's first concern, but she knew better than to cross her big sister, especially when she was hungry. *"I just hope we can help her, whatever is going on."*

"Of course we can." Laurel cuffed her sister's black-tipped ear. She might affect a certain nonchalance, a distance she thought was in keeping with her sleek Siamese appearance. In truth, she loved their person as much as either of her sisters. *"We're her cats, aren't we?"*

Neither of her siblings were going to argue with that. Besides, by that point, they all felt it. A ripple in the air, almost like a warm breeze. Becca, their person, was almost home.

"Finally!" Harriet was the first to greet her, Laurel and Clara acknowledging their marmalade sister's seniority. *"We've been starving!"*

"I think they missed you." Maddy, following behind her friend, made a wry face. "Either that or their gears need oiling."

"They're hungry, that's all." Becca sounded exhausted, and as Clara took her own turn around her ankles, she felt just how near collapse their person was. "Here"—Becca handed the small cardboard box she carried to Maddy—"let me open some cans, and then we can figure out the next step."

"There's nothing to figure out." Maddy held the box close to her body as she followed Becca, escorted by Harriet and Laurel, into the kitchen. Knowing her sisters would take first pick of any food, Clara hung back. And as she did, she picked up an unfamiliar vibration, almost like a purr...

"We're going to get you a lawyer," Maddy was saying as Becca scooped the contents of a moist and fragrant can into a dish decorated with a golden sun. "Ideally, this will all blow over, but I don't want you talking to the police without counsel."

"I won't, I promise." Becca placed Harriet's dish on the mat and then filled Laurel's, with its blue marble design, before looking around for their little sister. "Clara, are you okay?"

Tail up, the petite calico came forward. She didn't want her person to worry, and, in truth, she was hungry. Whatever was in that box could wait.

While the three dined, Becca stashed the box in the pantry with a suspicious amount of fuss. But by the time Clara had cleaned her own orange-and-brown spotted dish, their person had joined her friend on the sofa, where Laurel, lounging on the brown corduroy arm, appeared indifferent to the minor mystery. Of more concern to the sleek sealpoint, as she wet one chocolate paw, was her meticulous grooming. With a leap, Clara found her own perch on the sofa's back, washing her face out of habit even as her ears pitched forward to catch the conversation.

"If there was ever a time to convene a circle, this is it." Becca was staring at her phone, pecking at it as if she could summon a bug. Maddy sighed audibly, even to human ears, but Becca didn't look up.

"A lawyer would be the practical first call," the brunette said once she had her breath back.

"I'm not saying you're not right." Becca put the device down. "But I'm not going to reach a lawyer at this hour—not a reputable one. And, I know you don't believe, but a circle might do me more good."

Clara turned toward Maddy and saw the larger woman bite her lip. This was an ongoing issue between the friends. To Becca, Clara knew, a Wiccan circle was more than a meeting, it was a way to invoke the elements—all the powers of earth, air, wind, and water—as well as the combined powers of the participants. In addition to the regular cycle of holidays, circles were also invoked for healing, a way of concentrating everyone's best wishes, but they were useful in other crises as well.

To Maddy, as Becca's old friend had made abundantly clear, it was all superstition and wishful thinking. Clara, who had picked up some of what had happened, was inclined to agree, at least as far as human magic went. Clara and her sisters well knew that cats commanded great powers. In fact, it had been Harriet exercising one of her unique talents—the ability to summon objects out of thin air—that had set Becca off on her latest career move. As Becca had thrown herself into the role of witch detective, it was all the three littermates could do to keep Becca out of trouble, and if the slight buzzing that had Clara's guard hairs on alert was any indication, the cats were about to have their work cut out for them once again.

Oblivious to the concerns of the feline behind her, Becca continued talking. "Besides, I can use their help if I'm going to find out what really happened to Jeff."

"Oh, Becca, no!" Maddy's wail disturbed Laurel's bathing, and she shot her sister a look.

"Something's up." To human ears, the cat's warning sounded like one of the odd vocalizations that came with her part-Siamese ancestry. *"Something's happening."*

"You feel it too?" Clara flicked her tail. The humans paid them no mind.

"Maddy, between us we have sensitivities." Becca continued to explain to her incredulous friend. "We can find things. Anyway, if I'm the obvious suspect, why would the police look any further than the jilted ex?"

Maddy's mouth opened and closed twice before she found her next words. "You're not—it was an accident. And you've moved on."

"You mean Dr. Keller?" The name usually brought up warm associations for Clara. The new vet had kind eyes and a gentle manner, even when he was giving shots. Tonight, however, that strange buzzing had her on edge. "I don't know what's going on with him. In fact, I was thinking I should tell him when I see him tomorrow."

Maddy cut her off before she could go further. "You're going to see him? Great. Maybe he'd be willing to say he was with you today. Maybe he walked you home after you closed the store."

"I'm not going to ask him to fake an alibi just because—" She was interrupted by Harriet, who, having finally snuffled all the crumbs in the kitchen, had leaped up onto the couch. Considerably heavier and less graceful than her sisters, the hefty marmalade landed with a thud that made the sofa shake.

"Watch it!" Laurel dug her claws into the upholstery, though whether to keep her balance or out of annoyance, Clara couldn't tell.

"Aren't you listening?" Harriet stood between the two humans, her eyes wide with alarm. *"Don't you hear it?"*

"What are you talking about?" Laurel nearly hissed, but Clara already knew.

"Anyway, I'm not going to ask him to lie for me just because we've become friends." Becca laid a hand on the big cat's back to settle her, stroking the orange spot that saddled her creamy torso. "I'm more concerned that he check out my stowaway and help me figure out what to do with her."

"Your stowaway?" Maddy appeared momentarily confused.

"You know," Becca leaned forward over Harriet's back and lowered her voice, as if the three cats couldn't hear everything. "The kitten," she said, her words accompanied by the unmistakable sound of a mew.

Four

"I *say it's both prey and an intruder."* Harriet's deep rumble seethed with quiet fury, her fluffy white tail sweeping across the kitchen floor like a countdown to violence. The three cats were seated outside the kitchen pantry, staring at the closed door. Maddy had left, and Becca was sound asleep after her crazy day. Before she'd gone to bed, however, she'd revealed the kitten to the three feline sisters, holding the tan-and peach-spotted little floof up for them to see and, more important, to sniff, before closing it back in the pantry, along with a makeshift litterbox and, to Harriet's horror, a can of wet food.

"Are we even sure it's feline?" Laurel had her own tail coiled around her brown booties to restrain it. *"It is awfully funny looking."*

"It—she—is a kitten. A tortoiseshell kitten." Clara never liked to contradict her sisters. They were older than she was and due respect. Also, they were both bigger. But the little calico had been teased often enough for her own markings. Because of the orange spot covering one eye and the black over the other, Laurel had labelled her Clara the Clown, a nickname her biggest sister had picked up as well. Both Laurel and Harriet had eased off recently, as all three had come to work together to help Becca out of a jam.

Still, Clara was all too aware of how words could sting, and with Harriet lashing her tail like that, she couldn't be sure what exactly her sister would do. That closed door might be a bit of a hindrance—Clara was the only one of the three who could easily pass through solid objects, thanks to her particular magical gifts—but it wouldn't stop a determined Harriet.

"She's all alone." Clara did her best to evoke sympathy for the kitten, whom they could all hear exploring on the other side of that door. *"I bet she's scared."*

In truth, the tiny tortie hadn't seemed scared during their few minutes of interaction as Becca set up the makeshift quarantine. Clara had gotten a distinct impression of intelligence in those clear green eyes, and the mew that had announced her presence while the group had been clustered on the sofa had been one of annoyance, she was pretty sure. Although Clara could communicate with her sisters, and Laurel in particular was adept at picking up on and influencing humans' emotions, the kitten had remained a blank, only giving off that strange buzzing that had set Clara's whiskers on edge earlier. That, as much as her size and strangeness, upped Clara's anxiety. She didn't think Harriet had ever actually hunted or killed any prey beyond a catnip mouse. But she certainly didn't want her to hurt the kitten.

"We're royalty. We can afford to be gracious." She tried a last appeal to her sisters' vanity. It was true, the three littermates were descendants of a magical line, blessed by the goddess Bast. It was also the kind of flattery that Laurel, in particular, adored.

"She is just a stray." Laurel shrugged, her sleek cream shoulders, showing off the slim musculature of her Siamese forebears. *"And such a tiny thing."*

"We should make her welcome." Clara spoke softly, her voice the faintest mew. Neither of her sisters would take orders from the little calico, but really, she thought, this was important.

"As long as she's eating your cans." Harriet relaxed, her own tail curling around her mitten-like paws. *"Besides, you heard Becca. She's going off to the vet tomorrow."*

With that, the big marmalade flounced off, most likely seeking the gold-tasseled pillow that served as her special bed. Laurel soon followed, tail high, leaving Clara to hunker down by the pantry door. She didn't really know if the kitten felt lonely or scared, but she knew how she would feel if she were alone in a strange, dark place. Besides, she'd picked up enough of Becca's and Maddy's conversation to have a picture of what had happened earlier that evening. Becca sounded sure of herself, but just in case, Clara wanted to think things through and be ready to come to her aid.

Five

The next morning, Clara had to scramble. She'd fallen asleep eventually, once she'd heard the kitten settle down, and was still lost in a dream when Becca woke her, gently pushing her out of the way of the pantry door.

"Excuse me, Clara." Becca's apology broke into a dream of boxes within boxes as the calico found herself sliding across the kitchen tile. Blinking up into her person's sweet face, the gentle smile framed by a cascade of brown curls, Clara could see that her person already had her jacket on—and had the green plastic carrier in hand. "I need to get in there."

"Playing watch cat?" Laurel sat behind their person, an unreadable expression in her cool blue eyes. *"Are you sure it didn't sneak out during the night? Maybe cause more trouble?"*

"No, I don't think so." Standing, Clara shook herself awake and turned toward the door Becca was oh so carefully opening. Yes, she confirmed, that strange buzz—the kitten—was still within, sleeping as soundly as she had been minutes before. *Maybe my presence was a comfort*, she thought with satisfaction. But any warm glow was broken as Harriet barged by, licking her chops.

"You missed breakfast," she announced. Which meant she'd

eaten Clara's, her little sister knew, and while Becca was usually very careful to make sure each of the three sisters got their share, today she must have been too preoccupied to notice. Still, despite a rumbling beneath the white fur of her belly, Clara held her peace as Becca reached past her and scooped up the snoozing kitten.

"You're going to tag along, aren't you?" Harriet's question mirrored the one in Clara's own mind.

"I think so." She turned to look into her oldest sister's round golden eyes. *"I'm sorry I didn't yesterday, and I want to know what's going on."*

"Good." Harriet dipped her head slightly, giving her baby sister a slow blink of approval. *"You should eat up, then. You'll need your strength."*

Grateful, if a bit surprised, Clara trotted over to where the cats' three dishes had been set out on a mat. Sure enough, Harriet had made quick work of her own can, licking her dish so that the golden sun on its bottom shone. But while the big marmalade had started on Clara's multi-colored dish, she'd stopped herself before she'd finished, leaving almost a third of the can behind. With a flick of her tail, meant to convey gratitude, Clara dove in, not stopping even as she heard Becca come up behind her.

"Oh good. I was worried to find you sleeping like that." A soft hand stroked her back as she licked the dish clean. "I'll make sure to give you extra when I get back."

"Don't forget who saved that for you!" Harriet muttered as the three cats followed Becca to the front door.

"And let us know how that cute vet is doing too." Laurel pressed her brown muzzle against Becca's legs, the better to mark her as her own—and as a desirable female. Clara longed to respond. Laurel was always pushing their human toward romance, disregarding Becca's vulnerability or her own preferences. But just then, she had to concentrate. Becca had locked the door behind her and headed down the steps, with the kitten in the carrier by her side. If Clara was going to keep up, she had to move. Wiggling her butt and laying her ears flat against her head, she

jumped, passing through the closed door as if it were so much mist.

Bounding down the stairs after Becca, Clara was careful to keep an eye out for any of the building's other tenants, in particular Becca's downstairs neighbor Deb Miles. The brittle brunette—Clara couldn't help but think of the newcomer's careful coif and polished nails as hard—had hassled Becca about everything from her friends to her cats when she'd first moved into the apartment below over the winter. Since then, the well-to-do newcomer had come to appreciate Becca's sleuthing capabilities, if not her warmth and generosity, and Becca considered them to be on decent neighborly terms now, Clara knew. But the cat withheld judgment and carefully shaded herself before passing by the third-floor landing. Being able to fade her distinctive orange-and-black markings into little more than a shadow, along with her ability to pass through solid objects made up Clara's special skills. But Clara had learned that some humans were more sensitive than others, and so, despite her shading, the little calico was careful to stick to the side of the stairway as she scurried down after her person. Besides, the shadow that dulled her spots to a nearly invisible gray was strictly visual. If she ran into anyone, she could get kicked, and the new neighbor was prone to particularly pointy-toed heels.

But the annoying Deb was nowhere around, and Becca, luckily, was distracted, and so even though Clara, in her haste, nearly ran into her person, she remained hidden. Following Becca out to the street, Clara could hear her talking to the kitten in the carrier. Reassuring her, Clara gathered, although surely any cat worth her whiskers knew that trips to the vet were, in general, a sign that their people cared.

If only I could let her know that Dr. Keller was a good one, Clara thought, conjuring up an image of the tortie kitten, who was undoubtedly confused if not scared by all that had happened.

Clara was less concerned about Becca. Her person had come to accept that the three cats she shared a home with were special, her pet was pretty sure. Although she might not understand the extent of their powers—that Harriet could conjure items out of the ether or Laurel subtly shifted a human's perceptions—she had come to accept, as most humans did, that cats often simply appeared, seemingly out of nowhere. At the very least, Becca had developed the normal human trust that her cats were where they should be, evidence notwithstanding. Just last night, Maddy had commented on Clara's particular ability to pass through seemingly solid objects. "I'm so sorry," she'd apologized to Becca as Clara had sauntered out of the closet. "I could have sworn she was on the couch a moment ago." She had been, of course, but as part of her investigation into the day's events, Clara had felt compelled to examine Becca's friend's jacket before Maddy had left.

"Oh, that's just Clara." Becca, to her friend's great relief, had not been concerned. "She gets into the darnedest places, but she always comes out when I start to get frantic."

Out here on the street, Becca wouldn't be expecting to see her cat, and so Clara trotted alongside. Only when Becca descended to the T did her cat hesitate. She knew this was coming—the vet's office was across town—but the giant, rumbling subway still seemed a bit too much like a wild beast for her to be completely comfortable entering voluntarily into its gaping maw. Bound by love as well as duty, however, she steeled herself and bounded down the stairs, squeezing herself behind Becca's feet once her person had found a seat on an inbound train, only to let herself be lulled by the back-and-forth sway even as the metal monster roared on its way.

"Good morning." Clara had woken just in time to race after Becca as she exited the train and surfaced on a tree-lined street.

"Thanks for making time for us." Becca greeted the man at the door. Dr. Keller—Jerry, he'd insisted—had only just unlocked the front door of his office and stood back, holding it open for her to enter. "The shop's closed on Mondays, and I really wanted to get the kitten over to you."

"It's no problem." The tall, slender man smiled over at Becca, even as he raised the waiting room blind, the morning light playing up the creases in his friendly face. "I'm sorry it had to be so early. With kitten season, I've got my hands full."

With that, the vet ushered Becca into his examining room and, opening the carrier, gave Clara her first good look at the newcomer in the light of day. Jumping silently up to the table, Clara sniffed at the kitten, who turned toward her with those serious green eyes.

"Can you see me?" Clara murmured, trusting that her soft mew would be covered by the rattle as the vet tucked the carrier beneath the table. *"Who are you?"*

"So who is this little girl?" Dr. Keller's question echoed Clara's so closely that it spooked her, and she jumped back just in time to avoid his large, square hands, which dwarfed the kitten as he held her to listen to her heart and look into her eyes. "Where did you come from, huh?"

"You can tell me," Clara tried again. Something was getting through. Those green eyes were staring straight at her with such intensity that Clara peeked down at her own paw to confirm that she was, indeed, still shaded. It wouldn't do for Becca to suddenly see her own cat appearing here.

But the kitten remained silent, even as the vet looked over the tiny tortie, gently poking at her belly before lifting her to the counter-top scale. "You said you found her?"

Becca nodded. "She was running across Mass Ave, so I ran after her." The vet's bushy brows went up in surprise, but he didn't interrupt. "I was able to grab her," Becca concluded. "She didn't have a collar, and I didn't see anyone looking for her, and it was late, so...I took her home."

Keller nodded, his generous mouth set in a line as he turned his attention back to the kitten. Clara couldn't tell if he had heard the hesitation in Becca's voice. The calico could certainly understand why her human wouldn't want to relive the previous night's drama. Then again, there could be other factors at work. She didn't have to be Laurel to sense that there was still some tension between these two. Clara had followed them on one of their dates and had been pleased to see how respectfully the tall, quiet man treated her person. But it didn't take Laurel's sensitivity to feel Becca's reticence, the way she'd started like a spooked kitten when he'd reached for her hand. The calico knew the vet to be kind and sensitive, despite his size. But Becca had been hurt badly by Jeff, and it might take more than Dr. Keller's gentle touch to overcome her reserve. That didn't mean that Clara wasn't wishing for more. It would do Becca good to unload, if only the nice vet would draw her out.

"Did you look for any notices about her?" Not the question Clara had been hoping for.

"No." For a moment, Clara thought Becca was going to tell him about the night's horror, but she only shook her head. "It was late."

The vet nodded, accepting her terse response. "I'm asking because she seems clean and well fed. Well socialized too, so she's not feral. I'd say she's about eight weeks old."

"So you think she's someone's pet?" A softness had crept into Becca's voice, as if she was imagining losing her own cat.

"At some point, though, considering that she's a tortoiseshell..." He paused to give the kitten's left ear one more look, flicking the black velvet to peer inside. "Maybe she was dumped."

Only when he had examined the other ear did he notice Becca's confusion. "Because she's a tortie," he said, as if that explained it. Becca only shook her head. "Tortoiseshell cats are a genetic anomaly. They're almost always female. But beyond that, they can be a little odd. Some people say they're crazy."

Back home, a fraught subway ride later, Clara filled in her sisters. *"She's healthy and she isn't feral. She doesn't even have fleas."*

"I could've told you that," said Harriet with a snort. In truth, Clara thought her big sister seemed a little relieved. *"But how did we get stuck with her?"*

Clara sighed as all three cats turned toward the closed pantry door. With their sensitive hearing, it was easy to discern the slight purr as the kitten chowed down on a fresh can of cat food.

Following close behind Clara, Becca had swept in and immediately sequestered the kitten once more.

"She might have been dumped," Clara confessed. She wasn't sure how much else she wanted to share. After all, she and her sisters had been born on the street to a mother who willingly walked into a humane trap in order to give her kittens a better life. Although their mother had disappeared before they reached the shelter, Clara felt certain that she knew about Becca and how the kind young woman had fallen for the littermates immediately. The idea of someone adopting a kitten and then giving it up... No, it didn't bear thinking about.

Laurel, however, was pushing for more, reaching out to bat not so gently at her little sister's orange ear.

"Because she's a tortie," Clara confessed, lowering her own parti-colored head to the floor. The jibes would follow soon, with all the casual cruelty that a beautiful and, more important, symmetrical cat like Laurel could muster. She didn't know how they could hurt.

But what followed weren't jokes or insults. Instead, she was getting a distinctly quizzical vibe from her sealpoint sister, and when she looked up, she saw that Laurel's apple-shaped head was tilted in a curious manner, the tip of her tail twitching just so.

"A tortie, you say? Well, that could be useful."

Clara waited, hoping for an explanation. But any further conversation was interrupted by her sisters' sudden awareness of a ladybug. Unwittingly drawn in when Becca had opened the door, the poor thing had located the window. But the buzzing and tapping as it sought to make its own magical pass through the glass only served to draw Laurel and Harriet. The two pawed and batted at the beetle's hard shell, occasionally knocking it to the sill, until, her sisters tiring, Clara used a gentle paw to guide the bewildered bug to a small rent in the screen and freedom. By then, the sun was shining full on, and soon all three felines were lulled into a sweet, dreamless sleep.

. . .

Clara woke hours later to find Laurel bathing by the window, which now opened on a gray and drizzly evening, and Becca's keys at the door. *"Took your time, sleepyhead,"* her sister murmured as she trotted over to the door. Clara joined her, looking around for Harriet. But Becca had barely had time to shed her jacket and feed the three before the sound of the doorbell alerted them all.

"Cookies!" Harriet took off, trotting toward the front of the apartment, tail high. Becca's coven had arrived.

Six

"To start with, we should definitely do a cleansing circle." Ande spoke solemnly, her dark eyes shining as she unwound the scarf protecting her short, natural curls from the evening's drizzle.

"I could use one of those," Marcia chimed in, hanging her damp Red Sox hat on Becca's coatrack. "After the look I just got from that vile woman downstairs."

"Miles. Deb Miles." Becca did her best to suppress her smile. "And she's getting better. She actually said hello to me the other day."

"Okay, then we won't turn her into a toad."

"Wait, we can do that?" Tina, the newest member of the group, looked from one woman to the other two, her dark eyes wide.

"No." Ande hung her jacket. "And we wouldn't if we could."

"The rule of three," explained Becca, taking Tina's umbrella. "Whatever energy we put out into the world comes back three times."

"Still, if we could..." Tina tagged along after her host, even as Becca shook her head.

Tina's hypothetical was quickly lost as the friends followed

Becca into her apartment. Becca had texted her friends the rough outline of the events of the night before, and as she tried to set up, she found herself hugged and cossetted, and questioned as well.

"Hang on, let me get the tea." Becca rushed back into the kitchen. The kettle had begun to shriek, sending the cats fleeing. "Tina, would you plate those cookies?"

Harriet, ears flat against her skull, stopped short and turned, just as Becca grabbed the kettle, putting an end to the infernal noise.

"Got 'em!" Tina lunged for the plate, making her glossy black ringlets bounce in a way that Becca's refused to. Not much longer than Becca's, they set off her sharp features—a heart-shaped face and a nose best described as pointy—without the softness that, to Clara at least, made her person so appealing.

"Careful!" Taller than the other woman by several inches, Ande caught Tina as she stumbled over Harriet, righting her and removing the plate in one elegant move. Placing it safely on the table, and giving the big marmalade a look that she pointedly ignored, the leggy witch called back over her shoulder to Becca. "I'm wondering if we should smudge you tonight, even before we start."

"Surely, we need tea before anything." Marcia, one of the small coven's other two original members, answered for Becca. A sparkplug of a woman, her boyishly short brown hair still holding the imprint of that Sox cap, she reached to lift the fluffy marmalade from the table. "Not just yet, Miss H," she said, placing the cat on the floor. "Humans first."

"Humans first, harrumph!" Harriet grumbled. It was a token protest: Clara could hear that her oldest sister had a large bite of oatmeal raisin in her mouth. More interested in the conversation than the cookies, the calico took up a position on the back of the sofa, watching as the four assembled.

"This was someone you knew?" Tina gaped, even as she accepted a teacup from Becca.

"It was your ex, right?" Marcia filled in the blank. None of the coven had ever met Jeff, but Ande and Marcia had heard the stories.

Becca simply nodded. "I didn't recognize him. Not at first, but, well, that's why I asked if we could convene tonight."

"Of course." Ande reached for her hand. "That's why I was thinking of sage. An unnatural death carries bad vibrations—"

"I think you've got your terms confused." Marcia interrupted. "But I agree, and I could run back home—"

"And I'm grateful," Becca broke in, raising her hand to stop any further comment. "But that's not why I wanted a circle."

Six sets of eyes—three human and three feline—turned toward their host and human.

"Tina, I don't know if you know this, but in addition to my job at Charm and Cherish, I do a little, well, investigating."

The newcomer nodded enthusiastically. "I've seen your flier! I was so excited when Ande told me you were a member of this group—I mean, coven."

A hint of a smile lightened Becca's solemnity. "Thanks. I've only had a few cases, but I have had some success."

"Not this again." Laurel's low growl startled Clara. The calico had been focusing so intently on the humans that she hadn't heard her sister jump up behind her. Recovering, she flicked her tail in acknowledgment. Becca had first gotten the idea of a so-called witch detective from her coven. That group—Marcia and Ande were the only remaining original members—had been trying out the spells that had caused her initial misunderstanding when Becca had mistakenly taken Harriet's summoning as her own. It had been the untimely death of one of that first group's members that had led Becca to believe she could use her powers to solve crimes. Clara believed her person was capable of just about anything. Her human was unnaturally smart, the little cat knew, and she was certainly curious and persistent. But Laurel was most likely right: Any magic called for was going to have to come from the cats. Not Becca, who, she realized with a start, was still talking.

"I answered all their questions, more or less. But, well, I'm not entirely sure they believed me."

Tina, eyes like saucers, looked around at her colleagues. "But why? They can't think that you..."

"They were asking me what we were fighting about. At the time, I didn't know what they meant, but..."

"The victim wasn't only Becca's ex." Marcia's tone, as well as her screwed up half smile, signaled her feelings about the dead man. "He was kind of a jerk."

"That doesn't mean he deserved to be killed." Becca sounded pained at having to defend him, though that could have been a cumulative reaction to the situation.

"Well, he was." Marcia, who was happily coupled, crossed her arms in defiance.

"That makes it worse, don't you see?" Ande, as always, the voice of reason. "I mean, for Becca."

"Why?" Tina, confused, turned from one to the other.

"Because I'm the obvious suspect," Becca explained, sounding almost relieved to get it out. "Jeff had cheated on me, and I was really upset when we broke up. And when he sort of wanted to get back with me, I let him have it. Verbally, of course."

Becca hesitated, and Ande, clearly not convinced, jumped in. "There's something else, isn't there? What did you mean, you told the police everything more or less?"

"I told them I hadn't seen Jeff in ages, and that I certainly wasn't having a fight with him yesterday. But..." Becca took a breath. "I didn't tell them why I ran down there. I couldn't. You see, I'd seen a kitten, a tiny thing, crossing Mass Ave, and I was so worried, I took off after her. I don't know, maybe it was silly not to say anything. But I'd grabbed her just when they appeared, shining their lights into the alley. And all the time they were questioning me, I had her in my bag. I was worried they'd take her, like evidence or something. So when they went through my bag I just told them she was mine."

That kitten is a witness. The realization made the fur along Clara's spine begin to rise. *She could help clear Becca's name.*

"But it's all so silly." Laurel's hiss intruded on the calico's thoughts. *"The breakup was months ago—more!"* It had been a

little over a year, Clara knew, but time was too abstract a concept for most cats. *"If Becca was going to kill that faithless jerk, she'd have done it long ago."*

"That's not how they think." Clara wasn't going to take on her sister's suggestion that their person would ever kill. *"I don't know if Becca's really in trouble, but she thinks she is."* Knotting her furry brow, Clara admitted to her own fear. *"And I'm scared for her too."*

Although the sisters often communicated in audible tones, Harriet and Laurel were also able to read each other's thoughts—a skill they often lorded over Clara. This time, however, Laurel merely turned, her ears perked forward to indicate her assent.

"Well, let's think about it. That kitten ran down the alley before Becca, right?" Laurel's green eyes closed in satisfaction. "*Ipso facto, she saw more. Maybe even the killer.*"

A human voice interrupted the cats.

"I don't see why that's a big deal." Tina was trying to cheer Becca up, Clara could tell. In truth, she agreed. Becca had acted out of kindness, not cruelty. But the looks Marcia and Ande shot at the newest member gave the cat a sinking feeling.

"Because I didn't tell them I was chasing the kitten, I couldn't give them any explanation for why I was in that alley. And because I'd stooped to pick her up, I ended up with blood on my hands. Jeff's blood."

Clara swallowed, the full horror of the situation sinking in. Becca had thought she was protecting the little tortie. But it was the kitten who had dragged her into this mess in the first place.

Seven

Ande took charge: "First things first, what do we know about what Jeff was doing—?"

"Or who," Marcia broke in before turning to their host, shamefaced. "Sorry, Becca."

"It's fine." Becca managed a half-hearted smile. "Only, I'm not sure if this is the way we should be going about this."

"Are we going to do a circle?" Tina looked from one coven member to another. "I mean, shouldn't we start with a sage smudge to dispel any lingering evil?"

"Yes, yes, of course." Ande, ever so slightly cross at the reminder, reached for her bag. Clara braced, remembering the loud howling that had resulted the last time the coven had brandished the smoky bundle of herbs. Such ceremonies, she and her littermates had decided, did not belong in urban apartments.

Ande didn't seem to share the cats' concern. "We definitely should start with a smudging. Then we'll put our minds together."

"And start asking questions," Marcia chimed in.

"That's just it." Becca raised her hands to calm everyone down. "I do want a healing circle, and I'm really grateful that you're all here and want to help. But the problem is, I really don't know anything. I haven't spoken to Jeff in months, so I don't have any leads. Truly, I was hoping that if we got together, we could use our powers to try to find something out."

You could have heard a whisker drop as the three witches all stared at their hostess.

"Becca." Ande was the one who finally broke the silence. "You know we'd love to, but you're the only one who has had any success with a spell."

"And it wasn't even her." Laurel yowled, drawing a concerned glance from the newcomer, and Clara had to agree, even as another question was beginning to gnaw at her conscience.

"So far." Becca's enthusiasm wasn't catching, but she was certainly trying. "But I'm not even thinking of magic, per se. More like using our sensitivities. We've all spent so many hours attuning ourselves to the elements, right? And what could be more out of whack with nature than a murder?"

"Murder?" Tina was beginning to look queasy.

"Unless he fell on his own knife." Marcia, reaching over to take the other woman's hand, had to have noticed her recoil.

"Look, we don't know much. Only that there was blood and, yes, I did hear mention of a knife. What we do know is that Jeff's death was untimely," Becca emphasized the last word. "Which probably amounts to the same thing. So we can begin by looking for disruptions in...in the ether."

She was winging it, Clara realized with an outpouring of sympathy that pushed all other thoughts from her mind. If only she could help her person!

"What do you want us to do?" Tina was clearly still skeptical. "You don't want us to go to the crime scene, do you?"

Becca winced. "Well, I was thinking that we could do a circle in the alley. It would be a civic good." She glanced at her comrades, but no support was forthcoming. "As an alternative, I thought we could start with some of Jeff's belongings. You know, try to get something off of them."

"You still have Jeff's things?" Ande sounded more concerned

than Clara understood. Surely, a few old clothes didn't matter. "Becca, I didn't know."

"I don't have much." Becca waved her off. "There was a sweater of his that I liked and, well, I don't know if it's the same, but he did install some software on my computer."

"You let him?" Marcia had switched into protective mode.

"We were going out, and that was his specialty. It's not much. I mean, he gave me my malware protection, so that was useful." Becca must have seen Ande about to interrupt, because she kept talking. "And also one of those fun games where it looks like there's a kitten inside my computer, licking the screen."

General murmurs let Clara know that the women knew about the program, and Ande held her peace. But the room now quivered with a tension the feline couldn't decipher. She was about to ask Laurel her opinion—the sealpoint's sensitivity to human emotions could be a useful tool—when another voice broke loudly into the calico's head.

"Kitten in a computer! What about the kitten in the closet?" Harriet, who'd been oddly silent, sounded more aggrieved than usual. Clara looked around but her sister had moved on from her usual spot, beneath the table.

"Anyway, I want to examine the alley tomorrow. Would any of you come with me?"

"Becca, I don't think you should go there." The tension in Ande's voice had shifted into something sterner. Stern enough, at any rate, that Becca looked up at her in surprise. "Dear, I think you're still too close to Jeff, and, well, it's dangerous."

"You mean, the killer...?"

"I mean the police." The tall accountant was standing now, her hands flat on the table before her as she emphasized the last word. "Becca, I'm serious. You're a person of interest, and for you to go poking around the crime scene—"

"I'll do it," Tina chirped. "I want to help. But you'll have to tell me what I'm looking for."

"Tina, I don't know." Ande was shaking her head, even as Becca beamed at the newcomer.

"We'll talk," she said. "And, Ande, I'm going to call some of Jeff's friends. I mean, that's a perfectly normal thing to do."

"And I can ask around too," Marcia chimed in. "See what anyone heard. What? I'm a curious Sox fan. Everyone will talk to me."

Ande scanned the table, but it was clear she was outnumbered.

"Well, what if we start with a cleansing circle now, and then we can talk about the next step?" Ande, acting as peacemaker, was clearly trying to move things ahead. "In fact, Marcia, would you get that sage bunch? Becca, do you want to disconnect your fire alarm, just for the ceremony?"

"Well, that's a relief." Clara glanced back at her sister, only to see Laurel jump to her feet. As her sister ran toward the kitchen, Clara remembered her earlier concern and took off after her. That voice! She should have noted the frustration and rage in Harriet's complaint.

A loud crash interrupted Ande's instructions as all four women looked up in alarm.

"Is that one of your cats?" Marcia stood, but Becca was already ahead of her.

"Oh no!" She nearly stepped on Clara as she raced to the kitchen in time to see Harriet, just as the big marmalade managed to get one wide white paw over the latch that held the pantry door closed. "Harriet, no!"

"What's going on?" Tina asked, standing on her toes to see over the others.

"The kitten! Harriet." Becca lunged for Harriet as the fluffy marmalade fell back with a hiss, the pantry door swinging wide.

"She's eating my food!" Harriet howled, claws out, as she vaulted toward the open door, only to catch the back of Becca's hand as she reached for the stout cat.

"Harriet!" Becca drew back, blood already welling from the scratch.

"Sister!" Clara, fearing the worst, sprang forward, landing between her littermate and her intended prey. She needn't have

worried. Harriet, surprised by Becca's intervention—or by her own violence—was sitting back on her haunches, golden eyes wide. In the doorway, the tiny kitten, her spiked fur making her look even fluffier had her own minuscule paw raised, claws extended, while her pink mouth opened in its own nearly inaudible hiss.

"Is *that* the kitten you said needed rescuing?" Marcia had the grace to sound amused.

"Yeah." Becca, subdued, pulled the confused Harriet into her arms. All eyes were on the tiny tortie, who still held one paw up, ready to strike, as she hissed and spit.

"I'd say that little girl can take of herself."

Eight

Once peace was restored, and the pantry latch reinforced with a chair, the humans returned to the living room and their interrupted ritual. The cats, however, remained in the kitchen, where a quiet conversation was quickly growing heated.

"You can go in there. You should interrogate it." Harriet was positively bristling with frustration. *"Find out what it knows and what it's doing here. And then—"*

"No." Clara didn't need Laurel's skills to figure out the logical conclusion to Harriet's anger. The kitten might be an intruder, but it was a living creature. Besides, it—*she*, she corrected herself—hadn't come here voluntarily. *"I'll question her, but I'm not going to hurt a kitten."*

"Hmph." Laurel prided herself on her sleek, muscular form. *"As if you could."*

"I won't. And you won't either." Clara caught herself. It would never do for the baby of the litter to be telling her older siblings what they should or should not do. *"I mean, you wouldn't. That's a lost kitten in there. Scared, alone..."*

"Eating our food." Harriet grumbled, but Clara could tell she had won her point. *"You should find out what its story is, though.*

Granted, it doesn't seem very intelligent, but it might have seen something. After all, do we really think it found Becca by accident?"

Clara had no answer to that. Her own memories of their early kittenhood were vague, and while her siblings had filled in much of their family's history, other cats remained a mystery.

"I'll see if I can question her." Clara blinked up at her big sister. *"But, remember, we don't even know if she can talk."*

"Which is why I was trying to get in there." Harriet was almost growling. Behind her back, Laurel crossed her eyes at this dubious claim.

"I'll do it." Clara agreed before Harriet could turn to look. Besides, she had to admit she was curious. *"But let's wait until Becca's friends are gone."* The last thing they needed that night was another disruption.

The feline interrogation, as Laurel dubbed it, was indefinitely postponed, however, by Becca's coven. Thanks to Harriet's interruption, the humans forgot to disable the smoke alarm, which went off with a demonic wail, and as the humans rushed to air out the apartment, opening windows and, in Tina's case, furiously fanning the screaming device with a magazine, the cacophony was augmented by a pounding on the door.

"Deb, I'm so sorry." A breathless Becca opened the door to face her neighbor, impeccably dressed in a silk suit, four-inch pumps, and a scowl. "It's a false alarm, but I'm sorry."

"Got it!" Ande called from behind her. Standing on a chair, the tall brunette had been able to reach the device. "You're reset."

"Reset indeed." Shaking her head, the glowering neighbor retreated down the stairs.

"Maybe we should call it a night." Becca turned back to her colleagues. By then, the cats were all wedged into their particular hiding places, as far as they could get from the horrendous shrieking. Chastened, the coven agreed to postpone their ritual, and hold it outside, but for the felines, the excitement of the evening had the same effect as a rousing game of catnip mouse. By the time Ande, the last of the guests, had hugged Becca, all four of the resident felines were sound asleep.

. . .

"Okay, kitties, I'm off!" Becca's voice woke Clara, who had found shelter beneath an old sneaker in the back of the closet. It was early by her human's standards, easily an hour before she would usually leave for work. "I've left you breakfast."

She sounded worried, and Clara soon realized why. Harriet had only just appeared blinking from beneath the bed, and Laurel was nowhere to be seen.

"Don't give in." The distinctive yowling voice of the middle sister sounded in Clara's mind. She was beneath the radiator, Clara realized. *"She has to know that such loud noises are unacceptable."*

"But it's time for breakfast." Harriet's statement turned into an audible mew, and Becca reached down to rub the base of those wide white ears as the big cat bent her head to her dish.

"You'd better not eat mine." Laurel appeared, seemingly out of nowhere, to Becca's evident relief.

"Blessed be," she said, her brow smoothing out into a smile. "With what I'm going to do today, I didn't want to be worrying about you three."

Clara looked up at that, but Becca only chucked her under her chin. "Be good!" she called out, and was gone.

"You can question the pantry rat once we're done." Sleeping on the floor hadn't improved Harriet's temper at all, but Clara was in no mood to appease her.

"She's a kitten, not a rat." Clara couldn't stop her tail from lashing. *"And I'll talk to her later. But didn't you hear what Becca said? She's going to start investigating today, and I'm going with her."*

And with that, she leaped through the door.

Nine

Following Becca was the easy part. Although the night's rain had given way to a clear, warm morning, the early hour provided plenty of shadows to complement Clara's discreet shading, giving the calico an edge that would be hard to maintain once the bright June sun was at its peak. No, at this hour, not getting stepped on or tripping up some random stranger were what made Clara's mad dash through the streets of Cambridge more of a challenge. Although her person had only left the apartment moments before Clara's bold declaration, which had left Harriet staring in affronted outrage, Becca had already descended the stairs and pushed open the door to the street before the little cat could follow suit. Worse, the energetic young woman hadn't taken her usual route—left up the sidewalk and a turn at the corner where the young maple had begun to put out its fresh green leaves—a path that would have her heading toward Charm and Cherish.

"She's not going to her job." The realization hit the calico as she followed Becca out onto Mass Ave, away from the budding trees of their own street and away from the shop as well. Weaving through the commuter foot traffic that filled the urban center's

sidewalks, she struggled to remember Becca ever heading in this direction before. Granted, she didn't follow her person every time she left the house—a cat has her own life to attend to—but she knew most of Becca's usual destinations. Maddy's apartment was down in Cambridgeport, for example, and if she'd been going to her friend's, they'd have turned off the main drag two blocks before, following a downhill route toward the Charles that always had Clara sniffing for green, growing things. Even if Becca wanted the quickest route to the river—say, to hold a circle on the grass embankment—she'd have turned off by now.

This had to do with Jeff. The early hour and Becca's nerves made this the likeliest option. But beyond that, Clara was at a loss. The alley where Becca had found the kitten—and Jeff—lay in the other direction, toward Charm and Cherish. Maybe, the little cat told herself as she dodged a pair of scary-looking boots, she should be grateful.

When Becca took a sharp left into a paved courtyard, however, the calico felt the fur along her back start to rise. The bleak courtyard, still dark with shadow this early in the morning, filled Clara with a sense of unease, like the memory of a bad dream. Or no—it hit her like one of Laurel's lightning-fast slaps—a remembered trauma.

Could this sterile place have been where her mother had nursed her and her littermates? Clara eyed the few sad plantings that filled a corner, shrubs that would barely have provided cover for a family of mice, much less kittens, and tried to recall the wise, warm thrum of her mother's presence. Harriet and Laurel had recently shared with their youngest sister visions of their family's ancient origins, guarding the granaries of the priestess. But Clara's memories of her mother, that purr, the warmth of her tabby striped coat, and the welcome roughness of a tongue, those were her own.

A harsh buzz nearly made her jump. Distracted by her own musings, Clara had almost missed that Becca had ducked into one of the glass-and-metal doors that opened onto the sterile space and was now pressing a buzzer, summoning that awful sound.

"Hello? I'm here about Jeff Blakey." Only a cat, Clara suspected, would hear the quaver in her voice. But Becca was saved from having to say any more by the click of a lock, and with a leap, Clara followed after as her person pushed open the door to a small, stuffy lobby and entered an even stuffier elevator.

Now, cats may like boxes, but elevators were another matter. More akin to the cases used to transport them to the vet, these moving boxes gave even the bravest felines the creeps, and it took all Clara's willpower not to nuzzle up against Becca's legs as the enclosed space lurched and jerked its way up. Instead, she squeezed her eyes closed, laid her ears back flat on her head, and hunkered down in a corner until the elevator came to a shuddering stop, at which point she scurried after Becca, who was already heading down a carpeted hall.

"Becca, so good to see you again." The greeting didn't sound sincere, despite the wide grin pasted on the round face of the man who greeted her. Tall and bearish, with a flannel-clad midriff that a cat could knead, he ushered Becca into what Clara could only think of as a rabbit warren. Ostensibly large and open, the space they had entered was broken up by a series of carpeted walls and dividers, and Clara could sense movement inside pockets of the space, as if individuals, or perhaps entire families, had made their nests there.

"I'm Carl, Carl Rimsky," the bearish man said. "You probably don't have any reason to remember—"

"I remember you." Becca's tone sounded harsh, even to her loving pet's ears, and she smiled, as if to soften her words as the big man blinked in shock. "I'm sorry, it's been a crazy time," she said. "But, yes, you and Jeff were close. I remember him talking about...about hanging out with you."

"He knew about Jeff." Clara put two and two together. *"He might even have known that Jeff was cheating on Becca."*

"I am—was." The big man blinked again, his pink cheeks going pale. "Wait, you know? About Jeff, I mean?"

"Yeah." Becca nodded and turned aside, though Clara could

still see the brightness of the tears that had sprung into her eyes. "I heard."

Those tears, or perhaps it was the sudden roughness of her voice, brought the blood back to Carl's face. "I'm so sorry. Here, come in. Sit down."

Nodding, Becca allowed herself to be led around one of the carpeted dividers. As Clara suspected, a sofa and two chairs, their nubbly grey upholstery matching the dividers, would have made a perfect home for a nest of bunnies. Sitting on one end of the unprepossessing sofa, Becca leaned forward, her head hanging down, prompting a look of alarm from the looming man.

"Would you like some water?" He appeared to be looking for an excuse to escape, and when Becca choked out a short "Yes," he lumbered off rather quickly for a man his size. To Clara's surprise, Becca rallied as soon as he was gone, craning her head to take in her surroundings, her eyes once more clear and alert.

"Here you go." Carl returned, a *Star Trek* mug in hand. "It's only tap water, but it's cold."

"It's fine. Thanks." Becca managed a smile that brought even more color to the big man's cheeks. "I guess it all just hit me, being here, in his office."

She was hinting at something, though, what exactly, Clara couldn't tell. Neither, it seemed, could Carl. "Yeah, we really miss him. I mean, we did even before Gerald got the call this morning..."

Becca's confusion was clear on her face, and Carl reddened, stuttering.

"Renee, his—his friend, called Gerald. They used to go out before Jeff..."

Becca raised a hand to halt what was clearly an uncomfortable narrative. "Renee, that's right." She swallowed. "His girlfriend." That prompted another swallow, as Becca blinked up at the chunky computer nerd who had taken a seat by her side. "But what do you mean, you missed him even before?"

"Finding another software guy like Jeff isn't easy." Carl leaned forward, elbows on his knees, relaxing as he addressed his sneakers. "I mean, you know how inventive he was, always coming up with something smarter, cleaner, or faster. If he'd stayed with us, well..." He looked around the carpeted warren, his eyes following the fluorescent tubes that made their own maze across the ceiling. "I don't think we'd be in the armpit of Kendall Square anymore."

"Jeff left?" Becca sat up straight, drawing her host's attention back to their particular nest. "When?"

"Maybe a month ago? No, more like two." Carl grimaced at his own math. "Once he got that first hit of VC, he was out of here."

"Jeff got venture capital funding?" Becca might as well have been speaking Latin, but Clara could tell the words made sense to her. To her companion, as well. He was nodding, his wide mouth set in a serious line. "He went out on his own?"

"There was a little pushback, but there was no way the company could claim it was a work for hire," he said, more gibberish to the cat, but apparently logical enough to her human.

"What was his big idea?" Becca's question brought up an image in Clara's mind: a mechanical drawing of a kitten who romped around a computer screen, licking at imaginary spots. "Last I heard, he was really interested in malware."

"That's what got him started. Got us both started, really." Carl leaned in, as if confiding a secret, and Clara got a whiff of a bearish scent. Beef, she thought, with a trace of fries. "Look, we shouldn't talk here. Do you want to get some coffee?"

Thirty minutes later, Becca was speed-walking back to Central Square and nearly trod on Clara as she fished her phone out of her bag. Something about her pace made her cat wonder what the rush was. Was Becca about to go to the police? Was she simply late for work? But although the digits she punched into her phone meant nothing to the feline, the soft voice her acute hearing picked up on the other end put some of her worries to rest.

"Maddy, you wouldn't believe what Jeff was into." Becca spoke as she strode down the sidewalk, stepping into the street to avoid a cluster of tourists, all wearing orange badges, while Clara dashed after her. "I went to his office—his old office, it turns out —and talked to that beefy guy Carl. You know, the one who was always trying to get him to go out and pick up girls? Well, it turns out that Jeff dumped him too, kind of, and went out on his own."

"Wait, what? Becca, you went to his office? Are you crazy?" Maddy's voice rose to a squawk. "You shouldn't be anywhere near him—I mean, his old haunts."

"I have to, Maddy." Becca swung around a small oak that was budding optimistically in its small square of exposed earth, and Clara followed her back onto the sidewalk. "I've got to find out what's going on. I mean, it's my neck on the line. I told him I wanted to know about any memorial that might be happening, and I think he believed it. He was kind of a mess, but I think he just didn't want to break the news to me, and, honestly, I get the feeling he doesn't talk to women much. But, wow, you should have seen the place. I forgot how depressing an office can be. All those cubicles. Anyway, I couldn't really remember what Jeff did, but I pulled up that he was working on malware. Virus protection, you know? And it was the right answer. Carl must have thought I'd kept in closer touch with Jeff than I did. Hang on."

Without Clara even noticing, Becca had reached Charm and Cherish. Cradling the phone against her shoulder, she unlocked the door and reached for the light switch. "Anyway, Carl explained about some super-secret project Jeff was designing. All that time he spent working on protecting systems got him thinking about the opposite. I don't understand it all, but Carl said he was working on a skeleton key that would unlock any digital software."

"Like, a universal decoder of some kind?" Maddy's hardy laugh came through loud and clear.

"Yeah, I know." Becca chuckled as she flipped the sign on the door to "Open." "It sounds like science fiction, doesn't it? But Jeff was smart." She paused, and for a moment Clara was afraid she was going to start to cry. "Or other people are stupid, I don't know.

"Anyway, that program was going to be his golden ticket, Maddy. He'd gotten some crazy offer to go out on his own. It turns out my ex had suddenly gotten rich."

Ten

"Earth to Becca. Can you hear me?"

Becca started, but the older woman in the purple paisley caftan standing before her only smiled.

"I'm sorry, I was...I guess I was elsewhere." Becca returned the gray-haired woman's smile with a twinge of embarrassment. "You were saying?"

"I was talking about replenishing the touch stones." The colorfully clad woman reached out to run a knobby finger through the bowl by the register, stirring up the amethysts and rose quartz that reflected the hue of her gown. When she picked up the oddly shaped tiger eye, she glanced at Becca. "But what I really wanted was to ask for your thoughts about teaching."

"Teaching?" Becca hadn't realized how much she'd missed. What she did realize was that the woman standing in front of her, Elizabeth Cross, was not only her boss's sister and her sartorial opposite, she was Becca's ally, as well as an uncanny judge of character. "I'm sorry."

Elizabeth's eyes twinkled as her grin widened, their deep gray taking on an almost violet hue. While she shared the same facial features as her little sister, on her larger face the bushy eyebrows and prominent nose appeared generous, though her customary joy may also have played a part. "You're already on the case, aren't you?" Seeing Becca flush as she gasped for a response, she waved the younger woman's concerns away. "Online teaching. You'd be a natural."

"I've never taught anything." Becca protested. "And online? You mean, on the computer?"

"Unless you want to do the whole thing on your phone. Though, that's a computer too, at least to someone my age." The age of the elder Cross sister was actually a matter for speculation. Considering that Margaret, who owned the shop, was at least eighty, it would seem that her big sister was approaching ninety, except that the woman standing in the shop had the vivacity of youth.

"No, I know what you meant." Becca was at a loss. "It's just, I don't know if I'm the right person to do this."

"Of course you are." Elizabeth beamed at her. "You're our senior staffer. You know as much about the craft as anyone your age, and you certainly have more online experience than anyone *my* age."

She held up one finger, effectively cutting off any response. "Think about it," she said. Then, lowering her hand, she flipped a few of the bright stones in the dish. "Margaret wouldn't know a true gem from cut glass, but I do."

With that, and a swish of her long purple robes, she swept off toward the back room, leaving Becca more confused than before.

"If only I could do something." Clara, shaded into invisibility, looked on from her perch by the back door.

"You can," whispered Margaret as she passed, and then she shut the door.

Gripping her claws into the wood cabinet, Clara made a quick and quiet appraisal. Yes, she was still shaded, a process that should have made her appear no more than the faintest shadow and that only in full sunlight. No, Becca didn't seem to have heard. A quick glance over to the counter showed that her person was now staring into the shallow bowl of gemstones, rather than into space, but still seemed as distracted as before.

"What did that mean? What can I do?" She was talking to herself, mostly. Still, she wasn't entirely surprised to hear a response in the form of a familiar sound, the tinkling of the bells hung from the shop's door.

"Welcome to Charm and Cherish." Becca, roused from her reverie, greeted the newcomer, whose long, straight blonde hair and flowered blouse gave her a neo-flower child vibe. "Please let me know if I can help you with anything."

"Thanks." The slim woman flashed a smile as she slipped behind a bookshelf, but rather than browsing any of the titles or even reaching for the crystal and brass knickknacks that lined each shelf, she paused just out of sight. Clara, aware of the slightest movement, could see she was leaning forward ever so slightly, her eyes on Becca, palms pressed against the thighs of her fashionably faded jeans. Suspicious behavior, for sure, the cat thought, her tail beginning to lash. But before she could pounce, the young woman stepped forward, approaching the counter.

"You're Becca Colwin, right?" Blondie tilted her head, her blue eyes appraising. "You dropped by CodePhool this morning?"

"Yeah, I am." Clara's person returned the curiosity, but with her typical friendly tone. "And you are?"

"You were asking if anyone had planned a memorial for Jeff, right?"

"Yeah..." Becca drew out the syllable, waiting for an answer to her own question.

"The police aren't releasing the body yet." The other woman bit her lip and stared down at the ground. "It's kind of awful. So we don't know when we can even have a funeral, and his parents..."

"I know his parents are down in Connecticut. Or they were."

The stranger nodded, eyes still down. "His mother's been sick. I don't think they're going to want a big gathering even when..." She looked up, her big blue eyes taking in Becca, the shop. Even Clara, the little cat briefly feared.

"Are you okay?" Becca came out from behind the counter and looked ready to embrace the newcomer, or at least lead her into the back, where she could sit, when the other woman blinked and held up a hand, showing several silver rings.

"Sorry," she said. "I came by to let you know that some of us are going to be gathering tonight at the Plough after work." She shrugged, tucking her hair back behind her ear. "It was Carl's idea. I don't know if he was thinking of a wake or what, but he really wants to talk about Jeff and stuff. Maybe it'll be a good thing. Give everyone a chance to try to process."

And try to find out what happened. The thought sprang into Clara's head. From the way Becca straightened up, she suspected this had occurred to her as well. *Maybe Becca isn't the only one looking for answers.*

"Thanks. I'll be there." Becca eyed the stranger, her own brown eyes growing sharp. "I don't think I saw you at the office this morning."

"No." Her message delivered, the other woman sounded lighter, relieved of a burden. Or having achieved a goal of some kind. "I don't work directly with those guys. With Jeff." She headed toward the door and pulled it open, setting the bells jingling again.

"Wait." A sharpness had crept into Becca's tone. "What's your name?"

"Renee, Renee Wendig," the woman called over her shoulder once she was safely out the door.

"It's already working, Maddy." With nobody else in the little shop, Becca had pulled out her phone. "I'm shaking things loose, and I'm going to have a chance to question people too."

The response from the other end of the line wasn't audible to the cat, who now sat on the counter, watching her person with concern. It didn't have to be. The way the tone ratcheted up told the calico all she needed to know—specifically that Becca's friend did not want her to go to the nearby bar. Although the cat didn't understand all the implications of the visit, she couldn't help but share her concern. That name, Renee, had jarred Becca in a way that worried her pet, and the way the stranger had withheld her identity until she was done with her mission only worsened her suspicions. Tilting one ear toward the back room, Clara wondered if she could enlist Elizabeth's aid in dissuading Becca from attending the gathering. But the storeroom had gone quiet, even to the feline's discerning ear, and she remembered the older woman had exited via the back, leaving her to deal with Becca alone.

Or not. "You don't have to, Maddy. That's not why I called." Becca seemed to have moved on to another topic. "You never liked him, even when we were together. Besides, it's a get-together at a bar. I was asking about a memorial when I dropped by this morning so it would make sense I'd be there."

Clara was straining to make out Maddy's response, when the shop's bells began ringing again. She looked up to see a couple, who immediately headed toward the incense before popping up with questions.

Becca held up a finger to ask for a moment's grace. "Maddy, I've got to run." She nodded as her friend's voice broke through one more time. "I'm closing today, so I'll be heading over a little after seven." Becca nodded toward the tall woman to indicate that she was finishing up. "Okay, seven, then. But only if you want to, Maddy. Really. It's not like I'm going to be in danger."

Eleven

On the walk over, Maddy worked on her friend, urging her not to go.

"We could stop at that place on the corner and have a nice cup of tea. Or a beer, if you'd rather." Clara had rarely heard Maddy plead so ardently. "Talk about Jeff, if you want."

"I don't want to." Becca held firm. "I'm over him. I was months ago. Only, now he's back in my life, complicating my life."

"I think there's more going on." Her friend sighed. "This isn't going to help you resolve your feelings."

"It might keep me out of jail." Becca came to a halt in front of a green-painted door. "Besides, we're here."

Opening that door unleashed a roar of sound that stopped Becca in her tracks and nearly caused Clara to bump into her ankle.

"Good, let's go." Maddy could have been speaking for the shaded calico as she grabbed her friend's arm and pulled. But she may as well have been trying to herd a cat.

"No, I'm going in." Becca turned to her friend. "It's just...it's been a while."

Before the other woman could comment, Becca strode in.

The roar, she quickly realized, was general conversation, akin to the damp warmth of the crowded barroom.

"Do you want a drink?" Becca turned back to her reluctant friend. "Come on, at the very least, I owe you."

"I'll have a cider," Maddy said, her reluctance making it sound like a punishment. "But just one and then we're gone."

Becca nodded, a rather noncommittal response, her cat thought, as she made her way into the room, Maddy—and Clara —at her heels.

"We're early." Becca scanned the room. "Do you want to see if you can grab us some table space?"

With a grumbled, "We're not staying," Maddy peeled off. Pushing through the crowd standing by the bar and its overhead televisions—some kind of sports thing, Clara noted—she settled into a wooden chair in front of a table that still showed the wet rings of its previous occupants.

"Here you go." Becca reappeared, bearing two pint glasses full of golden liquid. "The bartender said they're going to turn the TVs down once this game is over."

"I'm sure that's going to go over well." Maddy eyed the crowd as she reached for her glass.

"I gather Jeff was kind of a big deal here." Becca followed Maddy's gaze, but it seemed to her pet that she was seeing something different.

"He drank that much?"

"No." Becca sounded as distracted as she looked, evidently missing the acid in Maddy's remark. "I gather they were in financial trouble, and he helped them out, acting like some kind of angel investor."

"Great." Maddy took another sip of her cider. "All the charities he could be giving to, and he decided to give money to a bar."

"I think it was an investment." Becca reached for her own drink. "At any rate, they're basically turning the place over to his crew when—oh, there's Carl."

Maddy looked up as Becca waved to greet the bearish software engineer. He'd changed out of his flannel button-down and into a green sports jersey. "Oh, hey, Becca." After an initial double take, he came over. "I didn't know you'd be here."

"Renee invited me." Becca put a little extra force behind the words. "It was good to meet her finally."

"I'm glad." Carl nodded as the pieces fell into place. "Yeah, she was asking about Jeff's other friends today, and I—well, I'm glad you're here."

What would have been an awkward silence followed, if it hadn't been filled with loud cheers from the bar. As soon as the noise subsided, Becca jumped in. "Is that a Plough shirt?"

He picked at his chest, as if to remind himself what he was wearing. "Yeah, we have a darts team. Had. Jeff was the organizer. He got us these."

"I gather he was helping out the bar."

Carl looked around, taking in the crowd. "Yeah, he really loved this place. And, you know, he was generous."

A grunt from Maddy could have been a comment. Instead, it prompted Becca to turn toward her friend. "Carl, this is my buddy Maddy. Maddy, Carl. He and Jeff work together at Code-Phool. Worked." She shook her head.

"Pleased to meet you." He held out his hand. "Are you also a...historian?"

The pause was telling, and Maddy jumped on it. "I'm a researcher, yes, and, yes, Becca and I used to work together too. I gather you and Jeff used to be close at one time."

Carl winced, and Becca moved to kick Maddy under the table. "We were partners back in the day. In fact, I helped Jeff with his big breakthrough."

"The unlocking software?" Becca chimed in, studying his face.

"Yeah." He shook it off like a bad dream. "I mean, that's a very simplistic take on what we were doing. What he was doing, but we started on it together."

"So who was working with him?" Maddy leaned over the table.

"Jeff? I think he was still assembling his team." Carl nodded at a far corner of the room and raised his hand. "Hey, I think we're going to start soon. Are you going to join us?"

"What was that about?" Becca hissed in her friend's ear as she maneuvered her way around the table.

"The killer could be someone he was doing business with—especially if big money is at stake." Maddy shrugged as she pushed the chair out of her path. "And you were asking about his project."

"I was," Becca conceded. "But I'm just fishing at this point."

The two had already fallen behind Carl, who, by virtue of his height or his gender or the fact that he wasn't trying to weave through the crowd carrying a nearly full pint, had already made it around the corner of the bar. By the time Becca and Maddy caught up—with Clara, unseen, at their heels—a group of about twelve had pushed several tables together.

"Here are two." Maddy pointed, but her face fell as she watched Becca's expression change.

"Hi, Renee." Speaking in an unnaturally high upbeat tone, Becca pulled out a chair.

Maddy caught on quickly. "Renee, so good to meet you. Jeff told us *all* about you." Becca shot her friend a glance, but Maddy wasn't done riffing. "Becca and Jeff were still friends, you know. Good friends."

Clara, who'd huddled beneath the table, dodged just in time as Becca kicked Maddy.

"I appreciate your inviting me." Becca ignored her friend's bug-eyed stare. "Honestly, we hadn't kept up."

"Really." The blonde sat back and looked from Becca to Maddy. "I thought you two had been in touch."

"Did he talk about Becca much?" Maddy leaned in, ignoring Becca's second kick.

"No." Renee had the grace to look at her lap, and when Clara peeked up at her, she thought she saw a deep sadness in the other woman's face. "But he was corresponding with someone. I thought, maybe..."

"Okay, everyone." At the other end of the table, Carl was banging a spoon against a pint glass. "Can we get some quiet?"

A general murmur of agreement as individual conversations broke down. Renee shifted her chair to face front.

"What was that about?" Becca hissed in Maddy's ear. "It sounded like you were trying to make her think Jeff and I were still an item."

"I didn't have to suggest that." Maddy's clipped tone carried easily to the cat at their feet. "She came looking for you because she was already suspicious."

Becca turned, shaking her head, like she was about to protest, when Maddy grabbed her hand.

"The cops told you that there were reports of a man and a woman yelling at each other, right? We've been saying that a business partner would make a good suspect." Maddy spoke softly but with intensity. "But nobody is more suspicious than an angry girlfriend."

"Maddy, please." Becca's warning came as Carl began to speak again.

"I think most of us have something to say, but I'm wondering, Renee, if you want to go first?"

The woman sitting next to Maddy stiffened.

"I don't think she expected that," Becca murmured. Maddy only raised an eyebrow.

"Thanks, Carl." Renee rallied, standing to address the table. "Hi, everyone."

"Hey, Renee." As the group greeted the blonde, Maddy surveyed the assembled crowd, eyes hooded with suspicion, and Becca too found herself looking around to examine the faces of the attendees, nodding at the few she recognized. Below the table, Clara listened for reluctance, or even hostility, but in the general rumble of response, any such off notes were hard to pick out.

"I guess I should start by thanking everyone for coming out tonight." With one thumbnail, Renee picked at the edge of the table. "I'm not really sure what to say."

"It's okay, Renee," said a chubby man whose curly beard

badly needed a trim. He sounded like he would have reached out to her, had Becca and Maddy not been in the way.

The blonde rewarded him with a tight-lipped smile. "Anyway, I know most of you through Jeff, either socially or because he brought me in as a designer." Her thumbnail pried at the table's edge. "He was really generous that way, always trying to bring people together. Always willing to share."

She bit her lip, and for a moment Becca thought she would start crying. "Maybe that's why I couldn't believe some of the messages he was getting. I mean, he'd moved on. People are allowed to move on."

Clara felt as much as heard Becca's quick intake of breath, but the other woman kept talking. "At any rate, I guess I'm angry that his last days were disrupted by such nasty, petty little digs. And I'm really sad that I'm not going to get to see what great things he would have done if he'd lived. That we're not going to get to share the life we planned. No matter what those messages said about me."

She sat down abruptly.

"You okay, Ren?" the bearded guy asked, leaning over Becca, his reddish-brown curls in her face.

"Excuse me," Becca pushed back her seat, and both Renee and her champion turned to face her.

"Thanks, Renee." Carl's voice interrupted Becca's neighbor's response. "I'm really sorry to hear that you've been having to deal with anything like that. As one of Jeff's oldest friends and certainly his longest collaborator, I know how much you meant to him. And I agree, Jeff was one of the most generous people I know. Whether it was helping you de-bug a beta or putting you together with a collaborator, he was there, easing the way with a bad joke and a smile. You all know this." He scanned the table, taking in all the bobbing heads. "Hey, I've already gotten a call from Jeff's VC guy, because of Jeff, and that's how so many of us know Renee now as well. Her designs have really helped take so much of what we do to the next level, and I'm sure we all look forward to working with her even more."

Renee was staring down at the table again, and from the way her foot was bouncing, Clara thought she didn't appreciate the attention. The chubby guy must have picked up on her discomfort, however, because he pushed his chair back roughly and started to speak.

"Actually, Carl, I think we should talk about something else." His soft voice had grown to a bark, serving to silence the table. "I mean, yeah, we all loved Jeff. Who didn't? He was a really fun guy. And, yeah, he was always willing to help out, but he could go overboard too. I mean, I remember when he came up with the beta for his malware probe. He put it on the server without telling anyone, and I know I had a hell of a time getting it off my devices when it automatically downloaded."

Voices around the table mumbled what sounded like agreement. "And his new gig? Well, that was great for him, and I believe you that he was hoping to take some of us along. But, well, I know I felt a little let down. We had projects really close to completion at CodePhool. Projects he would've been a real help with."

Now it was his turn to stare down at the table, dark eyes bright above that bushy beard.

"I don't know," he said after a prolonged pause. "I miss the hell out of him. Jeff was a fun guy, and, yeah, maybe brilliant too. And I certainly don't think he deserved to be stabbed to death in an alley, but since we all knew him, I just think it makes sense to remember him as he really was, warts and all." With that, he sat back down.

"Thanks for that." Becca leaned over. "I'm Becca."

"Theo." The chubby man nodded, taking her in. "Yeah, I know you."

"I think we met at an ultimate frisbee game." Becca's voice warmed.

Theo's did not. "Yeah, we did. Renee told me a little about you. I gather you two have been in touch."

"She told me about the gathering tonight." Clara could hear

the hesitation in Becca's voice. "And that someone was sending messages to him."

"She told you about those, huh?" An edge had crept into his tone, but before Becca could respond a general shushing cut them both off.

"When I think of Jeff, I think of respect." A new voice broke into the awkward hush, drawing everyone's attention. "I wasn't sure what to expect when I started at CodePhool. I'd come from an academic incubator, but I wanted to do something new."

Clara couldn't see who was speaking, but she heard something nervy in her tone. A little defiant. "As a person of color, I'm used to men, white men, being condescending. But Jeff wasn't like that."

"Probably because she's a looker." Maddy's sotto voce aside carried, making Becca squirm. Worried about her person, Clara missed some of what the speaker was saying.

"It was a silly thing, one of those early programs of an animated kitten, but I thought it was cute." Becca stiffened, as if in response. "But Jeff wouldn't give me the code. He said, 'You know how to do this, Zara. Make it your own. Make it better.'"

"Make it better." Theo echoed the words, as did several others.

"You okay?" Maddy's tone had become solicitous, reaching over to Becca as she slumped in her seat.

"Yeah." The one syllable didn't convince Clara, but there was little she could do as another of Jeff's former colleagues began to speak. As she listened, though, the little cat began to get an impression of Becca's ex, one that differed from the initially sweet but ultimately faithless boyfriend who had hurt her person so.

"Sounds like a jerk." Maddy's voice cut through her thoughts. Almost, the calico agreed. What struck her, though, was how confident he had seemed. Whether he was directing a project, like the one he had apparently begun with Carl, or helping a newcomer settle in, the Jeff who was being remembered here never seemed to doubt himself.

Carl, whose voice Clara remembered from when he opened

the evening, seemed to be doing his best to step into his late colleague's shoes, asking if anyone else wanted to speak, when a lull fell on the crowd.

"Does anyone know if they've caught whoever did it?" Renee asked finally, her voice tight.

"I don't think so." Carl, a slight tremor betraying his lack of confidence. "I'm sure the police are working on it, though."

"Someone should tell them about those messages." Theo, sounding gruff. "I mean, someone besides Renee. She's been through enough."

"Thanks. But I did speak with them, you know." The new girlfriend's voice had grown very soft, but there was an edge to it.

"Good! They questioned her too." Maddy's stage whisper was clearly audible to the cat at her feet.

Carl set about to smooth the waters. "I'm sure the authorities know what they're doing. And, honestly, I think we should leave this to them."

"But do they understand our world, our structures?" Theo sounded like he was going to say more, when another voice—Zara?—chimed in.

"What makes you think he was killed because of something at work, Theo? Is there something you're not sharing?"

"Okay, that's enough," Carl broke in. "We're here because of Jeff. This isn't the time to get caught up in conspiracy theories. I mean, we've all been drinking, and I'd like to buy one more round for the table. For Jeff."

"For Jeff." A general cheer, followed by calls for cider and beer, led to Maddy pushing her chair back.

"We should skedaddle," she said out loud, as if speaking for ears other than Becca's. "Becca, we've got that thing in the morning."

"What?" Under the table, Maddy grabbed Becca's wrist. "Yeah, you're right."

Becca stood, turning first toward Renee. "Thanks for telling me about tonight. It was good to hear everyone, and, well, this might sound odd, but I'd like to keep in touch."

"Sure." The blonde drew the word out. "You've got my number, right?"

"Renee..." Theo interrupted, but Becca turned to him next.

"I'd like to get your number too," she said. He hesitated, and Maddy reached once again for her arm. "Well, I can reach you at CodePhool, right?"

"For now," he said, his round face unreadable.

"What was that about?" Out on the sidewalk, Maddy turned to face Becca.

"Didn't you hear him?" Becca sounded more energized than she had at the table. "He resented Jeff for some reason. He couldn't resist taking a dig at him, even tonight, at what was supposed to be a memorial."

"I thought he was the only honest one of the bunch." Maddy shot a look back at the door, which remained safely closed behind them. "They were all talking like he was some kind of god."

"He could be charming." Becca sounded thoughtful, rather than sad. "And he was good at getting his way. Plus, it sounds like he was getting some big money. That could cause some hard feelings."

Maddy snorted. "You just don't want to blame her because you *do* blame her, and you feel guilty."

"What?" Becca's face scrunched up in confusion.

"Renee." Maddy spoke the name like it was obvious. "You're looking for motives in his work, but I'd look at the girlfriend. To me, it sounded like Jeff was cheating on her. We know that's his pattern, and we know the cops said there were reports of a man and a woman arguing."

"That's a stretch." Becca eyed her friend.

"Is it? She was talking about someone sending him messages. Messages that threatened *her*." Maddy stressed the last word. "Why do you think she asked you to come? Don't tell me you think she was just being nice."

"I wanted to think so." Becca shrugged. "But no. I think she wanted to check me out. Maybe she was just curious."

"She was jealous. You're twice the woman she is, and didn't you say Jeff had been in touch?"

"He'd texted, but we never talked," Becca mumbled, staring at the pavement. "He said something about wanting to look at my laptop. Check out my security."

"Your laptop, right." Maddy scoffed. "What do you want to bet Renee found out that he was trying to get in touch with you again? What if she knew something about what he really intended." She paused, turning to her friend on the sidewalk. In the dark, her expression was hard to see, but the tightness in her voice gave her away. "You didn't—you haven't been seeing him, have you?"

"No. Though I got his last message right before my last date with Jerry—Dr. Keller—and..."

"Great." Maddy sighed out her exasperation. "That vet is a nice guy."

Becca, clearly wanting to change the conversation, took her friend's hand and began to walk away from the bar. "You just hate Renee."

"Don't you?"

Becca smiled at her. "The whole 'jealous girlfriend' idea could include me, you know."

"The police are just being careful. And, well, you were there. But it should be clear to anyone you've moved on. We're talking a year ago. More," Maddy demurred. "And if it wasn't you, well, there was someone... I should have guessed. Jeff was always a secretive creep."

"Maddy,"

"No, don't defend him, Becca. You know I'm right. Even when things were good, he was always up to something."

"Maybe." Becca turned thoughtful, looking up to the night sky. "But whatever it was, he certainly didn't expect it to get him killed."

Twelve

"W*hat kept you?*" Laurel's distinctive voice rose in a querulous whine as she sniffed her baby sister. "*Why didn't you send word?*"

Clara had just popped through the door, rushing to beat Becca as she climbed the stairs. Their human would expect all three of her cats to greet her after an evening out, and the calico didn't want to give her cause for concern.

"*I'll explain as soon as—*"

The sound of a key brought Harriet from the kitchen, and the big marmalade pushed her way between her siblings.

"*Enough of that,*" she said in her no-nonsense mew. "*First things first. We haven't had dinner yet.*"

Aware of her big sister's priorities, Clara held her silence. There was so much she wanted to share, though. And she also wanted to know if anything had happened with the kitten, whose presence she could sense, moving around in the pantry.

"*Later,*" Harriet ordered.

Well, thought Clara, at least the kitten seemed unharmed.

"Hey, kitties." Becca dumped her bag and went straight into the kitchen, escorted by all three felines. "Let's try an experiment tonight."

"Experiment?" Even as she twined around Becca's legs, Laurel's voice rose in a peevish howl. *"She's not going to try a new food, is she?"*

"Isn't that your territory?" Harriet pushed her out of the way. Her comment wasn't exactly fair, thought Clara. Laurel did have a gift for implanting ideas in humans' heads, but she couldn't control everything their person thought. But as the evening routine unfolded—a can for Harriet, another for Laurel, and, finally, her own—the smallest cat had another thought: Harriet was not only her usual bossy self. She was extremely calm, as if she knew…

"Okay, kitten, would you like to join us?"

Clara started up in alarm. If her siblings attacked the kitten, she'd have to move fast. Becca alone wouldn't be able to save the newcomer. With Laurel's speed and Harriet's heft…

But, no. Harriet barely paused, lifting her head to lick her chops as the tiny tortie peeked out, blinking, before taking her first tentative steps back into the kitchen.

"Mew," she said.

"What did I tell you?" Harriet's aside to Laurel dripped with condescension.

Holding herself at high alert, Clara stared at her sisters, who, much to her amazement, simply sat there as the kitten stepped toward the cats' food dishes. Even when Becca turned toward the cabinet once more, her sisters didn't pounce. And as the kitten began to lap up her own can, served on one of Becca's teacup saucers, Harriet and Laurel only watched.

"What's going on?" Clara asked.

Harriet and Laurel exchanged a glance. *"While you were out, we were hard at work,"* said Laurel, wrapping her brown-tipped tail around her front paws. *"You could say we did a cat scan."*

A grunt from Harriet sounded more like disapproval than a laugh. *"What Laurel means is that I did a thorough examination of this little interloper, with your sister's assistance, of course."* That was high praise from the big cat, and Laurel's eyes closed in satisfaction.

"What did you do?" Clara's voice quivered. The tortoiseshell kitten appeared unharmed and had, in fact, at that moment, looked up from her plate, gazing at the bigger cats with unblinking green eyes. But Clara had been the butt of her big sisters' teasing often enough to know that they didn't always have the best sense of what could hurt a smaller creature.

"We are not monsters." Harriet didn't have to read her littlest sister's mind to understand her fears. *"We simply...asked questions."*

"Quizzed it a little." Laurel chimed in.

"Her." Clara corrected her automatically, and then nearly bit her tongue. The last thing she wanted was to get into an argument with her sisters. That would do neither herself nor the kitten any good.

"Her," Harriet conceded with a dip of her head. *"Not that it matters. She's as dumb as a human."*

Clara didn't respond, turning instead to the kitten. Clearing her mind, she tried to focus on the black fur between the tortie's ears. *"What did you see? What happened?"*

All she got was blackness, as dark as that fur. Though whether that was the kitten's response—the alley had been deep in shadow, Clara had gathered—or the little tortie wouldn't or couldn't respond was beyond her.

"See what I mean?" Harriet's voice broke into her mind, clearing the blackness away. *"It—she—is a simple creature, really. Just an ordinary cat."*

Clara dipped her head, acknowledging the marmalade's conclusion—and her own failure. But from the way the kitten was watching the three larger felines, she retained a sneaking feeling that perhaps her big sister was wrong.

Thirteen

"I know, Maddy. I do."

Clara woke the next morning to the sound of her person's voice. Even before Becca had gotten dressed, even before she had fed the cats, she had taken a phone call from her friend. Now she was nodding as she made her way into the kitchen, felines in tow, to properly begin the day.

"I let her out last night," she was saying. "And they all seem to get along, which is a relief. But, yes, you're right. I don't want to take her to a shelter, though. I'll ask Dr. Keller if he knows of anyone who is looking for a kitten."

"She's going to get rid of the tortie." For reasons she didn't fully understand, this was upsetting to Clara. Harriet, who was waiting for her dish, didn't respond, but Laurel provided the voice of reason.

"We were in the shelter, silly. It's how most cats find their people."

"Yes, I know." Clara couldn't shake the sinking feeling. *"But we were different."*

Was the tortie? Clara couldn't tell. Nor could she explain her unease to her siblings as, if on cue, the kitten emerged yawning from the now-open pantry.

Becca sounded like she was considering the same question as she pulled out four cans for the resident felines.

"She's a social little creature, and she seems to get along with my other cats. No, Maddy, I know. I'm not going to turn into some crazy cat lady. I'm just, well, I'm fostering her until I can find her a good forever home."

From the pinched expressions on Becca's face, Clara guessed that her friend had thoughts about this. But before she could try to eavesdrop further, or at least comfort her person with a soft rub against her bare ankles, her own dish was placed on the mat before her.

"If you don't want that..." Harriet's almost lion-like mane pushed over.

"No, I do, I do." And with that, Clara set to work.

Becca was still on the phone ten minutes later, as all three of the older cats were fastidiously washing their faces and forepaws.

"Honestly, Maddy, you sound like you don't believe me." She paused. "About the kitten at least."

Laurel had been working on her, Clara knew. Suggesting that the kitten had to go. That probably explained the note of tension in Becca's voice, her cat thought. Though it could also be the hour. While cats have no use for human timekeeping, the calico had lived with Becca long enough to know that her person was always concerned with what she called "running late," and the way she was grabbing at her coat suggested that this was one of those occasions.

Before Clara had finished with her whiskers, Becca was out the door. Conflicted, the calico turned back, toward where her older sisters lounged by the sofa, still bathing.

"Go." Harriet paused from her grooming to respond to the unspoken question. *"We're not going to harm that little thing."*

Laurel blinked slowly in agreement, and so, wiggling her butt, Clara leaped, making her way through the door and down the apartment stairs, in pursuit of Becca.

Her person was speed-walking down the sidewalk when her phone began to buzz again. Considering how rushed Becca seemed, Clara wasn't surprised when her person ignored it at first, only pulling it from her bag when the vibrating hum kept on, as persistent as a trapped bee.

Pausing on the sidewalk, she frowned at the tiny screen, before finally holding the device to her ear.

"Renee, hi," she said, beginning to walk again. "Thanks for inviting me last night. I'm sorry if I seemed to run out right when —" She broke off, evidently listening to the woman on the other end.

"No, I'm sorry. I haven't spoken to him." Walking this quickly had brought Becca in sight of the brightly colored storefront. "Look, I'm just arriving at work. I've got to go."

"That was weird," she said to herself as she fished the keys from her bag and let herself in. Turning on the lights and flipping the "Closed" sign to "Open," she seemed to regain her equanimity. "Maybe Jeff was cheating on her. But if she thinks I'm some kind of femme fatale..."

After hanging her coat in the back room, she grabbed a dust cloth and began to vigorously attack the front shelves, which had gone a bit gray. Clara had just settled on one of the clean shelves, watching as Becca reached for a crystal globe when a cheery jangling caught both their attention.

"Welcome to Charm and Cherish," Becca called, replacing the ball as she brushed the dust from her own top.

"And charming it is," replied the newcomer. Flipping a fall of auburn hair from his eyes, he scanned the shelves with a broad smile, apparently unaware of the dust Becca hadn't reached yet. As he turned, Clara noticed how short the rest of his hair was, only slightly longer than the neat beard, barely more than stubble, that covered a strong jaw. Taking in his jacket, a dark plaid with the same rust color running through it, her cat recalled that this was what her person would call a style choice. Something that signaled affluence, she remembered someone—maybe Maddy—saying. Whatever it mean, she felt a twinge of concern as Becca glanced down at her own hastily thrown together jeans and sweater outfit with a self-conscious frown before stepping forward.

"Thank you," she responded a tad belatedly to his compliment, brushing once more at her sleeve. "We do try to offer a full range of books, charms, and art pieces designed for the Wiccan or simply spiritually curious consumer."

Clara perked up. Becca never talked like this.

"The spiritually curious?" The stranger turned his smile on Becca, as if he sensed something off as well.

Becca blushed and ducked her head. "I know, that sounds weird," she admitted. "We're not supposed to say magic, because, well, you know. So many people don't believe."

"And you think I'm one of them?" A note of humor crept into the stranger's voice. "But, I'm sorry, I'm getting ahead of myself. I'm Darian, Darian Hughes."

"Becca Colwin." Becca took the stranger's outstretched hand. "How may I help you today?"

"You already have," said Darian. "I was told about the charming Charm and Cherish, and now I see that my colleague wasn't exaggerating."

"Your colleague?" Clara wasn't quite sure why Becca seemed on edge. While it was true that the newcomer wasn't the little shop's average customer, he didn't seem that odd. Increasingly, Becca's neighborhood, even her own building, had become populated by well-dressed young men, the kind that made Maddy cluck her tongue and roll her eyes.

"Carl Rimsky," Darian replied.

"Are you at CodePhool?"

"No." The handsome stranger chuckled. "I have an office nearby, though. Maybe that's why Carl suggested I come by."

"Funny, I don't think Carl's ever been in here." Becca crossed her arms across her chest and then, as if she realized what she must look like to a potential customer, apologized. "I'm sorry," she said. "Carl's a good guy. It's just been a rough week."

"I get it." Darian nodded, sending that shock of hair back into his eyes. "He told me about Jeff Blakey. I gather he was a friend of yours too? I'm so sorry."

"Thanks." Becca swallowed. "Jeff and I..." She broke off.

Only a few feet away, Clara longed to go to her. Her cat knew that appearing unexpectedly here, in Becca's workplace, would do more harm than the gentle pressure of soft fur would ease, but it was hard to feel useless when her person was in such obvious distress.

The stranger must have had the same instinct. "Oh, please, Becca. Don't cry." He pulled a handkerchief from inside his jacket and stepped forward. "I'm so sorry. I shouldn't have said anything."

"No, really. It's, well, it's just a shock." The stranger's solicitude must have done the trick, because Becca managed to summon a smile, wiping her eyes with the back of her hand. "And that was totally unprofessional of me as well. Now, what can I help you with? Were you looking for a particular book or a charm? Or maybe some incense?"

"Never mind that now." Tucking his handkerchief back into his pocket, he leaned in. "Would you be able to take a break? I think I owe you a cup of tea, at the very least."

"I just opened." Becca shook her head, the color rising to her cheeks. "But thanks."

"Very well, then. I was looking for something like this." He reached up to the globe Becca had been dusting. "In my line of work, I could use a crystal ball."

"Aren't you in software?" Becca's brows rose. That piece was one of the priciest in the store.

"More or less." He turned the ball over in his hands before handing it to her. "But that doesn't mean I don't believe in magic."

She took the globe and ducked under the counter, hiding her grin as she pulled out several pieces of tissue paper. But even as she bent over her task, wrapping the heavy piece, something of her smile, or maybe it was the color in her cheeks, must have communicated itself to the handsome stranger, because he perked up as well.

"Speaking of," he said as she handed him a paper bag with the shop's star logo on the side. "Any chance I could take you out for dinner tonight?"

Fourteen

"We sold the crystal ball!" Becca's excitement must have shocked Margaret. Her elderly boss stopped short as she stepped into the shop, her perpetual scowl transformed as her eyes widened in surprise. "I didn't even have to offer a discount."

"No discount?" Margaret's deep-set eyes took on a quizzical expression. "Are you sure?"

"I'm sure," Becca reassured her.

The polar opposite of her mystical sister, Margaret Cross was short, squat, and usually in a foul mood. But over her months at Charm and Cherish, and especially as her sister Elizabeth took over the day-to-day management of the little store, Becca had grown accustomed to the store owner's abrupt manner. At any rate, she was no longer put off by her borderline rudeness.

"Great, now I have to order another." The scowl returned. "Did she get you to throw in the stand?"

"He," corrected Becca. The proprietor's brows went even higher. Even Clara knew that most of Charm and Cherish's clientele were female. "And no. He didn't even ask how much it cost, just said he wanted it."

Margaret's lower lip jutted out in a surly pout exaggerated by her dark red lipstick.

"The payment went through." Becca anticipated her next query. "Darien Hughes."

"Sounds like a made-up name." The scowl deepened. "One of your warlock types, I gather."

"No, he's in software. And we say witch, even for men." Becca paused, as if she were about to say more, and then concluded limply. "He seemed nice."

"Seemed like he had money, you mean." Margaret's dark eyes turned on her employee. "Don't confuse the two, young lady."

"Well, he was a good customer." Becca, slightly cowed, didn't mention that she'd agreed to meet the good-looking redhead for a drink after her shift. It wasn't a deception, simply an omission, and Clara understood that Becca's boss was not as sympathetic as her sister.

Still, the little calico worried that something wasn't quite right, a suspicion that only grew as the day wore on. Even following Margaret's departure—the boss never stayed long—Becca couldn't seem to settle down. Whereas usually she'd pull one of the many thick tomes from the shelf and read at her post behind the register until a customer came in, today she kept walking around, following the dusting with a thorough cleaning of the window. Becca had just sprayed the display case below the register when her phone buzzed, and Clara looked on, hoping the call would break the cycle of nervous activity.

Instead, Becca tensed, and although her face relaxed as she listened to the low voice on the other end of the line, it wasn't enough to put her pet at ease.

"Thank you, Dr. Keller. When I saw your number, I was worried. I let the kitten out of isolation this morning, and I'd feel terrible if it turned out she was ill."

Clara paused, taken aback by her person's comment. Of course, the kitten wasn't ill. Clara and her sisters would have sensed such a thing. Once again, the calico was reminded of her person's shortcomings—and also her caring heart. It was nice to know she worried about them, even if such concerns were misguided.

But while she was thinking this through, the conversation had continued. "Dinner?" Becca appeared to be asking the air, rather than the phone in her hand. "No, I'm sorry. I can't. I've got a work thing tonight."

Even after hanging up, Becca appeared restless, gnawing at her lip as if it were a chew toy. Clara, watching as her person went back to her dusting, suspected she knew why. The person she loved was usually both honest and straightforward. Talking to the kindly vet, she had lied.

Clara was mulling over this unsettling development as Becca got ready to close, turning off lights and moving the most tempting pieces out of sight. With the longer daylight, she and Elizabeth had discussed keeping the little shop open, but the sisters hadn't yet hired another clerk. And while Elizabeth sometimes staffed the shop, and a sign on the door listed a phone number for after-hours access, as the clock ticked toward six, the older sister failed to appear.

"I wonder if I should wait." Becca checked the time. Usually, Clara knew, her person would linger in the shop, not even starting to turn off the lights until the posted closing time. However, she was already moving the magic mirror—a pretty piece studded with semi-precious stones—out of its place of prominence in the front window back into the storage room, when the hanging bells announced a late visitor.

"Be right out," Becca called from the back room. Laying the mirror on a shelf, she wiped her hands and headed toward the door even as Tina, from her coven, stuck her head into the back room.

"Becca! I'm so glad I caught you." Tina's cheeks were bright red and her chest was heaving. "You won't believe what I found!"

"Here, sit down." Becca beckoned the other woman to a chair. "Catch your breath. I'm going to lock the front door."

When she returned moments later, the other woman's

panting had normalized but her face was still bright. From excitement, Clara realized.

"Tell," Becca commanded, taking a seat on the break room's old sofa.

"Well, I didn't intend to go over there so soon," Tina began. "My team is finishing up a big project so we've been working late, but we'd actually gotten ahead of ourselves, and we need to wait for the hardware before we can—"

"Wait, you're in software too?" Becca looked a little flustered.

"Kind of. I'm helping out this mid-size startup that's got an incubator space over by Tech."

Becca held up a hand to stop her from saying more. "I'm sorry. I don't mean to be rude, and I shouldn't have asked. I'm actually supposed to be someplace in about twenty minutes."

"Oh, no problem." Tina shifted in her seat, shoving her hand into her pocket to dig around. "I just wanted you to know that I got over to the alley, like, ten minutes ago. The crime scene tape was ripped, so I figured there was no problem with me going in."

Becca bit her lip but didn't interrupt.

"Anyway, I went right to the back and used my phone light to go over every square inch. It was really disgusting."

Becca nodded but kept her lips clenched shut.

"And just as I was about to give up, I saw something reflect back." Pulling her hand from her pocket, she opened her palm to show Becca her prize: a key with a twist of red yarn tied on it, its broad brass head marked with a dab of bright red.

Becca gasped.

"Don't worry," said the other woman, poking at the red spot. "It's not blood. It's hard, like paint or plastic. I realized too late that it might have fingerprints on it. I wish I'd thought to wear gloves, but since I'd already picked it up, I figured I couldn't take the chance of someone else finding this, you know?"

"I do." Becca reached for the key, but paused. "Do you mind?"

Tina shook her head. "Do you think it's a clue?"

"I don't know." Becca spoke softly, her face unreadable. "I mean, I don't think so."

Her visitor looked at her quizzically, for once without words.

"Unless I'm very much mistaken, this is a key to my apartment," explained Becca, looking back up at her colleague. To explain, she turned the metal piece over before digging in her own pocket. "Yes, see? They're a match."

Tina craned over to look and sighed with what Clara could only assume was disappointment. "Oh wow. Maybe you dropped it, then? When you were in the alley?"

"No." Becca shook her head, her voice growing thoughtful once more. "This was Jeff's. The red dot." She ran her forefinger gently over the raised spot as if polishing its shiny surface. "It's nail polish. It was supposed to be a heart."

She fell silent, staring at the key, her eyes filling. More than ever, Clara wanted to go to her so she could headbutt those unshed tears away.

"I'm sorry." Tina's voice had grown softer too. "I got so caught up, I forgot you two were involved."

"No matter." Becca blinked back the tears back as she forced a smile. "We were over a year ago. And besides, you might have just saved me some trouble."

Tina shook her head.

Becca lifted the key by its yarn tail. "Well, if the police had found this, they might have wondered why he was carrying it around." Her voice grew thoughtful. "Though, come to think of it, I wonder why he was too. I mean, a lot has happened since then. He could have just tossed it."

"Maybe he didn't want to." Tina scanned her face.

"Nah, I don't believe that." Becca shook her off. "But it is something we should talk about. Maybe the circle will be able to raise some answers."

"We're not meeting tonight, are we?"

"No, tomorrow." Becca sat up. "But that reminds me, I should run."

"Are you doing more investigating?"

"Not really." Becca was reaching for her coat, so Tina couldn't see the faint flush that had colored her cheeks. "I had an interesting conversation with a client earlier, and he asked me for a drink."

"Good for you." Tina stood as well. "Get back on the horse!"

Becca rolled her eyes. "We've only just met, but Darien does seem like a nice guy."

"Darien?" Tina's eyes went wide. "Darien Hughes?"

"Yeah." Becca took in her colleague's shock. "Uh-oh, what should I know? Is he another serial cheater? He's not your ex or anything, is he?"

"No, he isn't. But," she paused, "you really don't know?"

"No, tell me."

"Darien Hughes is a legend. He invented that app that matches your personality with music. You know, Your New Favorite Song. And since he's sold that, he's become the principal in the biggest venture capital fund on the East Coast."

"Oh." Becca's brow furrowed.

"I don't know why you're looking so worried," her friend added. "You've got a date with the richest man in the city. And he's cute too."

Fifteen

Becca did not seem as pleased by this information as Tina seemed to expect. In fact, she responded to this news with a string of muttered words about what Bast should do that had both her coven colleague and her shaded cat reeling.

"I'm sorry." Becca caught herself, shaking her head. "You just caught me by surprise—or rather, *he* did. But maybe he has his reasons, and besides, there's always the rule of three."

Tina's wide-open face was blank with confusion.

"You don't remember?" When the other woman only shook her head, Becca explained. "The rule of three is simple: whatever energy we give out, we get back three-fold," she said. "Good vibes or bad. It's kind of the Wiccan golden rule."

"That makes sense." Tina smiled and nodded. "Thanks."

"I'm surprised you didn't remember us talking about it when we all met. But never mind." Becca must have picked up on Tina's embarrassment, as she bowed her head in a way that made Clara think she wanted to hide. At any rate, Clara's person had a date to keep.

"I should go," she said, donning her coat.

As she walked Tina to the front door, Clara trotted along behind, and as Becca paused first to unlock the door and then to flip its front door sign, she took the opportunity to thoroughly sniff the short brunette. She and her sisters hadn't paid much attention to the newest member of the coven when she had showed up at Becca's a few weeks before. The three cats found the gatherings generally annoying—too many feet and, too often, the disconcerting odors of incense or candles. Each had made their peace with the meetings: for Harriet, the cookies were key, while Laurel enjoyed the opportunity to implant ideas about the divinity of felines in the Wiccans' minds, and Clara appreciated the warmth their person got from her friends. But, in truth, they had begun to take the gatherings for granted.

Now, as she breathed in unfamiliar scents, Clara wished she had her sisters with her. Laurel might have been able to sense something in the newcomer's thoughts, while Harriet would certainly have found a way to distract her, even if only by conjuring a furball. Clara was grateful for her abilities, being able to pass through solid objects and shade herself into invisibility. But beyond that, she had only her heart to guide her. And both her heart and the common cat sense that their feral mother had licked into them all told her that a would-be witch who couldn't remember the most basic rule of all was either deluded about the coven and the magic it claimed to practice. Or she had joined the group for reasons of her own. Reasons, Clara feared, that might not have Becca's best interests at their core.

Becca didn't seem to be worrying about the coven's newest member, however, as she walked swiftly away from the shop. She and Tina had parted outside Charm and Cherish, both agreeing to bring up Tina's find and Becca's questions the next night, when the group would have its delayed circle. But by the time the other woman had disappeared into the rush hour crowd, Becca appeared to have forgotten her. Once again, Clara longed for her sister's telepathy. It wasn't that she wanted her person to worry overmuch about the delicate brunette, but she did wish Becca would be a bit less trusting of everyone who came into her orbit.

Maybe some of that desire communicated itself to Becca, because her person was clearly on full alert as she approached the end of the next block. Despite the flow of foot traffic, which threatened to sweep Clara along, Becca had stopped in front of a plate glass window. Inside, Clara could see a crowd of fashionably dressed young people, some sitting on stools by a bar backlit by colorful neon, others resting pints and martini glasses on a wooden shelf that seemed to span the length of the front window. To the cat, the movement and play of light were about as intriguing as a window on a flock of pigeons—tantalizing but, without scent, not terribly exciting. Becca, however, seemed mesmerized, and, tearing herself away from the sight of a nearly full tumbler that was just itching to be knocked on the floor, Clara made herself focus. Yes, Becca had located the handsome man who had been in the shop earlier. Darien Hughes, the VC millionaire.

"Becca!" The red-haired man rose from a barstool as Becca pushed the door open and entered, Clara hard on her heels. The sudden influx of scent and warmth almost overwhelmed the little calico's senses, and she had to move fast to keep from being kicked by some very pointy-toed pumps. But she managed to both keep her appearance cloaked and her tail untrodden as Darien signaled to a waiter and then waded through the crowd to greet Becca and escort her in.

"I got us a table," he said as the waiter signaled from the bar's end. "No pressure, we'll just have a drink. They know me here, though, and I thought it would be nice to be able to talk." He laughed. "Talk and actually be able to hear each other, I mean."

Becca's smile had a tight quality that made Clara think she didn't share Darien's sense of humor. "That's fine," was all she said as she followed the waiter past the bar to a cozy back room.

At this hour, most of the tables were empty, but Darien chose one in the corner, with a small vase of spring flowers livening its bare blond wood. Grateful for the quiet, Clara went to work, trying to sort out the various scents emanating from this man. Quickly filtering out the smell of that table arrangement as well as the tantalizing aromas from the kitchen—was that cheese? Chicken?—she did her best to sniff around the man's lace-up leather shoes. She got polish and a soft warmth, which made her think of a craftsman's careful hands. But the constant bouncing of one leg against another made her task difficult. Clara certainly didn't want to get kicked, and she also didn't want to give herself away by grabbing at those bouncing toes. That didn't mean she was going to back off. Something about that movement made her think this Darien wasn't right, and she needed to investigate. She wasn't sure how she would be able to communicate whatever she found to her person. It didn't matter: as Becca's cat, she needed to know who her person was dealing with.

"Would you like to hear our specials?" The waiter hovered.

"I think we're just going to have drinks, Remy," said Darien. "Unless?"

He turned to Becca, but she shook her head, that same tight smile still in place. "I'll have a cider, thanks," she said, and waited while Darien gave his order, one of the seasonal draft beers the bar apparently had on tap. As soon as their server had taken off, Darien turned to Becca with a smile. But before he could say anything, Becca leaned forward.

"Let's start over," said Becca, laying her hands flat on the table. "How do you know Jeff, for real?"

Sixteen

To his credit, the handsome financier didn't try to deny anything.

"I'm sorry," he said as soon as he'd caught his breath. "I didn't mean to deceive you. I'm—I *was*—backing Jeff. I mean, I *am* in software. That's true. I was a developer, but now I'm basically a venture capitalist. I gather you figured that out?"

Becca nodded. A certain stiffness in her legs told her cat that she wasn't entirely mollified by this confession, however. "Your name came up."

"Google." He sighed. "That *Boston Globe* piece was wrong, though. I'm not the richest man in Cambridge, or whatever it was they said."

"Boston." Becca had done a quick search on Hughes as she had walked to their date.

"Whatever." That foot was bouncing faster now, tempting Clara to swipe at it. Anything to alert Becca. "But that's not the point. I should have been open with you. My only explanation is that since that piece ran, people act differently toward me when I meet them. Money should make everything easier, but it doesn't."

"I get it." Becca appeared to be relaxing. Clara wasn't, and when Becca continued to question the man across the table, she felt a glow of pride. "But that doesn't really answer my question. How did you get to know Jeff, and why were you looking to speak with me?"

"Those are good questions." Darien paused and, to Clara's surprise, his foot stopped moving too. That might have been because the waiter had returned with their drinks, but the cat wasn't going to lower her guard just yet. "The best way I can answer is by talking you through what might seem like a long story."

"I'm listening." Becca's words sounded skeptical. Her tone, however, had softened.

"Jeff and I go way back." With that, the financier shifted, as if to hold off any objection, and Clara decided to try another tack. Rather than relying on scent alone, she would move to a chair at the empty table beside the couple. Sight isn't as important to cats as smell, but Clara wanted the advantage of both if she was going to suss out what was happening.

Darien, meanwhile, continued to speak. "We'd fallen out of touch in recent years, but in college, we'd collaborated on a couple of projects together. In fact, we'd worked on an early protection program, much like Jeff was doing for CodePhool. Then I took the personalization concept in a different direction and, well, I got lucky. But when Jeff came up with his new idea, he reached out to me."

"Okay." Becca sipped her cider.

"I thought it really had potential. Big potential. Plus, I missed working with Jeff. I like how he thinks—how he thought. I'm sorry." Another pause, less awkward this time.

Becca's voice, when she spoke again, had grown more relaxed, but no less urgent.

"But what brought you to me?"

"Jeff always spoke so highly of you. No, really." Darien fended off Becca's burgeoning objection with a wave. "I know you're not in software, but he really respected your intelligence. He said he could bounce ideas off of you, and you served as a reality check."

"Well, I might have idiot-proofed some of his work, but that's it."

"Don't put yourself down." Darien was sounding more confident. "His faith in you is why I decided to track you down."

Becca looked up, the question clear on her face.

"Jeff's project, his legacy, is too good to abandon. He had a smart idea that could revolutionize software. Only, he hadn't gotten his team up and running yet, which means that development is still kind of nebulous."

"But you're still going to continue with it, right?" This seemed to matter to Becca. "I mean, if it's that good."

"Yes, yes, of course." Darien brushed aside her concern. "Jeff had everything planned out. The only question is who takes his place at the helm."

He shifted, leaning over the table toward Becca. "A lot of people want in on this project, Becca. A lot of talented coders and software designers who could scale Jeff's project to the next level. But I wanted to talk to someone who knew him, knew who he was outside of work. I don't need help with the software part. I need help with figuring out who Jeff would trust, who he would want to carry on with his dream."

The table fell silent as Darien took a deep draft of his beer and Becca stared at her own pint glass, as if the golden cider held some secret she hoped to learn. When she finally broke the silence, Clara was struck by the quiet sadness in her voice.

"I don't think I'm the person you want to talk to." She could have been addressing the cider, but Darien leaned closer. "Jeff and I hadn't spoken in a while, and the way we left things... We weren't on the best of terms."

As if gathering courage, she took a deep breath and sat up straight. "You know he had a new girlfriend, right? Renee would have been much more up to date on whatever Jeff was working on. Besides, she's in that world, or at least she's software adjacent. I gather she's some kind of designer and worked with CodePhool. I think that's how they met."

That admission seemed to take it out of Becca, and she

slumped back in her chair. Reaching for her drink, she must have missed the gentle smile that spread across her companion's face.

"I knew you'd say that." He shook his head. "Jeff always said you downplayed your own comprehension, and now that we've met, I can see what he meant. Why he trusted you. But you're wrong on this. I know Renee, and I've spoken to her, but I'm not asking for her take on this. You could say it's because she's too close to CodePhool. I don't know, but I've done pretty well by following my instincts, Becca. You're the one I want to talk to. The person whose judgment I trust."

Seventeen

Two hours later, Becca was walking home when she called Maddy.

"I don't know, Maddy," she was saying. "He came on pretty strong."

As she detailed the evening to her buddy, Clara looked on with concern. On one paw, she was grateful for her person's apparent skepticism. Becca had been taken in by charming men before, and her pet knew she hadn't fully recovered from the breakup with Jeff. On the other, Becca had stayed with the wealthy investor considerably longer than she had originally intended, allowing herself to be talked into having dinner with him. While it was true that the talk had turned to Jeff's colleagues, with Becca giving the financier her limited take on the CodePhool crowd, as the meal progressed the conversation became less about Jeff's project and more like what one would expect on a first date, at least according to her cat's limited experience with those.

Clara couldn't fault her person for that. She'd been lonely for a while, the cat knew, and the red-haired man had been good company, asking Becca questions about her own work and interests. However, that meant that Becca was lying to Maddy, or at least not sharing the entire truth.

"He kept going on about how close he was to Jeff and how much he respected him." Becca was still talking. "But I don't remember Jeff ever mentioning him. Carl, yeah, because they worked together. And maybe even that guy Theo who was sitting next to you. But Darien? No.

"Darien? Yes, that's him. Darien Hughes." Becca seemed to be answering a question, and the cat looked up to gauge her person's reaction. "I don't know, Maddy. We talked about Jeff's project. He's really into it; like, he really believes it could be the next big thing in tech. But he's nervous about something. He says it's about who to hire to continue with it, but I don't know."

Maddy must have had questions, because Becca started nodding.

"Yeah, I told him. I think he wanted an outsider's take—an outsider who knew Jeff. But it must be a really big deal if he's that anxious about who to give it to, right?

"All I can tell you for sure is that he was super nice. He paid for dinner, and he asked me for my number. I mean, if it weren't for the whole thing with Jeff, I would've thought it was a date."

"A date?" Harriet was appalled.

Clara had reported the evening's events as soon as she had slipped into the apartment. Her sisters, alerted to Becca's imminent arrival, had been waiting by the door, Harriet's mood certainly not improved by the hour. The fluffy marmalade liked her meals to be served on time. But as the siblings listened in on Becca's call, the oldest sister soon had other reasons to be upset.

"Maybe he'll be nice." Laurel, who prided herself on her way with men, closed her eyes in satisfaction. She'd been wanting to match Becca up with someone for a while now, and although she'd begun to accept the idea of the kindly vet, she'd been quite vocal about her belief that their person could do better. *"More money means more treats, especially if he wants to endear himself to Becca."*

"I don't care!" Harriet caterwauled. *"She doesn't need anyone else. She barely has time for us as it is!"*

"I've got to run, Maddy." Becca, ending the call, scooped up the big marmalade. "Harriet, were you afraid I wasn't coming home?"

"No." The big cat struggled to be released, hitting the floor with a thud. *"You don't get to cuddle us until after we've been fed."*

"She was trying to comfort you." Clara understood her sister's pique, but she couldn't help but be moved by Becca's obvious dismay as their chastened person followed Harriet into the kitchen. As the small procession continued, Clara was seized by a growing sense of alarm.

"Harriet..." She did her best to keep her voice, even her inner voice, calm and gentle. It wouldn't help the situation if she sounded accusatory. *"Where's the kitten?"*

It was too late. Harriet was laser focused on Becca, who was in the process of opening a can.

"Laurel?" Clara could hear the urgency creeping into her voice.

So could her other sister. *"Cool your jets, Clown."* The familiar insult, Clara the calico, Clara the clown, sounded particularly snide in Laurel's Siamese drawl. *"She's here somewhere."*

Clara, ignoring her own can, began to search frantically, dashing back to the living room to peer under the sofa, wondering where a scared kitten would hide. Becca, either picking up on her pet's anxiety or her own growing realization that the smallest feline in the apartment was missing, followed, before turning on her heels and returning to the kitchen.

"There you are!" Emerging from the pantry, she held up the tortie. Blinking drowsily, the kitten yawned and looked around, apparently surprised to find herself being transported. "Look who I found sleeping behind the pasta sauce," Becca said as she lowered the kitten down to the cats' communal food mat and placed a fourth dish before her.

"Told you," Laurel murmured, her brown snout deep in her

own dish. Harriet only flicked her tail, and Clara, relieved, bent toward her own dinner.

"How was she today?" Ten minutes later, the three adult cats were grooming. The kitten, meanwhile, had trotted off after Becca, who had retreated to the bedroom to change. *"Did she say anything?"*

"Nothing." Harriet's tail lashed once as she ran a big white mitt over her ear. *"She's dumb as a post."*

"It is truly unusual," Laurel, who had bent herself into a corkscrew to better reach the small of her back, chimed in. *"Even with a creature that small, I'd usually get something."*

Clara mulled this over. In addition to her ability to read her sisters' minds, Laurel's sensitivity normally allowed her to pick up emotional states. And because the little calico knew her sister tended to exaggerate her skills, she also suspected what such an admission must cost her. No, if Laurel wasn't picking up anything, there was a good chance that Harriet's initial dismissal was correct.

Only, Clara couldn't be sure. There had been something, a flash, when she'd first met the kitten. It couldn't be that the tiny tortie was keeping silent for a reason, keeping silent and also blocking her older sisters' attempts to read her mind. Could it?

Clara's musings were interrupted by a cry from the bedroom that sent her running. She rounded the corner in time to see Becca bending over the kitten, who'd apparently chased, or pushed, something beneath the bed.

"If it's not live prey, why bother?" Laurel had come up behind her silently and now watched, bemused.

"What is it?" Clara, relieved that her person did not appear hurt or scared, watched as Becca bent to reach under the bed and emerged with a piece of metal in her hand. *"Oh, it's the key. She must have been going for the yarn."*

As Becca placed the key, which apparently had fallen out of her jeans pocket, on top of her bureau, Clara brought her sister up to date. *"I think Becca is wondering why Jeff had it on him,"* she concluded. *"I think she's wondering if he wanted to come back."*

"Too late for him." Laurel's ears flicked back. As much as the sealpoint might want their person to be coupled, she too remembered how badly the unfaithful programmer had hurt Becca. Clara agreed, but from the way Becca kept looking at the key with its red dot, she knew her person hadn't quite left the old romance behind.

Eighteen

"Rise and shine!*" Laurel was in a particularly chipper mood the next morning, even going so far as to gently cuff Clara's head as the calico stretched and yawned in the first dawn light. Hours before, the three cats had arrayed themselves around Becca's bed as their person slept. Harriet hadn't even complained when the kitten managed to make her way up to Becca's pillow, nestling down on top of her head sometime after midnight.

"You're up early." Harriet opened one yellow eye to glare at the sealpoint. At her low growl, Becca shifted in her sleep. It would be an hour yet before the alarm rang, but cats had no need of such devices.

"It's going to be a good day," Laurel replied, a certain smug tone creeping into her voice.

"Is the rich guy going to call?" Clara was used to her middle sister's priorities being slightly off, but after seeing Becca stay up way too late staring at that key last night and having waited her out as she tossed and turned, the calico almost welcomed the idea of a new suitor.

Harriet did not. *"No,"* she said, closing her eyes once more. *"We are not going to share our person again."*

There was no point in arguing with Harriet, ever, and certainly not when she was in this mood. Instead, Clara looked at Laurel, knowing that her sister wouldn't be able to resist sharing whatever insight had made her whiskers perk up like that.

"She's going to get a call," Laurel purred. *"From a new man."*

Clara ducked her head in acknowledgement and to hide her reaction. Laurel, she knew, could pick up her mixed emotions easily enough, but Clara hoped that her sister's self-satisfied contentment might buy her a little time.

A new man wasn't necessarily a bad thing, she told herself as she watched Becca sleep. Only, Clara was partial to the kind vet, Dr. Keller. With his slightly too large features, he might not be as handsome as Jeff was; even a cat could tell that Becca's late boyfriend had a boyish charm that the lanky veterinarian lacked. He most likely didn't have the resources of the handsome financier Becca had dined with only the night before either; Becca's few dates with the vet had been centered around coffee or burgers at a local pub. But Clara couldn't dismiss the care he took with her and her sisters, and with the kitten as well. Surely, that had to count for something.

Or did it? Clara was an honest feline, and as the spring sunlight leaked around the shade, she was forced to acknowledge that maybe she was just as biased as her sisters. Was she simply looking—or sniffing—for something off about this Darien because she didn't want him to outshine the gentle vet?

"I don't like any of them," Harriet grumbled as she settled back into the hollow she'd made in Becca's blankets. Laurel didn't bother to respond and instead jumped down to start her day, while the kitten slept on.

By the time Becca woke, the subject seemed to be forgotten. Becca appeared to be her usual self, at any rate, singing along with the radio as she dressed. She had already fed the cats, of course. The kitten had finished her half can, and Harriet was cleaning up the few remaining crumbs when a familiar rattle in the next room drew Clara's attention.

Leaving her own dish fairly clean, she peeked around the

corner to see Becca throwing a catnip mouse. The kitten took off after it, running in that awkward kitten style that soon had her moving sideways, her hindquarters moving faster than her forepaws.

"Is that my *mouse?"* Harriet had come up beside her, still licking her chops.

Clara couldn't remember the last time her hefty sister had chased the toy, not that she would say that.

Laurel, however, purred her assent. *"Remember the time you got so excited you fell off the—?"*

"No!" Harriet cut her off.

Clara began to wash her face, the better to hide her laughter as the kitten and the mouse made another headlong rush down the room.

The call, when it came, caught Becca at work, wiping down the small statuettes on display in the window. Clara, who'd been watching her person all morning, had almost come to believe her sister was wrong—until she heard the surprise in her person's voice.

"Oh, hi, Carl." *Carl.* Clara recalled the bearish software engineer, the one Becca had spoken with at Jeff's former workplace. Becca shifted, replacing a Bast whose ebony surface now glowed with a sheen that drew her cat's gaze. "No, I haven't heard anything yet. Why? Have you spoken to the police?"

Becca's voice tightened with tension, and her cat looked up from the shiny black figurine to see her person had gone pale.

"Oh, that's good." Relief then, and the little cat relaxed, silently thanking the cat goddess. "But, sure, I'd be happy to get together, though I don't really know what I can share. No, I'm sorry, tonight I'm busy." A pause, and Clara saw Becca's brows go up. "You are? Great, come on by."

Ten minutes later, the bells announced the arrival of the big programmer, clad in a fresh plaid flannel shirt, a plastic-wrapped bouquet of daisies in his hand.

"Hey, Becca." He held out the flowers with one paw-like hand. "These are for you."

"Thanks." Becca accepted the bouquet, burying her face in the fragrant spring flowers even as her forehead furrowed in confusion. Their scent was sweet and fresh, stronger, even, than the damp balm of the budding trees outside, but Clara got the sense her person was stalling, rather than indulging in what would, to a cat, be an intoxicating indulgence. However, before Becca could phrase a longer response or a question, her burly visitor rushed into an explanation.

"I saw them as I was walking past that florist, and I thought, well, Becca's had a loss." The blush creeping up his round face could have been due to that flannel—the bright June sun had warmed the crowded storefront—but Clara suspected a more personal motive. "Plus, it must have been so horrible, finding Jeff like that. I wanted to bring you something nice."

"Thanks." The word had more warmth to it this time, although it presented another dilemma. "Would you mind waiting for a moment?"

"Not at all." Carl had already started looking around the little shop as Becca ducked into the back. Unsure whether to follow her person or keep an eye on the newcomer, Clara jumped down from her perch on the shelf. Trotting over to the door, she saw Becca rinsing out a mason jar that had previously held Elizabeth's special blend of potpourri. Confident that her person wasn't going to need her help—and a little leery of that fast-running faucet—Clara turned back to the shop in time to see Carl as he moved from the front bookshelf to the window display, where he appeared to study first that Bast and then a flat object right nearby.

"There. That works." Becca emerged holding the makeshift vase with its bright bouquet, which she placed on the glass case by the register. "That was really thoughtful, Thanks, Carl."

"My pleasure." Carl turned a little too quickly, nearly knocking over a display of crystals.

"Careful." Becca leavened her warning with a smile. "I know, this place is kind of crowded."

"Honestly, it's great," he said, taking in the overpacked shelves and the walls hung with mandalas and charts. "I'm sorry I haven't come by sooner."

"I wouldn't have thought this was your kind of place." Becca leaned back against the counter. "I mean, I'm glad you like it, but, well, I know Jeff didn't think much of it."

"Jeff made some major mistakes," said Carl, his head bobbing.

"Oh?" Becca sat up. "In his programming? You don't think that's what got him—"

"No, no." The big man waved, as if to dispel the very idea. "I meant in terms of his life."

"I don't know. I know that it was a disappointment to you, but from what you've told me and from what I've learned from Darien Hughes, I think maybe he was making the right move."

"You've spoken to Darien Hughes?" Carl blinked in surprise.

Becca nodded. "He came by yesterday, and he told me more about Jeff's project." She gave a little laugh as she turned to take in the space on the bookshelf where the crystal globe had stood. "He seemed to think I knew more about it than I did. I mean, if you hadn't filled me in on what Jeff was doing, I'd have been totally lost."

"So he was asking you about Jeff's project?" Carl tilted his head, looking for all the world like Laurel inspecting a spider.

"Crazy, huh?" Becca didn't seem to notice. "I gather he wants to continue with it, but I gather everything is in disarray now, which makes sense."

Carl nodded sagely. "Jeff had great ideas, but as to writing the code..."

"Oh, I don't think it was that." Becca knew that much. "He was talking more about building a team, asking me who I thought Jeff would have hired. Things like that."

"So he's getting ready to hire." Another nod. "And he wanted your input?"

Becca ducked her head, the better to hide the pink creeping up to her face. "He told me that Jeff had spoken about me, which, well, I don't know. I think he might have me confused with Renee."

"No." Carl rejected the idea. "Jeff and Renee were on the rocks." He scanned Becca's face, as if he were waiting for a cue.

"You don't think Renee—I mean, she doesn't seem the type."

Carl's face went blank, his brows knotting as if he were confused.

"She wouldn't have hurt Jeff. Would she?"

"What? No." The big man scoffed, his lips pursing. "I only meant, well, I wonder if she was hanging around because she was hoping to cash in."

"I don't know. The police said they had a report of a man and woman arguing. I think that's why they questioned me," Becca said in a voice growing small.

That seemed to take Carl by surprise. "Wow, that's interesting. But it seems more likely it was just random street violence, doesn't it? I mean, wasn't he stabbed? The whole idea that someone who knew him could do that..."

"Yeah." Becca winced. After a moment's silence, she looked up again at her visitor. "So, I'm sorry, Carl, but why are you here again?"

"Well, I didn't know if you wanted to know more about Jeff's project. I figure I'm the obvious choice to continue with it, so I could explain it, if you're curious." He paused and seemed to dance on his toes for a moment. "I figure that's okay because I know he confided in you."

"But he didn't." She shook her head. "I don't know why people keep saying that."

"Well, anyway, if you want to know any more, the inside track, so to speak. You've been through a lot, so if maybe you'd like to get dinner some other night..." He tilted his head in what was probably supposed to be a boyish move and ended up looking rather like a confused bear.

"Oh." Becca seemed taken aback by the question, if not her visitor's ursine appearance. "Thanks. I don't—I mean, I do want to hear what's going on with the investigation. If you hear anything, that is."

"That's all I meant." The tall programmer rushed the denial out, waving away his earlier words. "I just want us to keep in touch, you know?"

"Yeah. Yes, I do." Becca, relieved, repeated herself. "And you have my number, obviously." She patted her pocket, a lost look suddenly replacing her friendly smile.

"Your phone?" Carl read her confusion. "I think I saw it over by the window. Hang on."

"Thanks." Becca gushed in relief as he retrieved the device. "Sometimes, I think I'd lose my head if it weren't attached to my neck."

"Don't even joke about that, Becca." The programmer reached out to place the phone in her palm, his hand warm over hers. "There are a lot of us out there who would miss you."

"Thanks." Becca studied the floor as he released her hand. "And thanks for the kind words. It's been weird, what with me and Jeff not being together and all."

"I get it," he said, his smile returning as he turned toward the door. "Unlike computers, humans don't run on only ones and zeroes. Speaking of, I couldn't help notice you're still on iOS 10. Do you want me to do an update? You should do those regularly, you know."

"Thanks, yeah, if it won't take too long." Becca shrugged, handing over the phone. "Jeff used to do that for me, and since then I haven't always kept up..."

"I get it." A few clicks, and he handed it over. "That should set you up. And, Becca? I know I'm not Jeff, but if you need anything. Any updates," he laughed softly, "please just call."

Becca watched in silence as her burly visitor ambled down the street, and then looked down at the phone, which was turning itself back on. When she turned to take in the daisies, sprouting like the spring sunshine from their makeshift vase, her expression grew pensive, and Clara didn't need Laurel's powers to make out what her person was thinking. Carl might have been Jeff's friend, rather than hers. He might have once urged her boyfriend to cheat on her. But now, in the wake of tragedy, he appeared to be courting Becca.

NINETEEN

The rest of Becca's afternoon passed uneventfully. As usual, browsers outnumbered buyers, although one young woman, clad entirely in black, did purchase three books on astrology and a package of incense. Clara was even considering a move to a sunny spot in the front window—a risk, given her desire to remain invisible—when she picked up the vibrations that signaled another visitor.

"Linda, right? How may I help you?" Becca prided herself on her memory for names, especially the names of good customers. But she wasn't quite sure which of the friendly couple from the other day had returned.

"That's right." The tall woman held up her conference badge in delight. "And you're Becca, yes?"

"And I'm not even wearing a name tag." Becca returned her friendly smile. "How's your conference going?"

"Kind of overwhelming, to be honest." Linda dropped her voice. "Everyone's got great ideas and most people are willing to share, but it's all about getting that unicorn investor, you know? And it's a very male energy."

"I do." Becca grew pensive, and then shook it off. "That makes me doubly glad you came back here. Is there anything I can help you with or did you just want to soak up some goddess vibes?"

That brought the grin back to the other woman's face. "Goddess vibes! Yeah, I could use some of those. But actually, yes. When we were here, Pam was looking at something, and I thought I'd surprise her."

"How nice. What was it?"

"A globe. Glass, or maybe it was crystal?" The tall woman scanned the nearest bookshelf, her plain face lit up with hope.

"A crystal ball?" Becca's own smile faded.

"I don't think it was, like, to tell fortunes." Linda sounded embarrassed. "I mean, not really. But it was pretty, and it had a nice wooden stand. I was sure it was on that shelf over here."

"It was, and it is. A crystal ball, that is." Becca rushed to explain. "But we sold it yesterday."

The other woman's disappointment was obvious.

"I'm so sorry." Becca was. "It's, well, it's a pricey piece, so we don't keep them in stock. But we should be able to get another pretty quickly, maybe within a week. How long are you in town for?"

"We're heading back to Des Moines right after the conference." From the look on Linda's face, the situation was hopeless, but Becca rallied.

"Let me get your contact info. If it doesn't come in time, maybe I could ship it."

Relief brought the tall Midwesterner's color back. "That would be great. Her birthday's not until next month, anyway."

The two moved over to the register, and as Linda jotted down her number and email, Becca looked on thoughtfully. From the way she gnawed on her lower lip, Clara knew she was mulling something over. "May I ask you a question?" she said finally. "Something's come up that's more your field than mine."

"Of course." Linda handed Becca back her pen.

"What usually happens with a startup once the founder is gone?"

Linda's brows went up. "That depends on what stage the startup was in and why the founder left."

"The project was fully funded and work had started," said Becca, ignoring the second part of Linda's question. "At least one other person wants to take it over, and the person funding it seems to want to keep it going."

Linda took her time before responding with some questions of her own. "And this wasn't just a theory or some pie-in-the-sky idea, right?"

"I don't think so." Becca shook her head. "It's really not my field, but from the way the people involved are talking, I'd say it's feasible."

"Then they'd most likely go ahead with it." Linda paused, her brown eyes focusing on Becca. "Is there some kind of problem?"

"I don't know." Another shake of the head. "It seems like there's some kind of hold up, and everyone seems to be asking me for input."

Linda took that in. "Well, it could be a couple of things," she said. "It could be that the person or persons who want to take it over aren't really qualified. Have they worked in the field? Ideally, with the founder?" Becca nodded. "That makes it harder, then. I mean, logistically, startups are crazy, and a million things can go wrong. Are people in touch with the founder? Is there an open line of communication?"

"I'm afraid that's not possible."

"Well, then, maybe the work is more complex than the new guy thinks. Maybe it's beyond him—I'm assuming it's a him." She paused for Becca's assent. "Or maybe it's simpler. Could they be missing some of the code, or the protocol, perhaps?"

"I'm not sure." Becca folded Linda's contact info and tucked it into her pocket. "It's probably not important. What is important is that I give our owner a call. I want to see how quickly I can get you that crystal ball. If it comes in in time, maybe I could even run it over to you."

"Oh! That reminds me." An impish grin lit up the older woman's face. Reaching into her pocket, she pulled out another badge. Pink, rather than orange, she held it out to Becca. "Our presentation comes with a couple of one-day badges, and we thought it might be fun for you to see a different kind of magic."

"Thank you. That's really considerate, but..." Becca looked down at the other woman's outstretched hand. "You've got to know I'm completely lost when it comes to computers."

"Take it." Linda held the badge up. "You don't have to use it, but check out the schedule online. There might be something that you want to learn."

"My boss, one of my bosses, was asking me about teaching online." Becca accepted the pass and examined the black type on its pink face: *One Day*. "Though that would probably just mean setting up a Zoom class."

"If you want, but there are a bunch of different platforms out there now. And even if you do, you might be interested in some of the tech for improved interaction."

"Thanks." Becca looked up at her benefactor. "Maybe I will. Are you and Pam giving a presentation?"

"No, but we have a booth, C326, in the exhibitor's hall." Linda beamed, even as she turned to go. "Come by and say hi. One of us is there most of the time. And, Becca?"

"Yeah?"

"A boss who's urging you to try new things is a keeper. It means she values you."

Twenty

Determined to get that crystal ball for Linda, Becca called the upstairs apartment as soon as her client left. But neither Margaret nor her sister were answering their phone, so Becca left a message and made a note to herself, which she pinned on the store bulletin board. *Get CB for L,* the bright orange sticky said, while the red thumbtack Becca pressed in served almost as an exclamation point. The reminder wasn't likely to make sense to anyone other than Becca, but that didn't bother her. If the clashing colors caught anyone's attention, maybe they'd skim the board—and see her older notice advertising her services as a witch detective.

"Maybe nobody believes I can solve their cases," she said softly to herself. There was a sadness in her voice that made the small cat watching her wish once again that she could rub against her person with comfort and love. It would have been dishonest to do more, Clara knew that. Becca had no more magical power than the thumbtack that held her note in place. In truth, all her previous success with her detecting ventures had been due to her own wits, with some circumspect intervention by Clara and her sisters. But Becca so wanted to believe that she had power. And also, her pet suspected, that she could find out the truth of what had happened to her late ex-boyfriend.

Whatever her disappointment, however, Becca had the sense not to dwell on it, especially when she had other things to do. The sun was still hanging low over the city when she locked up the shop for the evening, stepping out into a warm breeze that had her curls bobbing and freshened the usual city scents with the smell of new leaves.

Weather permitting—and the goddess herself seemed to have obliged—her coven had agreed to finish its aborted cleansing circle by the banks of the Charles. It was an auspicious choice: not only was the setting closer to essential elements—earth, water, and air—the clear, warm evening would counter the gloom of the occasion, contributing its own natural healing magic.

"Hi, Ande!" Becca greeted the tall witch, nodding to the large thermos she carried. The walk and the weather had already worked their own kind of magic, and her voice carried across the grassy riverbank with a chipper lilt. "I'm glad you brought tea," she said, hoisting a white paper bag. "Cookies!"

"Great. Is that a bag from Mike's?" Her eyes lit up as Becca nodded happily.

"Raspberry thumbprints. I couldn't resist."

Clara, shaded into invisibility at her feet, caught the trace of butter in the air in the humid air. *"Thank Bast Harriet isn't here,"* she mewed to herself.

"I'm sure you were prompted by the goddess." Becca's friend almost echoed the cat's silent prayer, her response leavened by an answering grin. "Speaking of which, I had some time on my hands, and I started checking around about Jeff's finances." Ande's tone grew serious as she spoke. "It seems like he had recently come into some money."

"Oh, I'm so sorry. I should have told you." Becca dismissed her friend's concern. "He'd gotten VC funding for a new project. He was probably rolling in it."

"Well, not exactly." Ande had on what Becca thought of as her serious accountant face. Still, her friend's expertise had served the coven before. "He'd made a four-figure gift to a local bar and applied for a car loan, but those aren't big ticket items."

"The money probably hadn't come through yet." Becca paused, considering. "Is there a way to check on something like that?"

"I can look to see if there are any announcements or SEC filings," said Ande as she spread a cloth on the grass. "There are different ways of doing funding these days, and I can try to see if there had been any announcements. Like, maybe, who exactly was backing him."

"Oh, that I know," Becca broke in. "Darien Hughes. Didn't I tell you? He came by the store."

Ande looked up, open-mouthed. "Darien Hughes?"

"Yeah," Becca chuckled. "Crazy, huh?"

"Interesting," her friend responded, before they were interrupted by a familiar voice.

"Hey, kids!" Tina called. Becca and Ande turned to see her descending down the grassy bank. "This is like a picnic," she said, setting down a bakery box. "Fruit jellies," Tina explained. "Because...water."

Marcia appeared on the rise. "Oh, what's this?" She descended to the blanket, placing her contribution, a thick candle set inside a lantern, at its center.

"Earth, air, water, and now fire." Ande summed up the offerings. "I don't know if any of these were strictly necessary, but it is rather like a picnic. Shall we?"

Raising her hands, she summoned the others, and as Tina and Becca took their places, Marcia lit the candle, closing the lantern door against the breeze off the river. "Well, we've got air joining us," she noted, as she stepped back into place. With only four members, the group had a hard time reaching around the blanket, and Marcia, shorter than the rest, dug her toes under it, moving in to reach out for both Becca's and Tina's hands.

"Welcome and blessed be." Ande made the greeting official.

Once all four witches had repeated the ceremonial opening,

they dropped their hands, and Marcia sighed audibly. It had been a stretch.

Becca raised the small brass bell she had bought the day before, using her employee discount, straightened her back, and in her most serious voice began to speak. "We four are gathered, facing the four directions to invoke the four elements." Voices from the path had Tina leaning forward to listen, so Becca raised her voice.

"Earth." She gestured toward her feet. "Water." Thc Charles behind her. "Air." She raised her face to the cool spring evening. "Fire." A nod toward Marcia's lantern. "These elements make up the natural world and all we are, and we look to them for cleansing and healing."

Becca was making up the ritual as she went along, her cat was well aware. The four witches had discussed the format at their earlier meeting, coming to a communal decision that they could incorporate whatever Wiccan practices felt right at the time. After all, they had agreed, it was Becca who had encountered the body, and that body had belonged to Becca's ex. Surely, she should be the one to channel the healing powers of earth and sky.

"In that spirit, we consecrate this beverage and the water within." Becca reached for the thermos. As she did, the voices behind her grew louder, and she turned to face the couple who had crept closer as she spoke. "Do you mind?"

"It's her!" A woman with jet black-hair and a nose ring was pointing at Becca. "The witch involved in that killing."

"Excuse me?" Ande, ever protective, stepped forward.

"We read all about it," the woman continued. Nearly hopping with excitement, she turned to her companion, whose own midnight hair matched his eyeliner. "The murderess."

"I am *not* a murderess—murderer." Becca protested. "I am a witch, and we are trying to do a cleansing circle here."

"Oh, I bet," the pale young man said, a sudden grin splitting his blackened lips. "Throw the cops off your trail."

"Hey!" Marcia stepped forward, nearly kicking over the

lantern, and Tina fell in behind her. "Where do you get off saying that?"

"Wicca isn't evil." Ande offered the voice of reason. "We follow the practices of nature."

"And I'm trying to solve Jeff's murder, not hide it!" Becca burst in. "I'm a witch detective."

"That's right." The goth girl nudged her colleague. "She works out of Charm and Cherish."

Becca's face fell. Ande kept speaking. "We're trying to do a nature ritual here. Now, if you'd like to join us, we'd welcome you. But if not..." She stepped toward the couple, and their faces fell. Clara knew Ande to be as gentle as Becca, but the Black accountant was significantly taller than the two pale, white goths.

"We were just passing through." The glee was gone from the raven-haired man's voice. "Blessed be." He pulled his girlfriend away.

"Blessed be," Becca answered automatically, even as her colleagues turned back to her.

"That was kind of awful." Tina stage-whispered to Marcia, who was walking back to her side of the blanket. "Do you think we can start over?"

"I think we could do with some cleansing after that." Ande tried for a lighter tone. "Becca?"

"Yeah, I guess so." Clara's human sounded both distracted and distressed. The four assumed their respective positions, and Ande handed a small cloth bag to Becca.

Becca cleared her throat and began. "Once again, we invoke the four elements." Pulling a handful of salt from the bag, she walked around the four, sprinkling it on the ground.

"That's protective," Marcia explained to Tina. "After all those bad vibes, it's super important."

"Fire brings cleansing," Becca continued. "We call on that element not to purge the darkness, for the darkness is always with us, accompanying the light. But to keep it from overpowering the light."

"Blessed be," her colleagues echoed.

"Water." She reached for the thermos and the four plastic mugs Ande had also unpacked. "The element that gives us life. May it share with us its clarity."

She poured the tea, which was not, her cat noted, clear. However, the minty steam that spread on the breeze was refreshing, and the four sipped carefully.

Invoking earth and air, Clara noted, Becca sounded a bit rushed. Perhaps, she realized, earth with its associations with the grave were not to her person's liking at that moment. When it came time for each member of the coven to speak, she saw how they all focused on Becca, calling on the natural world to bring her peace.

"I too ask for peace." Becca looked at each of her coven in turn when they had all spoken. "But in the sense of closure. While Jeff is at peace"—she swallowed, and for a moment it sounded like she was choking up—"we are not. The natural order has been disturbed, and while we seek to be cleansed of this violence and negativity, we also strive for clarity. To understand what has happened and why."

"Spoken like a witch detective," Tina whispered to Marcia as Becca ended the abbreviated ceremony. Nobody else had disturbed the small coven, but Clara could see that her person kept glancing around, anxious about intruders.

"Blessed be." Ande once again led the others as they reached around the blanket once more to take hands. "And now the circle is broken."

"Do you feel better?" Tina sidled up to Becca after, a cookie in her hand.

"I do." Becca bit into hers, licking the raspberry off her teeth. "Cleaner and maybe more sure of myself."

"I wasn't sure where you were going with that," Marcia came over, holding the box of fruit jellies.

Ande poured more tea. "Well, clarity helps us move forward," she said.

"It's more than that." Becca sipped the fragrant brew. "I really do feel like I need to understand what happened to Jeff, and why. And, also, where did that horrible couple read about us?"

"The *Globe*?" Marcia looked around. "I confess, I only read sports."

"Not likely." Becca shook her head. "I don't think they'd mention me without reaching out for a comment."

"Maybe they got it from the police." All eyes turned to Tina. "Sorry." She shrugged. "Just, well, it is an open investigation."

"They haven't asked to speak with you again, have they?" Ande's brow knit in concern.

"No." Becca shook her head. "They did say they might, though."

"Maybe I can find something." Marcia began to scroll through her phone. In the fading light, its glow made her face look paler and more serious, and Becca reached out to touch her arm.

"Please don't," she said. "We've just done a ritual to make us feel clean. I don't want to dive back into the craziness."

"You sure?" Marcia held up her phone, and for a moment Becca hesitated.

"Yeah," she said finally. "I'm sure. I'd rather focus on finding out what happened."

"Speaking of." Tina looked up from folding the blanket. "Did anyone else find out anything?"

Ande shook her head slowly, as if she were wary of dislodging a thought. Marcia too appeared distracted, until she latched onto Tina's words. "Anyone else? Does that mean you found something?"

Tina's head bobbed like an excited puppy's. "I guess Becca didn't get a chance to tell you all, but I went back to the alley. You know, the one—"

"We know." Becca looked away, though whether in distaste or discomfort, Clara couldn't tell. The interruption didn't seem to dim Tina's enthusiasm, however.

"Anyway, I found a key, a marked key. And Becca says it's hers and that she gave it to Jeff."

Ande and Marcia both stopped what they were doing and turned to the new member. "What? How did you know?" Marcia asked, while Ande merely turned to Becca, her dark eyes wide.

"Tina didn't, but I recognized it," Becca explained. Then she once more went into the nail polish and the heart that wasn't. "Maybe he meant to give it back to me. I don't know."

"Were you two planning on meeting?" Ande spoke softly, even as she studied Becca's face.

"No." Becca shook her head, her answer definitive. "We hadn't spoken in ages."

"Still, no wonder his new girl was jealous." All eyes turned to Tina again. "What? Didn't she say she was getting threatening messages or something? I mean, I don't know if we should believe that, but clearly something had gotten under her skin. Otherwise, why would she have sought out Becca? Maybe Jeff had been talking about her or—"

"Enough!" Becca raised her hands. "Look, I appreciate all your concern, but I think I really have to let this go. It's horrible and it's sad, and I had nothing to do with it, okay?"

"Okay." Tina, chastened, agreed, while the others simply nodded. By then the picnic/ritual had all been packed up, and as the dusk deepened, Becca stared out at the river.

"I'm just wiped," she said, her face in shadow. "I know we'd talked about getting dinner after, but I think I just want to crash and be with my cats."

"I get it." Marcia leaned in to give her a hug. "You're not heading toward the T, are you?"

"No, I'll just walk up Pearl." Turning, she took in Memorial Drive and the dark streets beyond.

"I'll join you," said Marcia, taking her arm. "I parked up there anyway, so I can give you a lift the rest of the way."

"Great." Becca took the blanket from Tina, giving the now silent woman a quick hug as well. "You've been great, Tina. Thanks," she said to the downcast newcomer.

"Thanks. I didn't mean..."

"It's fine, really." Becca managed one more encouraging smile before turning to Marcia. "How far up did you park?"

"A couple of blocks." As they crossed Memorial, Marcia glanced over at her friend. "I'm on Putnam, actually, but I wanted to talk to you."

Becca sighed, but nodded anyway. "I thought there was something besides that creepy couple."

Marcia took her hand. "It doesn't mean anything, Becca. Really."

That stopped Becca in her tracks. "What?"

"I told you I was going to ask around, right? Well, I did." The short Sox fan looked acutely uncomfortable, even as she forced herself to face her friend. "So, you know a few people heard a fight, an argument, really, right before, well, before Jeff was killed, right?" She took a breath, waiting for Becca's assent. "Turns out one of them is a season ticket holder, so we started talking.

"He wasn't the one who called the cops. Said he thought it was just a boyfriend-girlfriend thing. But I gather he hasn't been too hard to find." She swallowed. "Becca, he actually saw the couple. From across Mass Ave, but still—and he described the man and it sounds like Jeff. And the woman? He said she was short, with dark, curly hair. Becca, it sounded like he was describing you."

Twenty-One

By the time the smoke had cleared the next day, Becca knew her worst fears had come true—and she didn't have some strange goth couple to blame.

It wasn't just the fire alarm screaming so loudly that it made it nearly impossible to think, an unbearable screech emanating not only from Charm and Cherish's ceiling, but from the three floors of apartments above. Nor was it the two fire trucks that had arrived with their sirens wailing and were now blocking a lane of Mass Ave outside, their big-booted occupants thumping around the store with a cavalier clumsiness that threatened to knock every porcelain figurine and glass candleholder off the crowded shelves. Nor was it the lookie-loos, craning to stare into the little store and eager for disaster.

No, it was all of these combined, which the arrival of the Cambridge police only aggravated and which had brought Margaret down from the sisters' penthouse, descending into the shop like a small but furious thundercloud. As Becca closed her eyes, her resilient, if shaken, cat unseen by her side, she waited for the worst. The denouement to a disastrous day.

. . .

It had started so well. The morning had dawned bright with promise, that same fresh breeze now blending the perfume of early blossoms with the new greenery as it wafted into her apartment. Even Harriet had appeared in a good mood, waiting patiently for her breakfast and no longer glaring at the tortie kitten, who had taken to toddling along behind her. And with no feline drama, Becca, with Clara at her heels, had arrived at the store extra early, ready to start the day.

The morning had been so beautiful, in fact, that Becca had seemed flustered. At least, that was the best Clara could come up with as her person walked back and forth from the storeroom to the front door.

"Maybe I should anyway," she said, more than once, as her cat took up her usual place high on the bookshelf nearest the register. "What can it hurt?"

The first visitor seemed to decide for her. Because although Becca would usually welcome an early client—foot traffic didn't usually bring anyone in before noon—there was something off about this visitor. It wasn't her tri-colored hair or the oversized green glasses that made her eyes look enormous. Those were standard student fashion here in Cambridge. No, it was the way those big eyes lit up when she saw Becca, like a large fish intent on its prey.

"So you must be Becca," she said as she approached, her voice hushed and breathy. She'd already walked around the tiny shop, head swiveling to take in the shelves as well as the posters and other artwork that hung on the far wall. "Becca Colwin."

"Yes, I am," Becca had replied, her usual smile looking a bit forced.

The visitor had paused at the poster advertising Becca's skills as a witch detective, which had brought Becca the majority of her clients. Still, she seemed a bit tense to her observant cat.

"You're the one involved with the murder." The eyes behind those large frames looked ready to pop. "Can you tell me what it felt like?"

"What? No!" Startled, Becca had yelled, and the woman had

turned and fled, the front door slamming behind her, its bells, normally so cheery, jangling discordantly.

"That's it. I'm doing it." Becca had come out from behind the counter and, flipping the "Open" sign to "Closed," locked the door. "First instinct, best instinct, and all that."

Curious and a bit concerned by Becca's sudden mood swing, Clara jumped down and followed her into the back room. Surely, she couldn't think the rude visitor posed a threat, her cat thought. Like the couple the night before, the big-eyed woman had been misinformed and a bit of a voyeur. But as she watched Becca dig into one of the big storage boxes, the calico grew worried. Was Becca considering a weapon?

What Becca pulled out was worse. A bundle of gray twigs tied together with twine, the odor was already overpowering to the sensitive feline. Once she lit it, as Clara feared she would, the combination of its heady herbal aroma and the ensuing smoke would be nearly unbearable. Clara would stay with her person; she was too loyal to flee no matter how her nose and eyes would itch. But her ears went back at the thought of what was to come.

"I wish I had a spell." Speaking softly to herself, Becca took the bundle back into the shop's front room. When she left it on the counter, for a moment Clara dared to hope. But, no, Becca was only looking for a reference. As she leafed through one of the bigger books, Clara's optimism faded. Worse, she noted, if Becca did not, the small blinking red light almost directly above her person's head.

"Here we go." Becca laid the open book flat on the counter. "A spell for dispersing negative energy." Digging into her pocket, she fished out a book of matches marked, Clara noticed, with the logo of the restaurant from her dinner with Darien. Resigned to what was about to happen, Clara wedged herself deeper into her niche in the bookshelf, closed her eyes, and flattened her black-tipped ears firmly against her head.

It didn't help. Even with her ears back, she heard the *wisp* of the match being lit and smelled the funky smoke. And as soon as Becca started waving the sage around, calling on the original inhabitants of the land to help her dispel the negative spirits of anger and suspicion, she knew what would happen next.

The first alarm made her jump and sent Becca running, wild-eyed, for the front door.

"Do you need help?" An pink-haired woman in a purple sweatsuit reached out to steady her.

"No, just—can you hold the door open?" Becca spun around, searching the space before grabbing a small stone statue of Bast. "There, that should do—"

It was too late. Her spinning, while still holding the smoking bundle, had only sent more smoke into the crowded shop, and soon the building alarms began to wail as well.

"Oh no!" Becca ran into the back and pushed open the door to the alley. For a moment, the cat, who had followed to escape the awful howl, feared she was going to toss the smoldering sticks into the dumpster. But Becca clearly thought better of that impulse and ran instead to the small bathroom, where she shoved the smudge into the sink and opened both taps, producing a cloud of revolting steam that had her gagging and coughing.

"What the heck is going on?" Margaret's unmistakable voice cut through the smoke from the front room. "Becca, are you here?"

"Coming!" Becca ran onto the shop floor, the still smoldering smudge in her hand. "I'm sorry. Can we...?"

Climbing on the counter, she reached up and poked at the alarm with the stick end of the smudge. It fell silent, but by then they could all hear wails of the approaching fire trucks.

"Oh no." Becca looked down at her boss.

"Of course I called them. The alarm was going off and I could smell smoke." Margaret scowled as she offered her explanation. "I didn't know you'd be so...so foolish!"

"So conscientious." Her sister, Elizabeth, appeared at the door. "A sage smudge is a useful tool. Though perhaps it would have made sense to disengage the alarm and open the doors first." Reaching up, she offered Becca a hand.

"Thanks," Becca responded with an emphasis that implied so

much more. Turning to her actual boss, she adopted a more apologetic tone. "I am sorry, Margaret. It was foolish of me not to think the smudging through. But I did have my reasons."

Margaret raised one shaggy brow, fixing her with a gimlet eye, and even Elizabeth seemed curious.

"A woman came in earlier who, well, wasn't really interested in the store." Becca's narrative fell off as the firefighters arrived. Despite Becca's assurances, the first crew ushered Becca and the sisters outside, while another crew marched up to the apartments above. Only after all the alarms had been silenced were they allowed to re-enter the shop, where Becca continued her story.

"The woman—she wasn't really a client. She was only here because of something I stumbled into." It sounded unconvincing, even to her faithful pet. Seeing the skepticism in her boss's hawk-like eye, Becca took a deep breath and let it out in a rush with a version of the story that barely made sense, even to her pet.

"When I was leaving work the other day, I ended up chasing a kitten into an alley and finding the body of my ex-boyfriend who'd been murdered and now people are acting like I'm somehow involved." She looked from one sister to the other as the last of the firefighters emerged from the back. "But I'm not."

"All clear here," he yelled out to the street before turning to the women. "As soon as we get the all-clear from my partners, you can go back up to your apartments," he said.

"It's about time," Margaret grumped. "Now that your people have stomped all over my carpets."

Elizabeth reached to restrain her sister, but the firefighter merely winked at her. "Happy to be of service, ma'am."

Becca, for her part, smiled at the large man, though out of gratitude for his willingness to tackle a blaze or to divert her employer's pique, her cat had no idea.

As he left, Margaret turned her scowl on Becca. "I knew letting you advertise as some kind of unlicensed investigator was a bad idea."

"This wasn't because of that." Becca wasn't at her most articulate, stumbling through her explanation even as Elizabeth signed for her to stop.

"Excuse me?" The three turned in unison to see a tall, light-haired man with a face like a depressed basset hound standing in the doorway. "I'm Detective Scott Newsom, and I'm looking for Becca Colwin."

"If this is because of the fire alarm, I can explain." Becca stepped forward, ready to confess. "I'm really, really sorry the fire department had to come out, but it was an accident. I never intended to cause harm."

"Oh, don't worry," he said in a calm baritone. "I'm not an arson inspector. I'm here to talk to you about the murder of Jeff Blakey and your possible interference in our investigation."

Twenty-Two

Elizabeth had started to offer the sisters' upstairs apartment for the interview when Margaret shut her down.

"Bitsy," her sister had hissed. "We've already had hordes of strangers trampling through our home and now you want to offer it as a convenience for a murder suspect?"

"Nobody is a murder suspect," the doggish detective offered, a statement that appeared to cheer Becca until he followed up. "We're speaking with several people who may have had some involvement with the victim or with other persons of interest in the case."

"Persons of interest?" Becca parroted the words under her breath as both Elizabeth and Clara, who had been watching the interaction with growing concern, looked on sympathetically.

"Is there another place we can speak here?" Newsome ignored her comment. "Or would you like to come down to the station?"

Which was how Becca, with a vigilant Clara tucked beneath her seat, came to be in Charm and Cherish's back room, which still smelled of smoke and charred sage. And why she feared the worst.

"Were you cooking back here?" The detective sniffed as he pulled up the storeroom's other chair. "Is that what happened?"

"No." Becca shook her head. "I was smudging the store. It's a Wiccan ritual designed to dispel evil influences, and what with Jeff's death..."

"I get it." Newsom's long face lifted momentarily in what Clara assumed was a smile, before settling in as he pulled a notepad from his pocket. "Now, would you like to explain why you crossed a police barrier the other night?"

"What?" Becca sat up, startled.

"You were seen ducking under the tape to enter the alley between Pearl and Brookline." He consulted the pad. "Two nights ago at approximately six p.m."

"That wasn't me," Becca rushed to explain.

"Did you leave this store around that time?"

"Yes, we close at six, usually. I had plans to meet someone." She paused, and Clara could tell she wasn't sure how much she wanted to share. The detective must have picked up something from her hesitation as well, because he simply sat there, his long face growing more somber by the second.

"I met someone for drinks, and we ended up having dinner," Becca said finally. "If you need to, I can give you his contact info. But I think I know why..."

Her voice trailed off as Newsome leaned toward her ever so slightly.

"A friend of mine went into the alley," she said in a rush. "She wanted to see if there was anything there that the police might have missed."

Newsom's brows rose at that.

"We're, well, we are trying to be witches." Becca's explanation sounded more like an apology to her cat's sensitive ears. Becca herself must have been aware of how weak it sounded. "We thought there might be something, some trace, that would help us in a spiritual way." By the time she was finished, Becca was barely audible, her knuckles white from how tight she was clasping her hands.

"And did you find anything?"

Becca winced. The pronoun, Clara thought, until she remembered Becca's key. "Nothing we could use in one of our circles," she said, speaking so softly the detective had to lean forward even further to hear her.

Even after he had sat back, he kept looking at her. For Clara, who knew her person well, it was torture. Becca wasn't accustomed to lying, and while her answer hadn't, strictly speaking, been untrue, she could sense her growing discomfort as the seconds ticked by.

"Well, we can come back to that," he said at last, a trace of a growl in his voice. "For now, why don't you tell me about your relationship with Carl Rimsky."

"Carl?" Rather than relieved, Becca sounded confused. "You mean Jeff's friend from CodePhool?"

Newsom nodded.

"I just know him through Jeff. I saw him at a gathering at the Plough he organized as a kind of memorial."

"And he invited you?"

Becca frowned, and Clara could tell she was thinking of the coder's visit to the shop and his unexpected invitation. "No," she said at last. "Renee, Jeff's girlfriend invited me."

"So you were on good terms?" A half smile made it look like he found this a pleasant surprise.

"I guess." Becca shrugged. "Honestly, I hadn't met her before. I was kind of surprised."

"Did she tell you about the letters the deceased had been getting?"

Becca nodded.

"And did she tell you that these were from another woman in Jeff's life, someone who threatened them both?"

"Now, wait a minute. You can't think that I was threatening Renee or Jeff. We broke up over a year ago. We hadn't spoken in ages."

"And yet everyone from his life seems to be popping up in yours, Ms. Colwin. Wouldn't you say that's interesting?"

"Excuse me." Before Becca could come up with a response, the interview was interrupted as Elizabeth swept in, all six-foot-one of her in motion. "I hate to interrupt, but it just occurred to me that Ms. Colwin here should not be speaking with you without an attorney."

"And you are?" Newsom eyed her, clearly unhappy about the interruption.

"Elizabeth Cross. My sister and I own this shop."

"Do you really think that's necessary?" Newsom could have been responding to her statement, but Clara thought it likely he was reacting to her dramatic gesture, which concluded with the tall sister sweeping between the detective and her employee, her long purple robe spreading out around her like a cape. Whichever was responsible, Becca beamed up at her with relief.

"Yes, I do." The gray-haired amazon leavened her words with a smile but continued to stand between the two.

"Thanks, Elizabeth." With a moment of reprieve, Becca had rallied, and stood to take her place by the tall woman's side. "And actually, I think she's right. I want to help, I do, but if you need to ask me any more questions, I think I should have someone representing me."

"Good girl." Clara felt, rather than heard, Elizabeth's affirmation. Out loud, the towering senior draped one purple arm around Becca's shoulders, exclaimed with an alarm that sounded to the cat like she was reading from a script. A bad one. "Oh my! And nobody is watching the shop! Becca, you should get out there right away, lest some potential customer fails to realize we're still in business."

"On it, boss." Not even bothering to hide her grin, Becca headed for the door. The detective stood as well, but Elizabeth blocked him from following.

"I'd like to take down all of your information before you leave, Officer." Despite her smile, Elizabeth was not a woman to be trifled with. But despite her height and overwhelming manner, Clara couldn't help but wonder if there was some other power at work from the way the doggish detective paused, mouth hanging open but speechless.

"You must have a card, no?" Elizabeth raised one quizzical eyebrow.

"Yes, yes, of course." The detective fished his wallet out of his jacket pocket and offered the laminated rectangle.

Or tried to. As Elizabeth took hold of it, Newsom looked up, eyes widening in surprise.

"You can't really think our Becca is a suspect." Elizabeth spoke softly, but her voice resonated throughout the storeroom with a power that made the fur rise along Clara's back. "Surely, you know the girl is innocent of anything more than wanting to help."

Newsom's mouth moved like he was a fish out of water until Elizabeth pulled the card free.

"A person was murdered, ma'am." The words appeared to cost him. "I have to do my job."

She nodded, though whether in acknowledgment or agreement, Clara couldn't tell. "I know," she said, her own voice sounding more like that of a healthy octogenarian. "I simply don't want you to take the easy way out."

For a moment, the two locked eyes, before Elizabeth turned toward the back of the storeroom. "Speaking of," she said, reaching the back door with three quick strides. "Why don't you see yourself out this way? Something about the presence of the police tends to discourage our clientele."

Twenty-Three

"*I always hated that ritual.*" Laurel wrinkled her chocolate nose in disgust. "*Not just the smoke, but the noise!*"

"*Becca didn't mean to prompt the noise.*" Clara had arrived home moments before their person and was quickly bringing her sisters up to speed. "*She thought she would keep the loud people away.*"

"*Huh.*" Laurel wasn't buying it, perhaps because she sensed that her baby sister had substituted the word "loud" for "obnoxious and mean-spirited." But how else could Clara explain the visitors who had upset Becca so badly.

"*You could simply say that nasty visitor was...ratty.*" Harriet's deep rumble broke through Clara's musing, and the calico bowed her head. It always caught her by surprise when her sisters read her thoughts. Harriet was right, of course. Even for a feline who insisted on receiving her meals fresh from the can, there could be no greater insult than to be compared to a large, aggressive, and extremely unpleasant rodent.

"*It was worse than that.*" Clara flicked her tail, remembering the woman's strange excitement. From the way she was acting, it seemed she really did want Becca to be a murderer.

"*So many humans have no sense of propriety.*" Laurel's purr reached Clara's ears, and she flicked them, as if by doing so she could toss off the horrible memory. *"Although the desire to kill is natural,"* her sister drawled.

"I know." It wouldn't serve to annoy either of her siblings, Clara knew. Besides, for a moment there, Laurel's cool comment had sparked a thought. Something about killing being natural? Well, for a cat, at least. She thought of her favorite catnip toy, its felt ears long shredded and its tail a memory. No, that wasn't it.

"Do you think humans have the same predatory instincts?" Trying to recapture the thought, she turned to Laurel, who sat up.

"Some do." Her blues eyes crossed as she thought, although Clara had the sense not to point this out to the vain sealpoint. *"But that's not what you're asking, is it?"*

"No, I don't think so." Clara lashed her tail again, this time in frustration. *"Maybe it was about instincts and that we all hunt or hide when we're scared."*

"Speak for yourself, little one." Harriet puffed herself up. *"Some of us would fight back before we ran."*

Clara dipped her head, but before she could properly respond, the three heard the approach of feet and, moments later, a key in the door. Becca was home.

"Hey, kitties." Clara could hear the relief as well as the fatigue in their person's voice. Becca's feet had been dragging as she walked, even though Elizabeth had sent her home early, telling her, once that annoying policeman was gone, that she thought it best to close the shop for the rest of the day. It had been all the shaded calico could do to keep from rubbing against her ankles as she walked, and she'd only left Becca once their building was in sight, eager to fill in Harriet and Laurel on all that had happened.

"Feel how soft I am." Harriet stood as Becca reached to pet her, rubbing one velvet cheek against her hand. Behind her, the tortie kitten stared longingly at the flicking tip of Harriet's white fluff of a tail. Luckily for the kitten, Harriet was too focused on Becca, and the idea of food, to notice when she pounced.

"And how warm my fur is." Laurel pressed up against her leg

and stretched herself out to make figure eights around both Becca's ankles when Harriet did finally turn to swat the kitten. That left little for Clara to do except to stare up at her person adoringly, but she put her heart into it, hoping that at least some of what she felt got through.

"I can't tell you how glad I am to see you all as well." Becca rallied a feeble smile as she dropped her bag and keys. "And, yes, Harriet, I think we can have dinner early tonight."

"Why is she still fussing?" Ten minutes later, all four dishes were clean, Harriet was making extra sure her white mittens matched as well.

"She had a rough day." Clara had explained everything as best she could, but at times her older sister could be particularly dense.

"She thinks she had a rough day," Laurel scoffed. *"She should try babysitting this little troublemaker."* To illustrate, she put out one chocolate paw and, pulling the tiny tortie toward her, began to groom her, making the kitten squirm and squeal.

"She still isn't talking?" Clara watched as the kitten wiggled out from under Laurel's paw. To her credit, she then tried to continue the grooming on her own, falling over as she lifted one hind leg.

"She's just an animal." Laurel returned to her own toilette. *"You're too young to remember. Most cats have very few powers."*

"Maybe..." Clara knew her sister spoke the truth. While all cats have more magic than humans, most lacked the superior skills possessed by Clara and her sisters. True, the kitten was acting sillier than usual as she attempted to groom her own tail and ended up chasing it until she fell over once again. But in those few brief moments when the tortie was still, Clara was sure she picked up...something. A spark, maybe, in those round green eyes. But just as she was about to try an experiment—thinking a direct address to the kitten might answer a few of her questions—a cry of distress caught her attention.

"Becca!" Clara dashed into the living room, where she found her person perched on the old couch. She appeared unhurt,

despite the soft wail that had alerted her pet, but she was staring at the laptop before her in horror.

Jumping up onto the brown corduroy beside her, Clara tried to make sense of the scene. To a cat, an image without movement or scent is barely recognizable. And Becca, from what Clara could see, was looking at a page of typing. Words—without a bloody picture or angry predator among them.

"Who would write such things?" Becca seemed to be questioning her own reaction as well. Or, no, her cat realized as Becca began to type furiously and then scrolled down the screen. She was reacting with disbelief. Clara leaned closer. Whatever was on that screen had to be pretty bad.

"Oh, Clara." Becca reached over to stroke the calico's brown and black back. "Why are people so obsessed with murder? And why are they so sure they know what's going on, saying I've shown a 'desire to kill'?" She shuddered, then drew her hand back to type some more. "At the very least, couldn't they leave me out of it?"

Clara sniffed at the screen, Becca's words stirring a memory just below the surface. But Becca had already shifted, pulling out her phone.

"Hi, Tina? It's Becca." Closing the laptop, Becca stood and began to pace. "I was wondering if you could help me with something. There's this awful blog..."

Silence followed, and Clara crept closer to the closed computer. No, she realized with sinking spirits, it carried no clarifying scent. Whatever that lost thought was, she'd just have to wait for it to reappear on its own. In the meantime, she hopped to the back of the sofa to watch her person.

"It's just morbid. And mean-spirited," she was saying. "At first, I wanted to respond. I mean, it's basically saying I killed Jeff. That I had some kind of power over him through my magic. And then all these comments are adding to the fire—that we'd been seeing each other all along, and I was furious that he wouldn't acknowledge me now that he was about to be wealthy. It's all crazy, Tina. All of it. Well, except that maybe he was striking it rich. But that doesn't matter. We hadn't spoken in months. What? No, nothing. He hasn't called or texted or emailed or anything. Anyway, even though I really wanted to say that, to say that was all nonsense, I realized I probably shouldn't respond. Or, well, to be totally honest, I was going to if I could do it anonymously. But the site kept telling me I'd have to register, and I thought... I don't want to give these crazies any more ammunition."

Clara stared at her person. Becca didn't usually get so distracted. Her cat couldn't tell if her own concerted focus helped, but in a moment, Becca returned to her point.

"Anyway, Tina, I was wondering. You're in software. Do you think you could take a look and find out who's running this blog? The moderator calls herself the Dark Lady, but that could mean anything, right? If it wasn't so personal, I'd be wondering if maybe it was some kind of bot."

In the silence that followed, Becca seemed to relax. With a deep breath, she even leaned back against the couch, one hand reaching out to caress Clara's smooth head.

"Thank you so much, Tina." She fondled the base of Clara's parti-colored ears, hitting just the right spot. "It really makes me feel so much better knowing you, and the whole coven, have my back."

With one last gentle pet, Becca settled back onto the slightly frayed brown corduroy, disturbing Harriet, who had taken up her place of honor on her particular gold-tassled pillow. "Sorry, Harriet." Becca gave the big marmalade a conciliatory pet. "I've been so distracted I barely even saw you there. Speaking of..." She jumped up, but when the tortoiseshell kitten appeared, wrestling a paperclip, she sat once more, pulling the laptop toward her.

"She's spending too much time on that thing," Clara, looking over her shoulder, murmured to Harriet.

"I've told you that before," her sister grumbled. *"And you always go on about work and making a living, as if she got cans out of that thing."*

"This is different." Clara didn't know how to explain and instead jumped down to snuggle against Becca's hip.

"It was March, right? Or, no, February. Right around Valentine's Day." Becca's sigh seemed to deflate her. "I don't think I missed anything, unless..."

Rapid typing followed, and suddenly Becca sat up straight. "Straight to spam. I forgot I blocked him. I can't believe it's still here."

Speaking under her breath so softly that only feline ears would be able to hear, she read from the screen. "'It's been a while, Becca. That's my fault, I know, and I'm sorry.'" Becca paused, and for a flick of the tail, Clara thought she was going to close the computer. But she kept reading. "'And I'm sorry to bother you now, after everything. But I really need to see you.'" Becca inhaled, barely breathing out the last words. "'About the key.'"

Twenty-Four

The computer was not a friend. While Clara and her sisters had forged a tenuous peace with the metal creature, enjoying its warmth when Becca left it untended even as they resented the attention she gave it, what happened next confirmed that the object was hostile. Or, at least, not actively working toward Becca's advantage.

"What the...?" Becca had sat back so fast she dislodged Laurel, who had taken up Clara's perch on the sofa back. "No!" The distraught young woman slammed her hands on the keyboard, narrowly missing Clara's head. As she kept at the keyboard, poking it so quickly that, at the very least, her cats hoped to see some prey, a moth, perhaps, emerge and fly away. Instead, as the cats watched warily, their person took a few deep breaths and then started in on the infernal machine once again.

"I wonder..." As Becca tap-tap-tapped, Clara cuddled close once again. Trying to make sense of the images on the screen was difficult. Although she had a better sense of what her human saw than did her sisters, the constant stream of pixels didn't add up to much. A picture, maybe, of a face, or faces. Some color, that was it.

So intent was the little cat on the screen that she barely

noticed when Becca reached for another of her devices. Only her voice made the calico look up, whiskers bristling with curiosity.

"Maddy, it's been crazy." Becca shook her head as she talked, as if she could shed the day. "No, I'm home early. I tried to smudge the store and, well, it's a long story. But I found something. I told everyone—the police, everyone—that I'd had no contact with Jeff for months. But I found an email from him in my spam filter. He said he needed to see me."

Clara's ears perked up at that, and she could hear from the squeaks and squawks that came through the phone that Becca's friend had thoughts about this too.

"No, you're right. I wasn't lying. I never talked to him. I didn't even know he was trying to reach me." From Becca's response, her cat figured that Maddy was trying to talk her friend down. "Only, get this, the email said he wanted to see me about the key. Jeff was carrying my key with him when he was killed. The cops must have missed it, but Tina found it in the alley. So, was he trying to return it or what? It had been months. Plus, did I tell you? Marcia found one of the witnesses—no, not to the murder, but someone who said that they saw Jeff arguing with a woman. Not a blonde. In fact, she thought it was me. And if Marcia thought that was possible, well, no wonder Renee suspects me. I mean, it *wasn't* me. But if Renee knew that he was trying to reach me and that he was hanging on to my key, maybe that's what set her off."

Clara could hear Maddy begin to respond, but maybe Becca didn't.

"There's more," Becca cut off her friend, reaching for the laptop with her free hand. "I went to Jeff's Facebook page. Yes, I know."

Maddy, it seemed, had thoughts about that, and Clara could clearly hear the words "social media stalking."

"But I haven't, Maddy. Honestly, not in months, anyway. But I checked just now, and all I see are pictures of him and Renee. There's not even anything about the new job, but then I went to one of his favorite group pages, Cambridge Coders. I know,"

Becca seemed to be replying to something Maddy had said. "I joined back when we were together. It was social more than anything. There's nothing there either. No pictures of him with anyone else, and I didn't see any posts that looked flirty, though considering how cis-hetero male that group is, that's no surprise. The last thing Jeff posted was that he had an announcement to make and linked to an event page. Other than that, his life looks like it was totally normal."

She paused, and Maddy's voice came through.

"You're right, Maddy. If he was cheating on her, he wouldn't broadcast it online. He didn't with me. But if they were really on the rocks, I'd have thought there would be something. Photos or something. Though, let me check..."

She paused, one finger gently tapping at the edge of the machine. Maddy's voice had grown softer, and Clara assumed she was comforting her friend. Even the memory of a betrayal had to hurt.

"I think I'm going to call Darien," Becca said at last, her voice grown thoughtful. "No, not to ask him out. Please, Maddy, I don't even know if I'm interested in him. What I am is curious. I mean, yeah, Jeff could be super secretive, as you and I both know. But now I'm wondering about this press conference he was planning. I'm on the event page, and Darien isn't listed anywhere on the invite, and he's not a co-host. Maybe Darien isn't on Facebook or Jeff wanted to keep it all a surprise, but don't you think that's kind of curious? Like, shouldn't any press have been handled by Darien's company? And, Maddy, I just put it together. This event? It was supposed to happen on Sunday. The morning after Jeff was killed."

Maybe it was something in the long, squawking response that news provoked, but even after she got off the phone, Becca made no move to follow up with a second phone call. Clara didn't mind that her person didn't immediately call the handsome financier, but she was an honest enough kitty to admit she had her own reasons.

"You like that vet." Laurel's low hiss reached her from the back of the sofa. Clara looked up. She'd thought her sister was asleep, but even in the fading light she could see the blue glint of her half-closed eyes. *"Do you want her to be alone?"*

"She won't be. She has us." Even as Clara responded, she heard the hollowness of her words. Laurel was right. The kind vet had been friendly but shy, and with Becca's own reticence, they hadn't gone beyond a good night kiss. At least Darien Hughes seemed genuinely interested in pursuing Becca in a way that made his intentions clear. If she wanted another boyfriend, she should consider him.

"You see?" Laurel's hiss smoothed into a purr that made Clara's ears perk up.

"Are you influencing her?" This was exactly the kind of emotion Laurel was likely to suggest, her sister well knew.

Laurel's eyes had closed, though whether she had fallen asleep for real or simply decided not to respond, her little sister couldn't tell.

"You're not the only one who knows things." A grumpy snarl from the end of the sofa informed Clara that Harriet had woken. *"Clown."*

There was no good response to that, not if she didn't want her ears batted or to be pushed off the bed while she was sleeping. Still, Clara couldn't help that her ears went back slightly, the velvety black fur almost lying flat against her white and butterscotch fur. She knew she should be grateful that her sisters both appeared to be napping again and couldn't see what was really a largely involuntary reaction, just as she knew that both felines loved her and that Harriet's annoyance at being woken was probably behind the gratuitous insult. Harriet had taken over kitten-sitting duties, and although the little tortie didn't require much actual care, making sure she didn't get into more than the usual trouble—climbing the curtains to where she couldn't get down, for example, or wedging herself beneath the radiator—had kept her sister busy.

Maybe she should offer to look out for the kitten tonight, Clara thought. That would put her in a better position to say something the next time either of her sisters called her Clara the Clown. It would also give her some time alone with the tortie who still, she realized, lacked a name.

"I have a name." The words, little more than a thought, caused Clara's ears to perk up. Had that come from the kitten?

"Kitten?" She spoke softly, lest she startle the little creature. *"Were you reading my thoughts?"*

Silence, and Clara could have kicked herself. Cats are incredibly conscious of protocol and of their privacy. Even a kitten might find a question like that invasive.

"I'm sorry." She bowed her head slightly. *"I was surprised. But I'm glad to hear from you. Would you like to tell me your name?"*

Silence, and as she looked around, she saw that not only were her sisters sleeping – Laurel draped along the back of the sofa, her chocolate paws stretched luxuriantly along its brown spine, and Harriet snoring gently on her golden pillow—but the kitten had joined them too. Lying on her back, the butterscotch patch on her chest exposed and both her black and her peach front paws up in the air, the tortie kitten lay against Becca's other thigh, her slightly open mouth exposing two small fangs and, for all intents and purposes, out like a light.

"I don't understand." Clara was so fixated on the little cat that, for a moment, she thought she'd spoken her thoughts aloud. But, no, that was Becca's voice. Her person was clicking away at the computer again, when suddenly, a loud ping made her stop.

"Tina?" A few more clicks, and Becca was talking to her screen. "I got your Zoom invite. I'm sorry, I haven't used it in a while. Is that you?"

"Hi, Becca." The unmistakably girly voice of the other woman came out of the laptop. "Yeah, I wanted to be able to show you what I've found."

"Okay." Becca spoke slowly, as if she were uncertain. "I'm not sure I'm doing this right. Everything around you is fuzzy."

"That's my filter, silly." Tina giggled. "My place is always such a mess that I keep it on. I wouldn't want anyone at work seeing how I live!"

"I get it." Becca relaxed. "As long as it's not me."

"No way." The light on the screen changed suddenly, and Clara found herself looking at a different arrangement of colored squares. "I thought if I shared my screen, you'd see what we're up against."

"The blog." Becca sighed.

"Well, technically, it's more like a substack, with subscribers who are allowed to comment."

"I kind of don't need that level of detail, Tina. I've had a long day."

"Sorry." Tina giggled again. "I get into the weeds with this kind of thing, I know. But it kind of matters, because there are differences in moderation and privacy and that kind of thing."

"Okay."

Clara looked up at her person. In the light off the laptop, she looked pale, her eyes deeply shadowed.

"Anyway, it's being published under a pseudonym, The Dark Lady, from someplace in Cambridge. See?" With the click of a key, the light changed, switching from a sickly blue to an unhealthy pink, revealing a few lines of type. Becca nodded and then cleared her throat.

"Yeah, I see. Thanks, Tina."

Her friend didn't seem to notice how her voice dragged, but with a few more clicks, the screen changed back again. "You were smart not to register, but I figured I had to. I'm just an anonymous person, right? But I'm already getting emails. Whoever set this up wants everyone to comment. Whoever this 'dark lady' is, she's trying to make sure everyone knows your name."

Twenty-Five

Becca slept fitfully, despite the best efforts of her pets, who surrounded her on the bed. Wakeful herself, Clara thought about removing the kitten—the little tortie was still small enough that she could have easily lifted her by her scruff and deposited her elsewhere. But to her surprise, Becca seemed comforted by the bundle of fluff that had nestled under her chin. At least, as she lay awake, occasionally sighing with a vehemence that tore at her calico's heart, she seemed to enjoy reaching up and stroking the kitten's powder-soft fur.

The tortie, who Clara was now nearly convinced had not spoken, slept through it all. Granted, the kitten's strange coloring, the butterscotch running into the darker brown, made it hard to read the little beast. But even after Becca drifted off, turning on her side and sliding the kitten back onto the pillow, the tiny creature seemed oblivious. As Clara let her own eyes close—even when worried about their people, cats rarely suffer from insomnia—she could picture that one peach-colored paw sticking up into the air, the other, black, flung to the side, a portrait of feline contentment.

Her few hours of sleep didn't seem to do Becca much good,

however. Waking before the alarm, she puttered into the kitchen slowly, opening cans as if on automatic pilot.

"She's worried." Clara caught her sisters up. *"She didn't sleep well."*

"Tell me about it." Laurel, her brown muzzle deep into her dish, did her best to sound aggrieved. *"She rolled over on my tail."*

"Well, I did what I could." Harriet licked the last bit of her own breakfast from her gold-rimmed dish and looked around. *"I'm softer and warmer than that lumpy old comforter."*

"It isn't that." Clara licked at her own breakfast, conscious of her big sister's interest. *"She's thinking about Jeff and what happened."*

"She should move on," Laurel muttered, while Harriet bent over the kitten. Clara sat up, ready to protect the tortie's meal, but Harriet only began to groom the little creature. Who had, Clara could now see, managed to get wet food on her ears.

Becca, usually so involved with her pets, ignored all this, which made Clara sad. She had no idea what the future held for the kitten. But the fact that the three sisters had accepted the little tortie had to bode well. At the very least, Becca didn't have to worry about the kitten when she left for work.

The kitten's future seemed to be the last thing on her mind as Becca finished dressing.

"Uh-oh." Laurel dashed in front of her, before leaping to the top of her dresser. *"Not who I expected."*

"What?" Clara looked up from cleaning her own whiskers, but her sister was already doing her best impersonation of a bookend.

"Bother." Becca's pique echoed Laurel's as her phone buzzed, but with a sigh, she hit the speaker option. "Dr. Keller? Is everything okay?"

"Yes, yes. The last of the labs are back and as far as I can tell, all the cats in your care are in fine shape." Even over the tiny speaker, the vet's warmth came through. With, Clara realized, a slight bit of anxiety. "I'm sorry. I didn't mean to worry you."

"That's okay." Becca shrugged into her top and checked her hair. "It's just that I'm rushing off to work."

"I'll be quick, then. I've found someone to take the kitten. A lovely woman I know, her name is Leila, has recently lost an older cat, and her remaining cat could use the company. It would have to be a trial, of course, but I think it's a promising situation. I'm taking her to dinner next Wednesday, and I thought we could come by and meet the kitten first. And you, of course. Would that work?"

It was possibly the longest speech Clara had heard the vet make. Which might explain, she thought, why his voice had died off as he posed the final question.

"Oh." Becca seemed taken aback by it too, though whether because of the vet's proposal or the thought of escorting the kitten to a new home, Clara couldn't tell. She looked around and caught Laurel staring at their person with a startling intensity. "Look, can I get back to you? I'm running late."

Her caller barely had time to squawk out an assent before she reached for the phone, cutting off the call as she slid the device into her pocket.

"Good girl." Laurel's eyes closed as she wrapped her tail around her front feet.

"Really?" Clara wanted to question her more, but by then, Becca was at the front door. And in her current unsettled mood, there was no way her cat was letting her out on her own.

Sure enough, Becca didn't seem to be heading to Charm and Cherish, and Clara was glad she was with her person as she ducked into the Central Square T stop. The platform was quiet for the moment, but her cat knew what noise and terror awaited. Sure enough, within minutes a train came roaring into the station, roiling the air and nearly deafening the cat with its squealing brakes. It was all Clara could do to leap on after Becca as she boarded, apparently unfazed by the cacophony. Telling herself that she had done this before and survived, the calico took shelter under Becca's seat, watching warily as other humans entered and chatted casually. Braced for the worst, she was ready when it all started shaking and growling. By the time the train slowed and Becca stood, she raced to follow, grateful to have the opportunity to breathe fresh air once more.

Only, Becca wasn't going anyplace her cat recognized. The neighborhood was faintly familiar—something about the scents and the sounds, the faint hums of many small machines reminded her of Jeff—and at first she thought Becca had returned to CodePhool. But the sleek glass-fronted building her person was entering was nothing like the rundown former factory that housed her ex's former workplace.

"Excuse me." By the time the calico had slipped through the black glass doors, Becca was speaking to an older woman in a smart uniform who sat behind a desk of the same opaque glass. "What floor is Darien Hughes on?"

"Six." The woman looked up. "Do you have an appointment?"

"No, do I need one?" Becca looked concerned. "I can call Darien, if you'd like," she said, fishing out her phone.

"No need." The woman handed Becca a badge. "I just didn't know if anyone was up there today. I'll call so they know you're coming."

"Thanks." Becca clipped the plastic badge to her sweater. "I'm Becca, Becca Colwin."

Clara was ready for the elevator when Becca approached it, walking more slowly than she had all morning. As the machine hummed and purred, lifting them up through the innards of the building, she grew increasingly distracted.

"Becca!" Stepping out of the elevator, Clara's person turned at the sound of her name to see Darien coming down the hall. "What a surprise."

"Hi, I'm sorry. I didn't mean to catch you off guard. I should have called."

"No, no problem at all." The tall financier, more casually dressed today in a beige cotton sweater and jeans, bounced on the balls of his sneaker-clad feet. "What brings you to my neck of the woods?"

"I had a few questions, and I thought I'd drop by your office. But it looks like you're heading out."

"I just needed some air." He glanced back down the hall, with its array of closed doors, his usual grin fading for a moment. "Would you like to get some coffee?"

"Sure." Becca dragged the word out as if she were anything but, as Darien summoned the elevator once again. "I mean, I have to get to work too, but I was wondering. Can you tell me anything more about Jeff's project."

"Oho!" Darien raised his eyebrows as he gestured Becca into the elevator, his good humor returning. "Don't tell me you want in too."

From his smile and the lilt in his voice, Clara thought he might be joking. Becca, however, appeared to take him seriously.

"Me? No." She shook her head. "I meant it when I said I'm not a software person. If Jeff said anything otherwise, he was pulling your leg. But I was wondering if you could tell me something about how the project was developing."

"Oh." Darien sighed as the elevator pinged its arrival back in the lobby. "That's a story better told over caffeine." Holding that big glass door open for Becca, he waved over at the guard. "Thanks, Wendy!"

Ten minutes later, Becca had a cappuccino and a raspberry scone. What she didn't have were answers.

"I'm sorry I can't give you more details, but some of this is confidential." Darien lowered his voice and leaned in, elbows on the table. "There are security implications, as I'm sure you understand."

"I do." Becca nodded. He'd already repeated what she'd thought she knew: that after years of working on internet security, Jeff had come up with a way to unlock programs. "To start with, who would be the client for a program like this? Like, would it be ordinary people who forgot their passwords? Or are we talking about the police or governments?"

"Sorry, Becca." He pushed back, still smiling. "I can't even tell you who my other investors are."

"Other investors?" That made Becca sit up. "I thought you were the investor."

He laughed, rubbing his short beard. "That's what a lot of people think, that we venture capitalists single-handedly fund everything. And I am invested—I think Jeff was brilliant, and he had a once-in-a-lifetime idea. But I'm more like a cheerleader or team organizer for backers. Does that make sense?"

"I guess so." Becca appeared to be chewing over more than the scone. "So how close were you to launching?"

"A few months. Maybe more." Darien exhaled, his handsome face looking suddenly tired. "This has really set us back."

Becca didn't seem to notice. "I wonder what he was going to announce, then?"

"Excuse me?" Darien sat up, his eyes wide.

"Jeff was planning some kind of announcement before he died." Becca considered the man in front of her. "Could it have been about the project?"

Darien shook his head. "Maybe it was something personal? I gather he and Renee were really close."

"You mean, like an engagement announcement?" Becca winced, and her cat's heart went out to her. "I don't think so. It sounded like a press event."

"That's impossible. We hadn't authorized anything." Darien paused, brow furrowing. "Where did you hear about this?"

"He put it on this Facebook group that a bunch of his old friends share. It's funny, 'cause it wasn't on his own page. But it made me wonder."

"I don't blame you, but it sounds bogus. Maybe one of his friends posted it under his name. Those kinds of groups are easy to hack."

"Maybe." She paused. "Do you know Carl Rimsky?"

Darien nodded thoughtfully. "He's contacted me, I think. One of this group?"

"Yeah. I think he was hoping to come in with Jeff."

"He's not on our business plan." Darien's smile turned rueful. "I think a lot of Jeff's old crew hoped to come along, but..." He shrugged. "Maybe once we've launched."

"So you are still going ahead with the project?" Becca wasn't sure what she expected, but Darien only laughed.

"Of course!" His voice softened in apology. "I'm sorry. I know Jeff was one of a kind, but this is a business. You could say this project is his legacy. He'd want us to go forward with the work."

"I guess you're right." Becca finished her coffee. "And speaking of, I should get to work too. Thanks for the coffee and, well, for answering my questions. I didn't mean to grill you."

"I didn't feel grilled at all." He stood and reached to help her with her jacket. "But while I have you in my debt, might I ask you out for something more substantial than a scone? Maybe dinner, a proper one this time?"

"That would be nice." Becca flushed just a little. "I'm sorry I keep coming at you with these questions."

"Please don't apologize." His hands rested on her shoulders for a moment, his face close to hers. "You two were close. I think it's natural that you want to know what happened."

"Told you." Laurel's voice drifted into Clara's ears. Her sister was back at the apartment, Clara knew that. But whether because of their emotional attachment or the sealpoint's ability to read the calico's mind, she seemed able to pick up what had just happened. *"I knew there was another man interested in our Becca."*

"Maybe." Clara still had her doubts, even though the kind Dr. Keller seemed to have moved on. But Laurel's presence was fading, and if her sister had a comeback, it was lost in the noise of the traffic as Clara followed Becca back out onto the street and toward Charm and Cherish.

Twenty-Six

Clara didn't know what Becca expected when she got to work that day. Or rather, she did, but she wished she didn't. So much of her person's magic was wishful thinking, ignoring Becca's real powers of kindness and friendship. If only, she thought, good intentions counted with people like Margaret Cross.

As it was, Becca's boss looked like the living embodiment of her name when Becca arrived at the shop. Before the bells hanging from the door stopped their tinkling, the widow was stalking toward her.

"What are you doing here?" Her scowl accentuated by blood-red lipstick, Margaret crossed her arms as she came to a halt. Although shorter than Becca, she was wide, and with her teased-out hair, she effectively blocked her from coming deeper into the store.

"I'm working." Becca eyed her boss warily. "I'm on the schedule to work from ten 'til closing."

"You were." The widow's bushy brows came down for emphasis. "But that was before you nearly took the building down yesterday."

"I made a mistake." Palms out, Becca apologized once again,

sounding to her pet a little more sure of herself. "But the smudge did no lasting harm. There was no smoke or fire damage."

"There could have been. Or water damage, if the fire department had opened their hoses."

"You didn't have to call them." Becca was losing patience, the strain clearly audible to feline ears. "If you had waited a minute, the alarms would have stopped."

It was the wrong tactic, and Becca fell silent as her boss took a deep breath, visibly expanding like a furious toad.

"If I had waited a minute, I could be *dead*!" An unhealthy dark red that clashed with her lipstick began blotching Margaret's cheeks. "And you, young lady, cannot be trusted."

"You're not...firing me, are you?" Becca's voice fell to a whisper.

The scowl deepened. "Not yet. I can't run this place alone, you know. And don't look to my sister to rescue you again. I gave her a piece of my mind after you left yesterday. Reminded her who owns this shop and the penthouse. And to have you as a teacher, representing us? Ha!"

Clara lashed her tail. While it was true that the diminutive harridan owned Charm and Cherish and the apartment the two sisters now shared, she had inherited both from her husband, whose murder Becca had solved.

"I promise to do better." Becca had to have remembered her service to the Cross family too, her cat thought. And, really, neither Margaret nor Elizabeth were likely to become online ambassadors for the little shop. But maybe it was just as well if she went with conciliation right now. "I'll be more careful."

"I'm not taking any chances." The scowl eased slightly as Margaret eyed her employee. "We'll talk about the teaching if we don't have any more incidents. In the meantime, I don't want you alone in the store."

"Okay." Becca looked thoughtful. It was the end of the standoff. It had to be. Following some unpleasantness a few months past, Becca was currently the store's only employee, and while Elizabeth Cross was truly interested in Wicca and the occult, her sister, Becca knew, was not. There was no way Margaret would want to spend even a few hours in the little shop. "So will you be working with me this morning?"

"Yes, I will." A statement as stout as the speaker. "But only until noon. That's when my new employee comes in."

Becca swallowed, her eyes going wide. But she recovered quickly. "That's great, Margaret. It'll be good to have another person on the team. And, I promise, I'll win your trust back."

A decided sniff let Becca know her boss's thoughts on that. However, she did turn at that point and, stalking off into the back room, let Becca get on with the ritual of opening the shop.

Twenty minutes later, the bells announced a visitor, and Becca peeked from around the bookshelf she'd been dusting.

"Good morning. Welcome to Charm and Cherish." Standing, she dusted herself off and walked forward to greet the visitor.

"Hi." The visitor, clad all in black, looked around. "I didn't know this place was here."

"For a few years now." Becca smiled, making sure her answer didn't sound like a criticism. "We have a full library of books on Wicca, magic, and the occult, as well as incense, figurines, and a variety of tarot decks. And, well, you see."

As she'd been talking, the visitor had gravitated toward the nearest shelf and was examining a black statuette of a cat.

"Bast." Becca didn't think she needed to say more. The visitor smiled in response, her black lipstick parting to reveal an uneven grin that made her look years younger.

"I have one of these at home," she said. "And my own little Bast. She was a street cat when I found her."

"My cats were rescues too." Becca relaxed, even as she heard the door to the storeroom open. "Is there anything I can help you with?"

"Nah." The woman—girl, really—replaced the figure on the shelf, though she did run one finger longingly down its smooth back. "I just wanted to drop by and meet the witch who killed her scumbag ex."

"I—no, I didn't," Becca sputtered as Margaret rushed forward.

"You! Get out. Get out now." She shooed the goth girl as if she were an errant pigeon, sweeping at the air to drive her from the store. "We don't want your type. Get out!"

Wide-eyed with surprise, the girl retreated, and Becca turned to her boss in gratitude.

"Thank you, Margaret. That was awful. I don't know what to say."

"Don't say anything. You've done enough."

Becca inhaled, and for a moment Clara was afraid Becca was about to try to explain. The blog, the smudging...from her cat's eye perspective, the calico couldn't see this helping anything.

"This is what your so-called witch detective work brings in here. Thrill seekers, all of them." Margaret turned to stalk off to the back room. "More and more I'm thinking of closing this stupid place. Now, a yarn shop with knitting and crochet classes, that would have potential."

"No, please," Becca squeaked. She could have said more: Margaret had been one of Becca's first clients, coming to her with questions about her late husband, whose wandering eye undoubtedly contributed to his wife's foul temper, but the older woman was already gone, the storeroom door banging closed behind her.

The rest of the morning passed without incident. Without sales as well, as Becca was all too aware. Having thoroughly dusted the figurines of Bast and Hecate, she eyed the store's big front window. As she took down the dream catchers, their rawhide and silk weavings looking a little tired after the long winter, and replaced them with jewel-toned stained-glass hangings, each depicting a different astrological figure, Becca appeared to relax a little, and Clara dared to resume her usual midmorning nap.

"Welcome to—oh, hi!" The sudden lift in Becca's greeting woke her calico, who peeked over to see a familiar face. "Tina, good to see you."

"You too." The petite brunette beamed at her friend as she bounced into the shop. "I'm so excited about this."

"Excuse me?" Becca trailed after her as she shed her coat and looked around.

"Can I hang this in the back room?" Tina pushed open the door, Becca hard on her heels. Margaret, who had been reclining on the sofa, sat up with a start.

"I'm sorry, Ms. Cross. Did I wake you?" Tina nodded to the old crow, as Becca's head swiveled, taking in the scene.

"I was resting my eyes." Margaret rose and brushed down her suit jacket. "Now that you're here, though, Becca can show you the ropes. And tell you what not to do as well." Squinting into a particularly ferocious scowl, the elderly matron straightened her skirt and, without any further greeting, walked past Becca to the shop. A moment later, the bells announced her departure, and the two young women were left alone in a back room now faintly fragrant with a powdery-sweet floral scent Clara's sensitive nose identified as L'Air du Temps.

"Tina, are you—did you take a job here?" Becca's face showed her confusion.

Tina nodded enthusiastically. "Just part time, of course. But I'm so excited. I love this place!"

"But I thought you were a software developer."

Another vigorous nod. "Yup. I code, but these days so does everyone. Plus, I'm only a contract worker, and the first rule of coding is always have a backup." She snorted as if this were a joke. "But I'm not full time, not like you. I'm just going to be helping out. Mrs. Cross said she needed someone on a casual basis, and I was so excited about the idea of working here with you that I told her I could start immediately."

"When was this?" Becca seemed to be having trouble taking this all in.

"Late yesterday. I came by to talk to you, but you had already left."

"I see." Becca nodded slowly. "Well, we shouldn't leave the storefront unattended," she said at last. "Let me show you how to use the register and card reader, and then I can walk you through what I usually do. Do you know if you'll be opening or closing?"

"Mrs. Cross didn't say," Tina chirped as she followed Becca back into the front room. "She didn't tell me much, to be honest. Like, do we get an employee discount?"

Becca sighed, and Clara knew. It was going to be a long afternoon.

For a little while, Clara was concerned that Becca was going to lose her temper. The unpleasantness with Margaret had left its mark, and Tina's relentless questions, as well as her gushing enthusiasm, were irritating her just when she craved some quiet to think things through. At one point, when Tina came up behind Becca wanting the backstory about their boss and her sister, Clara half expected Becca to swat at her, much like Harriet would the kitten. Seeing how her person restrained herself—making herself respond in a calm, if strained, voice, that, yes, Margaret Cross was the proprietor, but it had been her sister who had convinced Margaret's husband, the late Frank, to use the ground-floor space for the shop—had Clara purring with pride. It also made her a bit more sympathetic to her own oldest sister, who had at least refrained from more than gently cuffing the enthusiastic, some might say indefatigable, kitten.

Within a few hours, however, the two had hit their stride. Once the shock of having a coworker—one with such effusive energy—had worn off, Becca appeared to enjoy the company. At some point, the newcomer, turned her curiosity on the craft, and Becca, seeing an opening, pulled a few of her favorite books from the shelves.

"Do you ever use these?" Tina appeared more interested in the tarot cards, examining a colorful oversized deck.

"I don't," said Becca, resting the books on the shelf. "Ande does, though. That's the Ryder deck, the most common. It's got some great history, and it's most people's go-to. But we also carry a range of newer designs, including a few where the major arcana are all people of color."

"Cool." Tina replaced the cards and began looking through the other options. "I'm going to ask Ande about those. Does she use the BIPOC deck?"

"I don't know." Becca paused, musing. "We should ask her. Maybe we could incorporate the cards into our circle."

"Or more African or African American rituals."

Becca nodded. "That's a great idea, Tina. You're good for us."

"You, the whole coven, have been great for me," the other woman replied. Now that her gushing had calmed down, she seemed calmer around Becca too. "I'm so glad you let me join."

"I am too." Becca laughed. "And for helping with the investigation! I still don't know why Jeff had my key, but I'm so glad you found it rather than the police."

"It was nothing." She tilted her head to take in her colleague. "How did you two meet, anyway?"

"Me and Jeff?" Becca blew out her cheeks. "College. We started dating senior year, and then..." A wave encompassed Charm and Cherish and, Clara assumed, the world beyond. "I guess we just grew apart. I mean, I took it really hard, but he and Renee probably have a lot more in common. She's in design, but she does a lot of work for tech firms, I gather."

"Renee Wendig." Tina huffed. "That's not going to work out."

"You know her?" Becca did a quick double-take. "Did you know Jeff?"

"A little," Tina admitted. "I mean, I did a short stint at Code-Phool when they were both working there. I didn't mention it at first because I didn't put two and two together when you first told us." She spoke quickly, staving off Becca's questions. "It wasn't until recently that I realized that the guy who was leaving was your Jeff. But him and that blonde? No."

"Actually, I've heard they were serious." Becca still didn't sound thrilled by that. "In fact, they might have been planning on getting married."

"What?" Tina reared back. "No way."

"Way." Becca managed a lopsided grin. "In fact, he posted on social media that he was about to make an announcement."

"It could have been work related. The new job and all."

"I don't think so." Becca didn't seem to want to mention Darien, and Tina wasn't convinced.

"It can't be," she said, shaking off the idea. "Now that I know who they both are, it was clear he was done with her. Besides, I think she was flirting with someone else in the office. Maybe she was trying to make him jealous."

Becca rejected that idea. "She was worried about something. She said someone was sending threatening messages."

"She said that, huh?" Tina was staring at Becca like she'd just solved it all. "Doesn't that make you wonder? Everyone's looking at you because they think you were the jealous girlfriend. But she was the one who was about to get dumped. I'd say spreading rumors about threats is just so much smoke. If I were the police, I'd be looking at Renee Wendig right about now."

Twenty-Seven

"Renee, it's Becca. Would you give me a call?"

By the time Charm and Cherish closed that evening, Becca was exhausted. Tina had pushed for the two to go out for dinner, but Becca had begged off. And although Clara knew that her human had other things on her mind, she also suspected that the kittenish colleague had worn Becca's patience thin. That was probably why Becca had had some difficulty placing the call to Renee Wendig, her cat surmised—not that felines know much about phone technology. And why she looked at first frightened and then relieved when the device started humming once again in her hand.

"Hey, Maddy. What's up?" Clara could see how her person relaxed, her stride lengthening, as she recognized her friend's voice. "I'm so glad it's you. My phone's on the fritz. I've been trying to leave a message for someone, and the display's all messed up."

The last of the tension evaporated into a smile as Becca listened to her friend's response. "Sounds like you've been busy too. Do you want to grab some dinner? I've got a few things on my mind that I'd love to get your take on. Mary Chung's? My place? I'll pick it up and be home in a half hour."

Thirty-five minutes and one more call later and Becca was unlocking her own door, a fragrant takeout bag under one arm.

"Be gentle, please." Clara had rushed ahead of her, wanting to warn her sisters. *"Becca has had a difficult day."*

"Becca?" Harriet, who had plopped herself right in front of the door, barely glanced at her little sister. *"What about all I had to go through today?"*

"That kitten has been getting into mischief," Laurel explained as she sidled up to Clara, before assuming her own waiting-for-Becca pose.

"What? Where is the kitten?" Clara craned her head and cocked her ears, trying to locate the infant. *"Harriet?"*

"Relax." Laurel batted Clara's ear to get her attention. *"She's in the pantry."*

"That poor child..." Clara turned tail just as the door opened.

"Hey, kitties. What a nice welcome! But, Clara, aren't you happy to see me?"

Clara looked up at her person, doing her best to convey her love. But just when Becca started to smile down at her, she heard it: the faintest *mew*. The tortie kitten might be safe, but she was trapped and lonely, and that was unbearable.

"What's wrong?" Knowing how difficult Becca's day had been, it broke her cat's heart to worry her, and Clara hesitated before turning and racing toward the kitchen.

"Clara?" Much to the calico's relief, she soon heard Becca following her, with Harriet and Laurel close behind.

"If you delay our dinner for that little pipsqueak..." Harriet was nearly growling as she and Laurel lined up by their mat.

Clara didn't care, and, instead, began scratching at the pantry door.

"Can't you simply walk in?"

Clara froze, one paw reaching for the doorknob. The question had come from inside the pantry, and in a higher pitch than either of her sisters'.

"Kitten, is that you?" But any response was lost as Becca exclaimed and then lifted Clara so she could open the door.

"How did you get yourself trapped in here?" Still holding Clara, Becca knelt as the tiny tortie came forward, blinking in the light.

"Mew," the kitten said.

"So, I think I still have a job, but I don't know how long the store is going to be open." By the time the four cats were finishing their dinner, Maddy had arrived, and Becca was filling her in on the day.

"Good." Harriet looked up from her spotless dish, liking her chops. *"Better she should stay home with us."*

"She needs a job to feed us." Clara knew from experience that any other tack, like, for example, suggesting that it was good for their human to have other human contact, would be batted away like a pipe cleaner.

"Not if she let that someone take care of her." Laurel's voice was slightly muffled as she licked the last of her wet food.

"That's not how she works." Clara looked over at the kitten, who was focusing very hard on cleaning her one peach-colored paw.

"You say that like it's a bad thing." Laurel looked up, her long tongue reaching from whisker to whisker. *"It's how we work, isn't it?"*

Clara had no answer, and so when the kitten trotted off to the living room, she followed, determined to get some answers.

"You know I could get you a position, right? You're a trained researcher." Maddy was focusing on the dumpling in her chopsticks' tenuous grip, so she didn't see Becca roll her eyes. "I mean, Becca, it might be time to get serious about your career."

"My career?" Becca's exasperation would have been obvious to her friend, had the dumpling not chosen that moment to splash into the dipping sauce. "Maddy, that's what I'm working on. You know I've solved some cases."

Maddy bit the dumpling rather than responding. Clara,

meanwhile, was searching for the kitten, who had disappeared once more.

"I already feel like I know more than the police." As Becca spoke, Clara shimmied under the sofa. No kitten. "Like, did I tell you that Jeff was about to make an announcement before he was killed? I asked Darien, and he said it couldn't be anything with the launch. They're not that far along yet, but even if they were, any announcement would have come from his firm. Then I thought that maybe it was personal, that he and Renee were getting married. But Tina hinted that they were breaking up."

"Wait a minute." Maddy swallowed and reached for her tea. "You've been talking to this Tina about the case?"

"She is in my coven." Becca took a smaller bite out of her own dumpling. "And she found my key too."

"And she knows Renee and Jeff?" Maddy was studying her friend, and so Clara passed through the closed bedroom door. No kitten. "All this on top of her coming for your job?"

"She's not coming for my job." By the time Clara had returned, Becca had put the dumpling down. "She earns a lot more as a contractor. She just loves the store, and she wants to learn more about witchcraft."

Maddy's eyebrows rose eloquently as she reached for another dumpling, and Clara, exasperated, collapsed on the rug.

"You suspect her of being involved." Becca sighed. "I confess, it did surprise me to hear that she knew Jeff and Renee. She even worked at CodePhool for a while. But what she says about them fits with what Renee told me."

"That she was getting nasty letters?"

"*Threatening* was the word she used, and it wasn't only Tina: Carl hinted that what Renee was really worried about was that Jeff was cheating again. Or, at any rate, that their relationship wasn't as sound as she let on. And it would explain why Renee reached out to me."

"She thought you'd have some insight?"

"No." Becca scooped some of the eggplant onto her rice. "I think you were right. She was worried he wanted to get back with me. Anyway, that's what I'm trying to get to the bottom of before the police come to talk to me again."

"Wait, what?" Chopsticks stopped mid-air, Maddy stared at her friend.

"A detective came by the store, but then he left. I think they're fishing."

"Becca..."

"It was nothing."

The two friends ate in silence for a few minutes. But it was obvious to Clara that Becca's friend was becoming increasingly agitated.

"Becca," she said finally, pushing her own rice bowl away. "There isn't something you haven't told me. Is there?"

Becca looked up, her mouth full. Clara, alerted by Maddy's tone, did too.

"I know you've been lonely, and the key... You weren't seeing Jeff again, were you?"

"No." Becca put her own bowl down. "But that's one of the reasons I want to talk to Renee. I want to hear more about what these letters really said. Because, Maddy, Tina might be clingy, but she's right about one thing. If the police are looking for a jealous girlfriend, Renee might fit the bill."

"You should just tell all this to the cops. Leave it to them." Maddy was still harping on this as they cleared the table, flanked by Clara and her siblings.

"I don't know. I don't want to throw another woman under the bus." Becca poured the leftover mapo tofu into a container and pushed Harriet off the counter with one sweeping gesture. "Not until I know what's going on. Besides, she might have information. I've left her a message, and I'm going to call Carl in the morning too. I want to follow up on this announcement Jeff was going to make. Someone has to know what he was going to say."

"It might have been nothing." Maddy reached down to pick up Laurel, who had been gently pawing at her leg.

"That's how you do it," Laurel purred, glancing down at her siblings.

"Most leads don't go anywhere." Becca directed a stern look down at Harriet. "No, no leftovers for you three. I mean, four."

"Four?" Maddy turned around, even as Laurel reached for the counter. "You still have the kitten?"

"For now." Becca washed her hands. "She got herself stuck in the pantry today, but she's basically no bother. The other cats seem to have accepted her."

"Ha." Harriet began washing in a sulk.

"Four cats, Becca. I don't know."

Laurel squirmed and jumped to the floor in protest.

"Like we don't have everything in hand," she sniffed. *"And that little creature is barely a cat."*

"I heard her talking. But then she managed to disappear." Clara leaned forward, hoping to impress her sisters with the import of this discovery. From the living room, a soft thud announced another absolutely ordinary kitten-sized misadventure, and Laurel flicked her ears.

"Sure," she said.

"Dr. Keller has someone who wants to take her. Some woman he's dating. A Leila something." Oblivious to the feline conversation happening at her feet, Becca was toweling off her hands. "I just want to make sure it's the right place for her."

"Becca, if Dr. Keller found a home for that kitten, it'll be a good place." Maddy spoke with a deliberate emphasis. "Or isn't that what's bothering you?"

"Nothing's bothering me."

"Then I think you should let this happen. I don't want to worry that you're becoming a hoarder."

"I'm not a hoarder," Becca scoffed, much as Laurel had only moments before. "It's one little kitten."

"A kitten who is hiding more secrets than we know," said the calico at her feet.

Twenty-Eight

Becca was up early again the next morning, and not because of the kitten. Although Clara had kept an eye on the little tortie half the night, only letting herself drift off once the kitten was clearly down for the count, she had gotten no further response from the little cat. If anything, the kitten was maturing. She'd stopped batting at Becca's feet under the covers as soon as it was clear that the human really did want to go to sleep, for example. And while she chased her own tail enough to provoke giggles in both Becca and Maddy, she had left Harriet's fluffy white appendage alone.

"It's almost like she wants Becca to keep her," Clara mused, watching the little cat. While the other felines were enjoying their breakfast, the tortie was grabbing at Becca's ankle, distracting their person as she listened to a message on her phone.

"Nonsense," huffed Harriet. *"She's simply responding to my training. Not all of us choose to gallivant all over town when there's work to be done."*

Clara ducked her head, accepting her sister's judgment, but privately she wasn't sure. Becca had seemed disturbed by the vet's message, and the kitten had only begun her playful leaps when she had appeared about to return the call. That had led to her pocketing the device, and Clara and her sisters had followed as their person headed to the door.

"Don't worry about us." Harriet must have sensed Clara's uneasiness, even if she misinterpreted the worries behind it. *"We're quite capable of handling one fuzzy mite."*

"We can always lock her in the pantry again," Laurel purred, with just enough of a wink so that Clara suspected she was joking. *"Now, go! I'm getting an uncomfortable vibe too, Clown. Becca's got some strange ideas, and she's more headstrong than that kitten!"*

Blinking in acknowledgement, Clara turned and leaped through the door, flying down the stairs before her person could hit the street.

Which was a good thing, she quickly realized. Once again, it seemed her person wasn't heading straight to work. As Clara trotted beside her, mindful of the busy rush hour crowd, she did her best to remember what the two women had discussed the night before.

"You can't go to his apartment." That much Clara remembered: Maddy had said it repeatedly and with rising volume. When she had gone on about police and the appearance of guilt, Clara had begun lashing her tail, hoping her person would take notice. But as Becca turned a corner that her cat vaguely remembered from the year before, Clara began to fear that her person had not listened to her friend's advice.

"Hello." Becca greeted an older woman as she crossed a familiar courtyard. The woman was carrying several packages and smiled gratefully when Becca grabbed the building's heavy outer door, holding it open.

"Thanks." She scrutinized Becca, as if fishing for a memory.

"No problem." Becca, usually so polite, ducked into the building's tiled foyer before the inevitable question could arise, and Clara slipped in beside her.

"That was easy enough." Becca spoke as if she were cheering herself on, and as she mounted the steps, her cat found herself torn. Even without Maddy's protests—and she had elaborated on all the risks Becca was taking—the cat knew this was not a great idea. And despite Laurel's encouragement, Clara didn't think she could have Becca seeing spiders or suddenly longing for a cup of coffee and a croissant. As it was, she felt as insubstantial as she was invisible. If someone interrupted Becca now, it might lead to trouble. But better out here in the stairwell than inside the apartment of her dead ex.

At least at this time of the morning the building was quiet. The morning rush was over, and Becca made it to the third floor without running into any other residents. After taking a moment to catch her breath on the carpeted landing, she tried the knob to the first door on the left, apartment six, only to find it locked. That wasn't enough to make Clara relax, though, and even as she did her best to envision a carrot muffin, studded with raisins, staring hard at the curls at the back of Becca's head, her person pressed herself against the doorframe, reaching up to its top sill. But whatever Jeff might have hidden up there was out of Becca's reach, and Clara began once more to hope. The door to apartment six looked solid enough: old wood, with brass furnishings that glowed from years of wear. And while Clara could have passed through easily enough, she knew Becca would need a key.

At one time, this had been a sore point for Clara's person. Back when they'd been going out, Jeff had used his odd hours as an excuse to cadge a copy of Becca's, explaining that he wouldn't want to wake her if he came by after working late. But he had never reciprocated, arguing that her research job was pretty much nine to five. In retrospect, Clara knew, his odd ideas about fidelity were more likely the issue, as she was once again seized by the memory of her dear person bereft and sobbing.

This morning, though, Becca's loyal pet found herself thanking the late coder for his unwillingness to hand over a key as she prepared to herd her person safely out of the building. But, for once, Becca proved to have sharper eyes than the calico. Behind them both, by the door across the landing, an empty plastic bucket was serving as a catchall for newspapers and fliers. Carefully placing its collection of takeout menus on the mat, Becca brought the bucket over to Jeff's apartment, turned it upside down, and climbed up, this time easily reaching the top of the sill.

"Gotcha!" A key flashed in the light as it fell noiselessly to the carpeted floor.

Stepping down, Becca retrieved the key, which fit smoothly into the lock, and the door responded by clicking open a nudge. At that, Becca paused, but when no alarm sounded or occupant yelled out in shock, she replaced the key and then the bucket, slowly opened the door, and stepped inside.

Clara didn't know what her person was looking for. Neither, it appeared, did Becca. As her cat watched with growing trepidation, Becca walked around the one-bedroom as carefully and quietly as if she were a ghost. In the living room, newly assembled cardboard boxes sat open on the floor, with books stacked beside it.

"The police must have allowed the family in," Becca said, gingerly opening an anthology of Kliban cartoons. "Unless Jeff was moving."

Moving on to a battered wooden desk, Becca opened the top drawer. "I guess it was too much to hope for a day planner," she said as she began to sift through the loose papers inside. "Or one of those threatening letters."

With that, Becca froze, apparently transfixed by the contents of that drawer. Moving silently, Clara jumped to the desktop and, stepping carefully so as not to dislodge any of the loose papers piled on top, crept over to where her person was staring. A yellow sticky note, the kind Becca used to remind herself to pick up cat food, had come free from the pile. As Becca reached for it, Clara got a fleeting scent of a once-familiar presence: Jeff.

The memory of Becca's onetime beau flooded the cat's senses, bringing with it the sounds of laughter and, too soon, tears. Clara closed her eyes as she recalled how helpless she had felt, leaning against her person as she wept, unable to comfort the crying girl or even distract her from her pain.

The sound of sliding metal jarred the little cat back to the present, and made her person jump as well. Grabbing the yellow sticky, Becca slammed the drawer shut with her hip and turned to face the door as the lock slid closed and then open again.

"Hello," a familiar male voice called out. "Is anybody here?"

"Carl?" Becca stepped toward the bedroom door, pocketing the sticky note as she did.

"Becca?" Clara whirled around to see the programmer in the doorway, a strange half smile on his round face. "I didn't expect to see you here."

"I know. I'm sorry to have startled you." Becca looked around, as if surprised to find herself in her ex's apartment—or looking for an excuse. "It's kind of a long story, but I saw something on Facebook that made me curious. Jeff posted a note to alert bloggers and the media about some kind of press conference he was planning to hold the day after he was killed. I know it could have been a coincidence, but I thought it might be important." She concluded her ramble with a shrug. "Anyway, I was trying to find out what Jeff was planning on announcing."

"Well, he had the new project." Carl pointed out the obvious in a tone that would have set Maddy off. What he didn't do, Clara was relieved to note, was ask how Becca had gotten in.

"No," Becca said, her voice reflecting her growing confidence. "It's not that. If it was about the launch, he would have done any press through Darian's company, not on a private Facebook page." Carl opened his mouth, but Becca had only paused to take a breath. "Just to be sure, I checked. Darian said he didn't know anything about it."

"You've spoken to Darian?" Clara didn't think that was what he had originally planned on saying, but Becca nodded vigorously, happy to have a question she could answer.

"He came into the store the other day and—and introduced himself." Carl might not have noticed the pause in her answer, but Clara did. It was all she could do to keep her tail from lashing, aware that such a movement would rustle the papers she sat on. "Anyway, what brings you here?"

Carl frowned, looked past her toward the desk. "I've been

asked to clear some things up. Locate some early papers." He gestured, and Clara carefully stepped aside.

"So you are going to be working with Darien?" Becca sounded relieved, though Clara suspected that had more to do with the end of the programmer's questioning. "I'm so happy for you. When I spoke to Darien, I thought—"

"It's not official yet," Carl cut her off. "But Darien needs me." He spoke with a quiet intensity that had the hairs along Clara's back standing on end.

Becca seemed to notice too. "I know you want to be part of the project, Carl." She spoke gently, as one would to a kitten, Clara thought. "Maybe it's just too soon?"

The programmer shook his head. "He can't get started without me. Not now."

Becca's eyes widened, and Clara felt a growl beginning deep in her chest. Did the chubby programmer realize he had just given himself a motive in Jeff's murder?

"I'm sure that in the coming weeks, he'll be in touch." Becca eyed the door to the bedroom. Clara, with a growing panic, realized that the stout man was blocking it. "This has got to be a crazy time."

"Indeed." Carl nodded toward the desk. "So, did you find anything?"

"To do with the announcement?" A nervous giggle bubbled up in Becca's throat. "No, nothing that makes sense. In fact, the more that I think about it, the more I think it was something personal. Maybe he and Renee were going to announce their engagement."

Carl dismissed that idea with a shake of his head. "No, they were through."

"I'd heard rumors, but who knows what goes on inside someone else's relationship?" Becca's voice had taken on a high, tight quality that made Clara's fur rise. "She told me she'd been getting nasty letters, so maybe he wanted to make some kind of public statement about that."

She inched toward the door. Carl, glowering at the desk, didn't move. "That doesn't sound like Jeff," he said.

"I know." Becca chuckled, but the sound was fake and thin. "Not the Jeff that I remember, anyway. But what else could it be?"

She took another step toward the door, as if to sidle by the large programmer. But even as she spoke, using that calming voice that Clara associated with visits to the vet, her cat saw a shadow pass over her face. A sudden thought had surfaced, her cat thought, making her reevaluate her own conjecture. "I know the launch was considered a done deal. But what if—?"

The rest of the question was squelched as Carl reached out and, grabbing her upper arms, pulled her close and kissed her.

"No! Carl!" Becca pushed the programmer away.

"I'm sorry." He reached out, but Becca was already heading toward the exit. "Becca, please."

To her cat's dismay, Becca paused, one hand on the knob. "I'm sorry too, Carl. Maybe I should have been more clear when you gave me those flowers. But I'm not interested."

"Of course not." He managed a pained smile. "You can't blame a guy for trying. But how can I compete with someone as handsome and rich as Darian Hughes?"

Twenty-Nine

"What in Bast's name was that?" Becca was walking quickly, her breath still coming hard. "I'm sure I never gave him any encouragement. And he was the reason Jeff was always going out..." Becca didn't finish the thought. She didn't have to. Her cat was simply relieved that she was clear of that building and the man who had confronted her there.

Blowing out her lips as if the last twenty minutes had been so much bad air, Becca slowed, sticking her hands in her pockets as she relaxed into a steadier pace. When she pulled them out a moment later, she was holding the yellow sticky.

"*Get k from b*," she read, stopping on the sidewalk. "What the...?"

"Excuse me!" As Becca was jostled from behind, she almost dropped the note.

"Watch it," she yelled at the hurrying pedestrian who had pushed by. Tall, slender, and clad in the kind of slim-cut suit she'd been seeing more and more of in Cambridge these days, the man didn't even turn. Clara noticed the ear buds that were probably obscuring Becca's peeved outcry, but to her person, she knew, he was just another example of a clueless male.

"Men," Becca grumbled, as if on cue, and, once more pocketing the note, continued on her way.

"Hi, Tina." If Becca's greeting was less than enthusiastic, Charm and Cherish's new employee didn't seem to notice. She had been leaning against the window, basking in the morning sun, as Becca walked up.

She jumped at the greeting. "Good morning!" Tina's broad grin couldn't hide how pale she looked or the rings under her eyes, and Clara wondered if she'd been catnapping in the June warmth.

"Late night?" Becca gave the other girl a knowing glance as she unlocked the door.

"Oh, I'm fine." Tina waited while Becca turned on the lights and then followed her into the back room, shedding her jacket along the way. "Mrs. Cross said that Sundays were usually quiet, but she wants me to learn the ropes, so I figured I'd be here when you open."

"That makes sense." Becca nodded, accepting the new reality. "I mean, if you learn how to cover, I can take some time off, at least on weekends."

"I can work evenings too. Maybe some afternoons."

Becca hung her own jacket and turned a quizzical look on her companion.

"The contract work is kind of drying up." Tina shrugged.

"I'm sorry." Becca handed the tray of semi-precious stones to Tina. "Here, would you take these out?"

"Sure." The sight of the colorful stones seemed to cheer Tina. "They're lovely." She poked at the brown-and-gold striped trapezoid. "Though that one doesn't seem to fit."

Becca looked over at the tiger eye. "Yeah, it looks like a collapsed cardboard box, doesn't it? I like it, though. It makes me happy every day I come in and see it there."

"Why don't you buy it? Is it really expensive?"

"No." Becca laughed, following her with the change and small bills that had also been locked away overnight. "None of them are worth much. Not really. But I kind of like that it's there every morning to greet me. You know? I figure the right person will recognize how special it is and buy it, and maybe I'll help that happen. In the meantime, it doesn't make sense to leave them out where they might tempt someone to do a smash-and-grab."

"I hear you." Tina cast a worried glance at the big front window. "I hadn't thought about street crime here. Though, at night—" She stopped cold and, still holding the tray, turned to face Becca. "Do you think that's what happened to Jeff? A robbery gone bad?"

Becca sighed as she fit the cash tray into the register. "I almost wish it was, but the police seem to think something else was going on, and I figure they should know."

"But not better than the witch detective!" Tina's cheer was contagious, at least enough to win a smile from Becca. "Have you made any progress?"

"Not really." Becca reached into her pocket, and Clara knew she was thinking of the note she'd found. "I think the biggest breakthrough has been you finding my key, and I still don't know what that means."

"I think it's more proof Renee is involved." Tina leaned back on the nearest bookshelf, crossing her arms. "I mean, they were fighting. She found out he still had your key. The relationship was clearly falling apart—"

"Was it?" Becca interrupted. "I mean, I know someone was sending her nasty letters."

"So she says." Tina emphasized the last word. But before she could present any proof, they were interrupted by a familiar jingling.

"Welcome to Charm and Cherish." Becca turned to the visitor and caught her breath at the sight of another pale young woman clad all in black. "Tina, would you?"

"Sure." Tina stood to greet the customer, and Becca slipped away to the back.

"Hey, Maddy." Even facing the corner of the storeroom, Becca kept her voice low. "Do you have a minute? Yeah, I'm at work, but another goth girl just came in, and I'm really not up to being interrogated."

By jumping up on the back of the breakroom couch, Clara could just make out the voice of Becca's friend. "... the blog?"

"Tina's done what she can. I gather they're pretty well hidden," Becca said. "But I did find something this morning. I went over to Jeff's apartment—"

Clara didn't need her feline sensitivity to hear Maddy's response to that.

"I had to, Maddy." Becca barely raised her own voice. "I've been stymied, and that detective called. He left a message that he wants to speak with me. It didn't sound urgent, but I feel like the smudging didn't do anything. Probably because I was interrupted."

Maddy's own interruptions were growing louder.

"No, I haven't returned his call yet, Maddy. I'm not saying I believe there's a curse on me, but I do feel under the gun. And that blog? It's almost like someone wants me to be the murderer." Ignoring the frantic complaints of her friend, Becca kept on. "Anyway, I found something. A note."

Reaching over for her jacket, she fished out the yellow sticky. "*Get k from b*," she read. "I figure 'b' has got to be me, right? And 'k,' well, he had my key on him. Only, Maddy—"

"Excuse me?"

Becca whirled to see Tina in the doorway.

"I'm sorry, but the customer wants to buy a book, and I'm not sure how to ring it up."

"I'll be right there." Becca breathed a sigh of relief before returning to her call. "Sorry, Maddy. A customer, a regular old customer. I'll tell you the rest later."

"Sorry, folks." Becca stepped back into the shop to find the goth girl running one black fingernail down a page. "Ah, a protection spell. That's a good one."

"Does it work?" The girl looked up, her kohl-rimmed eyes wide. "Some of my friends have been acting weird."

"It can't hurt," Becca replied. "Though if you feel like you're not safe in any relationship, I can help you find some other resources."

"No, this'll be fine." Her pale cheeks warmed a bit. "They're just on a weird kick. Besides, I've been wanting a good guide to the craft."

"I've got a copy of this one myself."

The young woman beamed. "I'm so glad you're here. Charm and Cherish, I mean."

"We're here because of customers like you," responded Becca. Clara had often heard her express similar sentiments. If this time she placed a bit more emphasis in it, her cat knew why.

"Wow, you're so good with the customers." Tina watched the woman retreat, bag clutched to her chest.

"Well, I started as one. You did too, I think."

Tina's broad grin was her answer. "Hey, I couldn't help but overhear what you were saying on the phone." Becca's raised brows registered her shock. "I'm sorry, I didn't mean to eavesdrop."

"No, I get it. We had a customer. I shouldn't have left you alone."

"It was fine." Tina waved off Becca's apology. "But I heard what you said about that note and that Jeff was looking to exchange keys. That fits with me finding that key, right?"

"I don't know." Becca sounded skeptical.

"But it makes sense," Tina warmed to her narrative. "If Jeff was getting serious about another relationship, he'd want to clean up old loose ends. You know, clear the deck."

Becca winced at that but quickly recovered. "I thought you were making the case that he and Renee were through."

Tina nodded vigorously. "Yeah, but maybe he wasn't thinking of Renee. And maybe this time he *was* serious. Didn't the cops say there had been reports of a man and a woman fighting right before he was killed? Maybe Renee found out that he was getting ready to move on."

"There's one big problem with that." Becca spoke softly, pain pinching her face once again. She was thinking of what Marcia had told her, her cat guessed. That the woman in the argument looked like her. What she said, however, took a different tack. "I don't know what that note means, what 'k' is. I never had a key to his place."

"Oh." Both women fell silent, Tina's face growing thoughtful as she absorbed Becca's words.

Becca, meanwhile, walked over to the bookshelf and began straightening the volumes arrayed there, pushing in a pensive gargoyle bookend to fill the gap. Clara watched as she worked, aware that her person was barely registering the titles she was lining up. Although she'd been willing to discuss the latest with her coven mate, it had clearly raised some painful memories. And while Clara understood Tina's high regard for Becca—at times, it seemed almost like hero worship—she wished the new witch would have a better sense of Becca's vulnerabilities. Once again, the calico conceded, humans' inability to accept that they had no magical powers at all had wound up hurting Becca, to her pet's lasting dismay.

Thirty

"Do you want to talk about him?"

Tina was trying, Becca knew. Two hours later, she'd agreed to share a small pizza for lunch in the back room. That didn't mean she had much appetite for this discussion. After taking an inordinately long time to chew a bite of pepperoni and mushroom, she sipped her diet cola and, taking a deep breath, turned to her colleague.

"No, I don't," she said. Moving on before Tina could respond, she explained. "I really appreciate you asking and, yeah, it's just horrible and weird. But I feel like I went through this all already, back when we broke up."

Tina nodded and reached for another slice. "I didn't know if this had brought up unresolved feelings. I mean, having to deal with Renee and all."

With an audible sigh, Becca took the last slice. "I know. Who'd have thought she and I would be chatting like old friends?"

"You've become friends?"

"No, I misspoke." Becca dabbed at her mouth with a paper napkin. "But she's the one who came by and invited me to the memorial. Like she was finally acknowledging that I'd been part of Jeff's life at some point."

"Unless she was looking for someone to take the fall for his death."

"Ugh, I hope not." Becca put down her unfinished slice. "But I just don't know..." She stared at the shelves that lined the wall, as if the answers could be found in the bulk boxes of incense labelled "Sandalwood" and "Cedar." "At the very least, she probably knows what that announcement was about. I've left her a message, but I should try her again." She paused, considering her colleague. "Do you want to join us?"

"Me? No." Tina pushed her empty plate back. "For better or worse, you two have a bond, and she's reached out to you already. I do want to hear what she says, though."

As Tina cleaned up, Becca made the call, her eyes widening in surprise when the other woman picked up.

"Hey, Renee. It's Becca." Pitching her voice slightly higher than normal made her sound more frantic than friendly, her cat thought. Then again, human ears were much less sensitive than cats'. "I was wondering if you'd be free to chat."

As Tina—and Clara, hidden beside her—watched, Becca rolled her eyes.

"Just, I don't know, to touch base.

"This afternoon?" Her voice hiked up an octave, a furrow appearing between her brows as she listened to the woman on the other end of the line. "Well, I'm at work now. But let me see what I can do."

She hung up, shaking her head. "Renee's busy tonight and tomorrow, but she said she could meet me for coffee. I don't know, though."

"Don't know what?" The two turned to see an older woman with a mass of gray curls sweeping through the back door, today's caftan, a brilliant turquoise, backlit by the afternoon light.

"Elizabeth!" Becca lit up at the sight of the owner's sister. "Tina, have you two met?"

"I don't think so." Tina came forward, hand outstretched. "Unless it was back when I was simply a customer."

"So you're the new girl." Elizabeth tilted her head, taking in the shorter woman with a gimlet eye. "I'm Margaret's sister. Her older sister."

"As in older and wiser?" Tina ventured, winning a smile from the senior.

"In some ways," she said. "Margaret told me she hired you. Though I disagree with her reasoning"—a quick glance at Becca —"I'm glad we can afford Becca some flexibility. She's really kept this place going."

"Elizabeth is being modest," Becca demurred, following the turquoise caftan into the front of the store, closely followed by her shaded cat and the other clerk. "Margaret owns the shop, but Elizabeth is the one who cares about the craft. Some of our best purchases have been her finds, like the antique Bast in the corner."

"Pieces like that make Charm and Cherish." Elizabeth ran her hand down the black statuette's smooth back and spun around so that her caftan puffed out like a cloud. "Bast deserves to be venerated," she said. Although Clara was shaded—she'd double checked as soon as the older woman had appeared—she was sure that as Elizabeth had turned, she had winked at her.

"Now, what was that about taking a break?" As her voluminous skirts—and Clara's startled fur—settled, she walked up to the tray of precious stones and began flipping them with her outstretched finger.

"There's someone I'd like to talk to, but she's only available this afternoon."

"I can stay here with Tina." Elizabeth turned her smile on the new clerk. "In case she needs any assistance."

"Really? Thanks, Elizabeth." Becca grabbed her phone, punching in a text before either woman could complain. "Damn."

"What's wrong?" Tina stepped forward.

"It's fine." Becca raised her hand to stop her. "Renee? Sorry, I just tried to text but my phone's wonky. Are you still free? Great."

"Might want to have that looked at." Elizabeth eyed her device.

"I know. I probably need a new one. It's been happening more and more," said Becca, pocketing it. "Anyway, I'm off. I'll be back in an hour."

"Take your time," Tina called as Becca grabbed her coat and headed for the door. "We'll hold down the fort."

"Yes, we will," affirmed Elizabeth. This time the wink was unmistakable.

Thirty-One

"Thanks for meeting with me." Becca scraped her chair up to the table, shedding her jacket as she sat. "It sounds like you're really busy."

"It's crazy." The blonde facing her sighed, brushing her long hair back over her shoulder. "I meant to take some time off after—because of Jeff. But maybe it's good to keep busy."

"You're getting more work?" Becca was only making conversation. That much was clear to Clara, who had dashed in behind her person and now crouched under the coffeehouse table. Even if she hadn't witnessed the earlier discussion with Tina, she'd be able to hear the forced lightness in her tone.

Renee didn't. "Yeah, it's weird. I'm getting all these offers now. Like losing Jeff freed something up. Or, no, it's more basic than that." She looked down at her own mug and then back up at Becca. "Do you want something?"

"I'll get a coffee in a minute," she said. "But you were saying?"

"At first, I thought maybe it was sympathy. But now I'm wondering if it was just that people thought they could only reach me through Jeff, and he was so busy. Plus, you know, maybe there was some resentment..."

Becca waited.

"Supposedly, CodePhool wants me to come back in. Carl told me." Renee played with her hair, twisting a strand around one ringed finger. "Despite what everyone was saying the other night, I think there might have been some hard feelings there with Jeff leaving and all. But maybe people are remembering the work I did before Jeff. I even got a call from Darien Hughes, the investor who was backing Jeff."

"He wants you to do design work?" Clara could feel Becca tensing slightly.

"I guess so." Renee shrugged. "We haven't really spoken yet, but I think everyone knows I was involved with Jeff, so, you know, it makes sense. I'm sure Jeff talked about me, about my graphics work."

"Already? I thought the project hadn't gotten off the ground yet."

Another shrug sent her hair cascading forward again. "That's what I thought too, but it sounds like he's looking ahead. When he called, he really seemed to want to hear my ideas. Or, okay, Jeff's ideas. He kept asking what Jeff had told me about the project. How he saw it moving forward, and the like."

Becca nodded, her face growing thoughtful.

"But then he asked me if I'd meet to talk about it. Over dinner." The blonde flashed a look at Becca, before letting her long hair fall once again over her face. "I mean, I'm not ready for something new yet, but, well, maybe he's just being supportive."

"Maybe." Becca's voice was unreadable as she changed the subject. "I confess I wanted to ask you about Jeff's thoughts too, Renee. Specifically, I was wondering if you knew about some kind of announcement he was intending to make."

"An announcement?" She looked up, blue eyes wide.

Becca nodded. "He posted in a local programmer's Facebook group that he was getting something together and was going to make an announcement the next day." She paused, taking in the woman seated across from her. "He posted that the day he was killed, Renee. I can't help but wonder if there was some connection."

"That's crazy," the other woman scoffed. "That's like blaming him for being killed." Before Becca could protest, she offered an alternative. "Maybe he was getting ready to hire? That would merit a big announcement, and posting it in a programmer's group would make sense."

"That was my first thought too, but I don't think so." Becca paused before adding, "I've spoken to Darien too, and I gather they weren't that far along yet. Besides, something like that would have gone through Darien."

"Maybe." The other woman chewed that over. "But Jeff was working really hard those last few weeks. He and Carl pulled some all-nighters."

"Carl was working with him?" Becca leaned in.

A nod. "I can't imagine what else they would be collaborating on. I mean, unless Jeff was finishing up some CodePhool project before he left. Why?"

"Carl hasn't been signed up by Darien. At least, not yet."

"Well, there you go." Renee sounded convinced. "That's probably what the announcement was about. Jeff was probably going public about Carl being his partner."

"Maybe." When Becca didn't continue, Clara looked up at her person. Surely, she remembered that the moon-faced programmer had denied having an offer. Instead, Becca pivoted. "I confess, Renee, I was wondering if it was about something personal. Maybe about your plans?"

Renee blinked. "My plans?"

"Like, that you were getting engaged?" Clara could hear the strain in her person's voice.

"No." Renee examined her cup, apparently finding something there. "We'd talked about getting married, of course. But, no." The admission seemed to cost her.

Becca swallowed as she nodded. "I was wondering, especially because you told me about those letters..."

"That was nothing." She shook off the idea. "He, well, you know. Women like Jeff. Liked him. In fact, at first, I thought that you..."

"I know." Becca said. "Or, I should say, I suspected as much when you came to see me. But it really wasn't me."

"I know that now." Renee had the grace to sound abashed. "It's only, well, he did talk about you a lot. Not to me, of course. But to Carl."

Becca's expression must have registered her shock.

"They talked a lot late at night. Jeff would go in the other room, but I could still hear him." Her voice dropped with embarrassment. "I'd hear your name a lot."

"That could mean anything." Becca found herself in the odd position of comforting the other woman. She didn't, her cat noted, bring up the bearish coder's attempted embrace. Though she did appear to be about to say something, when Renee kept talking.

"Yeah, I should ask Carl tonight."

"You're seeing him?" Becca's voice went up a notch.

Renee nodded vigorously. "He's been a total doll. He's taking me out to dinner, just to get my mind off things."

Thirty-Two

"She's involved." Becca called Maddy as soon as she stepped back out onto the sidewalk. "I don't know to what extent, but I can't imagine why else both Carl and Darian are courting her."

Her friend's response was lost in the roar of the city, but Clara could fill in the blanks.

"I know, Maddy. She's blonde and skinny and..." A sigh filled in for the ineffable. "But both of them? At any rate, she's sure not acting like she's in mourning."

The briefest of pauses as Becca crossed the street.

"There's something creepy going on with Carl as well. Darien, I get. He's a handsome, smart guy, with money too. I might even have gone out with him again. I mean, that was a nice fantasy, but you were the one who told me: cute guys know they're cute. He probably asks out every woman he meets, and he's probably only recently met Renee. But Carl and Jeff were friends, and now he's hitting on his ex *and* his latest girlfriend? I could almost understand if he were obsessed with Renee. But me? He could have asked me out any time over the last year. Not that I'd have accepted."

Whatever Maddy said was overwhelmed by the roar of the traffic.

"It'll be interesting to see what happens if they both end up pursuing Renee. But maybe that's it." Becca stopped short. "Didn't I tell you? Before he grabbed me, Carl was talking about how Darien needs him for this project. He wants to be hired so bad it's, well, honestly, it made me wonder. It's almost like he wants to take over Jeff's life."

Whatever Maddy's response was, it had Becca nodding along in agreement.

"That's a kind interpretation, Maddy. Maybe he was jealous of what Jeff and I had, but he sure had a crazy way of showing it. And trying to take his place?" Becca chewed on her lip. "Though, speaking of, Renee had another idea about Jeff's post. She thought that Jeff might have been about to make a public announcement about how he and Carl had worked together on the project in order to force Darien's hand. And if that's the case, then Carl didn't have any motive. In fact, he's out in the cold because Jeff didn't get a chance to make it official."

Still half a block down from Charm and Cherish when the call ended, Becca shoved her phone in her pocket as if it were to blame for her current agitation. The way she chewed on her lip was the giveaway of some kind of internal debate, her cat thought. Kind of like the way the calico's tail lashed back and forth in agitation just when she was trying to appear most calm. Pulling her phone out again, Becdca poked at it quickly.

"Meant to ask," she spoke out loud. "I'd love to see those letters. Can we talk?" And with that, she headed back to work.

"There you are." Tina greeted her with a big sigh of what sounded like relief. "It's been nuts."

"Oh?" Becca walked by to hang her coat in the back. "Where's Elizabeth?"

"She went up to their apartment." Tina tagged along behind

her. "She's funny, isn't she? She said I could handle everything myself, no matter what her sister said."

"I trust her." Becca turned to take in Tina's drawn face. "What happened?"

"The craziest thing." She collapsed on the sofa. "Everything was going well. I had two customers, older women. They asked for you. They looked really happy, but they didn't buy anything. Then this other group came in, two guys and a girl. The kind of friends who look like they all shared the same hair dye, you know? I figured they were regulars, and I was determined to make a sale. But all they wanted was to ask about you too. Only, well, they wanted to know if you practiced the dark arts."

Becca sighed and nodded knowingly. "It's that blog. I'm sorry. Elizabeth never should have left you to deal with everything alone."

"I know! It was odd, right? And the way she put it was kooky too."

Becca waited. Clara did too, the fur beginning to rise along her back.

"She said I should always remember to look to the light. That the light would always flush out the dark. It was like she knew what was going to happen!"

"Maybe she did." Becca took up her position behind the register, and Tina tagged along. "Elizabeth is an unusual woman, Tina. I think she has more powers that any of us."

"But you're a witch detective. You've actually done a summoning." Tina seemed to place a great weight on this, but Becca only shook her head sadly.

"That was months ago," she said. "These days, I don't know. I can't even ward off the negative spirits in my own workplace."

"You can't think that those three weirdos... They weren't spirits." Tina browsed the back bookshelf, the stress of the encounter gone. "They were real, just kind of freaky."

Becca wasn't listening, however. Instead, she stared down at the counter before her. "How long were they in the store?"

"I don't know. A few minutes." She pulled a book from the

shelf and began to thumb through it. "When they found out you weren't here—"

"Were you watching them the entire time they were here?" A new edge in Becca's voice caught Tina's attention. Replacing the book, she came over to the counter.

"Yeah, as much as I could. Why?"

"The tiger eye." Becca pointed to the tray of semi-precious stones. "It's missing."

"Are you sure?" Tina tilted the tray up, sending the pretty stones sliding.

Becca ran her hand through the gems, revealing pink and purple quartz and the smooth black tourmaline that had been there for months. But all these stones were round or oval, their cabochon curves polished to a fault. None of them had the rounded trapezoid shape of a squashed cardboard box, and none the black-and-caramel colors of a classic tiger eye—or of a tortoiseshell cat, Clara realized with a start. Becca's good luck stone was gone.

Thirty-Three

Elizabeth did not seem overly upset by the theft, but that didn't make Becca feel much better. She had come down to the store after Becca called and found the two women searching for the missing stone on the floor around the front counter.

"Sometimes things go missing," she said, addressing Becca's back.

"It's my fault." Tina hung her head. "I should have been more careful."

"No, it's my fault," said Becca, rising and brushing her knees. "I never should have left in the middle of my shift."

"If you recall, I gave you permission." Elizabeth held out her hands in absolution first to Becca and then to the new hire. "Such things happen. And tiger eye? Well, it has a will of its own. I wouldn't count that stone out yet."

Becca refused to be mollified. "Everything has gone wrong since I chased that kitten down the alley. Jeff and the police, and then the fire department."

"But you didn't kill Jeff, and you did save that kitten." Elizabeth waved the rest away, and for a moment, Clara was sure the gray-haired woman was staring right at her. "Remember the rule of three."

"I know." Becca forced a smile. "So, theoretically, I should have three good actions coming my way?"

"That may be a bit simplistic, dear. But remember, you do have three cats."

"I also have a job, and your sister is my boss." Becca's eyes grew big with tears.

"Leave her to me, Becca." With that, Elizabeth turned to Tina. "Anything you want to learn about the craft, you can. But never forget the basics. Blessed be."

The rest of the afternoon passed uneventfully, leaving the two clerks calmer if a bit forlorn. Tina clearly felt guilty, Clara thought, and kept trying to cheer Becca up with a series of nonsensical pronouncements.

"Maybe they wanted an excuse to come back," she said at one point, causing Becca to roll her eyes.

"I don't want that kind of customer. They're not going to buy anything. They're just vampires."

That shut Tina up, and Becca rushed to explain. "Not literally. They're just bloodthirsty. If they knew I didn't kill Jeff, they wouldn't be interested in me."

"But you have power, I know it."

Becca sighed, and her cat didn't need any of Laurel's particular power to know that her person couldn't wait for the day to end.

It wasn't that she had anything special planned. In fact, to Clara, it seemed like Becca was falling back into old habits, tap-tap-tapping away at her computer until late. Leaning in, she heard her saying Jeff's name more than once, but looking at the screen, all she could make out were lines of type or maybe numbers. Nothing like the images that had once made her cry.

"She's not looking at him, silly." Laurel had jumped up to the back of the sofa. Although Clara knew her sister couldn't make any more sense of the computer screen than she could, Laurel's ability to read emotions lent her words some credence.

"She keeps saying his name." Clara wasn't sure how long her sister had been up there, or what she had picked up with her unique skill.

"It's his tracks." Laurel's ears flicked back and up again. A sign of frustration, her sister knew. *"Where he was."*

"His work?" Clara asked, earning her a cross-eyed glare. While neither of them understood anything about software, the calico's experience in the outside world had exposed her to more of how humans spent their days.

"Maybe." Laurel's ears flicked again, though that could have been annoyance at her sister's superior knowledge. *"She's not getting anywhere, though."*

"No, she wouldn't." Clara looked on sadly. Becca had said often enough that she didn't understand Jeff's work. No matter what Carl and Darian claimed they'd heard the dead man say, Clara believed Becca, if for no other reason than that she appeared so lost now. As Becca sighed, Clara rested her head against her leg, closing her eyes to better concentrate on a comforting purr.

"Oh, that's good!" Laurel's excited yip woke Clara from her doze.

"What?" Blinking, Clara looked up at her sister, upright on the couch's back, ears on alert. Behind them, she could hear Laurel's tail thudding against the upholstery.

Laurel didn't respond, but her laser eyes were fixated on the screen. Cats have trouble with flat images, but movement always translated. As Clara followed her sister's gaze, she saw what had transfixed her sister. A game, one that Becca hadn't played in a while, now filled her screen. As the two cats watched, a simple drawing of a kitten, its fur dark and splotchy, darted around the display. Responding to Becca's fingers on the keyboard, it moved up and then across, stopping occasionally to lick at the screen as if cleaning it.

"It's inside the machine." Laurel's gurgle of a mew was fraught with excitement. *"There's something inside that machine, and it's trying to get out!"*

Thirty-Four

Charm and Cherish was closed on Mondays, and so usually Becca slept in, especially when she stayed up as late as she had the night before. This was greeted with mixed reactions by her cats, of course. Harriet, for example, couldn't understand why their person couldn't rise at her usual time and serve breakfast and then retire for a mid-morning nap, as any sensible creature would do. Clara tended to be more protective of their human's rest, and for Laurel, everything depended on what she had done the night before or had planned for the day ahead.

The arrival of the kitten just over a week before had disturbed all of their sleeping patterns, however. Although the kitten had pretty much accepted that, like Becca, the household went quiet during the night, she had inserted herself into the cats' bedtime routine, upsetting the three sisters' hierarchy by choosing a prime sleeping space on a pillow by Becca's head as her own. Until she got too big, Harriet had shared that pillow with their person. Only after Becca began waking with a start, sneezing and pulling cat hair from her mouth, did she give it up, as much, Clara suspected, out of fear of the mortifying possibility that Becca might actually physically remove her from the pillow as concern for their person's comfort. Still, neither Clara nor her other sister would have dared to settle into the soft warmth of that spot, maintaining the illusion that Harriet might return to it one day.

The kitten, however, had no such qualms, but since Harriet had surrendered it voluntarily, all she could do was grumble and roam. Add in the usual kitten clumsiness that had her sliding off the pillow, and often the bed, only to clamber back up once or twice a night, and Becca's tendency to toss and turn since her unsettling discovery the week before, and the little family's nocturnal routine had been upended.

All the more reason for Clara to purr her sisters to sleep, lulling them both while she kept watch. Harriet and Laurel could nap, and the kitten's energy seemed boundless, up until the very moment she dropped off, but Becca was flagging, her fatigue only adding to the sadness and anxiety. Becca needed to sleep.

Alas, it was not to be. Although Clara had kept herself up half the night, even after Becca had finally put her laptop away, keeping watch over the kitten and gently nudging her back up onto the pillow at crucial moments, Becca was up not long after sunrise, when even Laurel was stretching, eyes half closed.

"What is she doing up at this hour?" Laurel yawned, her pink tongue extending from between her fangs.

"Breakfast?" Harriet snorted, although Clara suspected her big sister was dreaming.

"'Scuse me, kitties." Becca poked her head back into the bedroom. "I didn't want to wake you, so you've got dry food. I'll give you fresh cans as soon as I'm back."

"Breakfast..." Harriet was definitely dreaming.

Laurel looked at her sister with one brow raised, lashed her tail, and rolled back over into slumber as the kitten gently snored. For Clara, though, a return to the still-warm bed was not an option. Instead, she trotted behind Becca as she carefully closed and locked the front door before, shimmying herself into invisibility, she leaped through the barrier and joined her person on the stairs.

Once on the street, Clara was careful to stay close. For once, she knew her person wasn't going into work, and while she toyed with the idea that Becca was off for breakfast with Maddy or one of the coven, she had a sinking feeling in her whiskers that nothing as benign was planned.

It was a relief, then, when Becca didn't turn off toward Jeff's old apartment. A few blocks later, the scents became familiar again, and Clara realized they were headed instead to his former workplace.

"I hope they're open," Becca muttered to herself, causing her cat to look up at her in alarm. Of course, Clara realized. Jeff and his colleagues tended to keep feline schedules, rather than the regular human hours of the shop. When Becca paused at a corner, one block from the CodePhool offices, Clara thought she must have remembered this about her ex and his peers as well. Then again, it could have been the intoxicating aroma of cinnamon and butter that had stopped her person. Either way, the little cat was grateful when Becca pulled open the door to the bakery café, releasing even more of the heady perfume, and went inside.

"Cappuccino, please, and one of those cinnamon buns." Becca ordered at the counter, her cat tucked close to avoid all the feet.

Retrieving her order, she set off toward the back of the café, searching for a vacant table. When she stopped short, sloshing the milky drink into its saucer, Clara looked up in concern. The room was crowded, but she hadn't seen anyone jostling her person. Her sharp ears, both the orange and the black, soon identified the reason for Becca's startled stop. Carl's broad back might be to the room as he sat at a corner table, a tall latte cooling in front of him, but his voice was as recognizable as his vintage *Star Trek* hoodie.

Resisting the urge to press close to Becca's ankles, Clara waited while her person took a deep breath and then strode forward. She was going to confront the programmer, her cat realized. In fact, it hit her as she trotted close behind, this had been Becca's aim all along.

"Carl." Nerves made Becca's greeting softer than usual, and a little frayed. She cleared her throat and started again. "Carl, you never really answered my question about the announcement."

"No, you listen!" The big man seated in the corner gestured wildly with his free hand, his raised voice causing patrons at the nearest table to turn in alarm. "She's not in any position to refuse me."

Clara felt Becca freeze, and she remembered the man's awkward advances.

"The cops have asked her to come in again, and she already thinks she's a suspect."

Becca gasped, momentarily distracting her cat.

"Don't you start too," Carl was saying, his voice hushed to an urgent whisper. "As I see it, you don't have any choice either. The quicker you get used to that, the better it will be for everyone."

He must have disconnected at that point. At any rate, he sat, reaching for his coffee. Becca, however, remained transfixed. *The cops have asked her to come in again.* That had to be Becca, her cat realized. More ominous was his earlier statement: *She's not in any position to refuse me.* Clara's fur bristled as she considered the implications, and as she crept toward the seated man, she felt her ears flatten against her skull, a low growl starting in her chest. If he thought he could pressure Clara's person, he'd better think again. He might not see her—Clara knew she couldn't risk unshading herself where Becca could see—but he would feel her claws and her teeth. She only had to clear one more table...

"Carl!" Becca had found her voice, calling loudly enough that the seated man straightened and turned.

"Becca?" His confusion quickly masked with a smile, he motioned to an empty chair. "I didn't expect to see you this morning."

"I know." She pushed her way through the crowd, placing her drink and bun on the table with a disregard that would have made Harriet furious. "But I was looking for you."

"Great!" He must have thought his expression of happy surprise charming, Clara realized. She'd ceased her stalking once

Becca spoke, but the low growl continued as she eyed his bare hands and throat with longing. "Please have a seat."

She did, looking down at her cooling coffee as if reading her next move in the foam. When she looked up again, her voice was calm. "I have some questions."

Good, her cat thought. *Ask him what he meant when he said you couldn't refuse him. Ask him why he was talking about you, and to whom!*

To her dismay, Becca took another tack entirely. "I realized after I saw you yesterday that you never told me what you thought about Jeff's announcement."

This seemed to take Carl aback as well, Clara realized. At least, the way his mouth hung open seemed to imply confusion.

"When I asked, you responded with a question. Not an answer."

Under different circumstances, Clara would have been so proud of Becca. She was speaking calmly, but she wasn't letting up. Only, right now, her cat didn't understand why her person wasn't asking him what mattered: why had he been talking so rudely about her?

"So I'm asking again: what do you know about Jeff's announcement?"

Carl sputtered, and Clara waited, her tail lashing. The discomfort was good for him. Unfortunately, her person lacked that feline killer instinct, and after finally taking a sip of her cappuccino, Becca broke the silence.

"Were you involved in whatever it was?"

"Yeah." He exhaled with relief. "I was."

Becca took another sip. Clara, now seated between espresso pots on a nearby shelf, looked down with growing curiosity. It was unclear to her whether the sigh that had lowered his shoulders had sprung from his confession or because Becca had asked a softball question.

"It was about Jeff's project." His voice had an earnestness that the little cat didn't trust.

Becca nodded for him to continue, taking another sip and finally breaking off a piece of that cinnamon bun. Was it possible that she couldn't see the possibilities that were so clear to her cat?

"Why didn't Darien know about it, then?"

"Good girl!" Clara could have purred.

"It was kind of a surprise." Carl regarded his own coffee. "Okay, it was kind of in defiance."

Becca's brows rose over her mug. She was learning to wait him out, Clara realized with pride.

Carl inhaled, the Star Fleet logo on his chest rising as if to take flight. "Jeff was going to announce that he and I were partners in this project," he said. "That we always had been, and that I had to be part of any deal. Jeff might have sold a bill of goods to Darien, but the truth was—is—that it couldn't happen without me."

"And Darien doesn't know this?" Becca sounded shaken, or skeptical. It was hard for her cat to tell.

Carl nodded. "He does now. We were just going over the details when I saw you."

That explained a lot, thought Clara. Becca, however, still seemed confused.

"I thought I heard you talking about me." She spoke slowly, watching his face for a reaction.

"I know you were part of this project from early on." He leaned in, the hint of a leer sneaking into his smile. "Jeff shared everything with me."

"No." Becca shook off the implication. "You don't know anything about me."

Carl responded by raising his hand before she could object more. "I know, I know," he said. "I misread your signals, and I'm sorry. I got that wrong. But I thought, you know, you showing up like that?"

"No." Becca was not going to be misunderstood. "I didn't know you were going to be there."

This got Carl's attention, and he regarded her with what could have passed for thoughtfulness.

"So, why were you in Jeff's apartment yesterday?" Carl leaned back, as if to take her in anew. "Were you looking for something, Becca? Or were you looking to put something back?"

Thirty-Five

"I don't know what you're talking about." Becca leaned forward, her eyes wide. Her initial outburst—"*What?*"—had drawn the attention of the café's other occupants, and she spoke now in a hushed but urgent whisper. "Are you calling me a thief?"

"I'm just saying I know you weren't supposed to be in there." The patina of concern gone, Carl's wide face looked particularly self-satisfied, undoubtedly aware of all the attention. "And I'm sure the police would like to know why too."

"I've been cooperating with the police." Becca's voice faltered a bit. "In fact, I was going to talk to them again today."

Carl's brows rose in an unspoken question, and with that, Becca pushed back her seat and rose, holding her chin high as she walked out of the café.

As soon as she was around the corner, however, her façade crumbled. Clara looked on in dismay as Becca's shoulders slumped and she dug her hand into her pocket. When she pulled out the yellow note, which had gotten stuck onto a rectangle of pink plastic, her cat knew she was thinking of Carl's accusation—and of what that cryptic note could mean. But as she stood there, staring at the note, she did something her cat didn't expect. She peeled the note off the pink plastic and, with a new determination in her step, set off down the street.

Twenty minutes later, she was climbing the broad steps of a large, domed building, but once inside, she faltered, coming to a halt amid a stream of pedestrians, their conversations echoing through the hallway.

"Excuse me." She approached a guard who was busy looking at his phone. "I'm looking for the exhibit area."

"Down the hall and to the right." He had the grace to look a tad embarrassed. "But I think they're packing up today."

"Thanks." Becca sighed as she took off through the throng. "Wish me luck."

Sure enough, nobody even asked to see her badge as she entered a large room divided by screens. People were folding or rolling up banners as she quickly made her way down the first aisle and loading crates onto dollies as she went up another. By the third aisle, Becca had almost given up. Craning her head over the crowd and their products, she started to move on to the next aisle, when a familiar voice stopped her.

"Becca, hey!" A tall woman waved from behind a table piled with boxes, her pale face lighting up with joy. "You made it."

"Yeah, finally." Becca made her way over, dodging a cart piled high with fliers. "You're packing up?"

"Yeah, the hall closes at noon. You missed most of the presentations, I'm afraid. There was one on online teaching—I bet we can get you a recording." The tall woman turned to call behind the screen. "Pam, come on out."

"Becca, good to see you again." The shorter woman placed a cardboard box on the table and reached for Becca's hand. "And, yeah, I'm sure I can download that session and send you the link."

"That would be great. But, to be honest, I'm here because I wanted to talk something over with the two of you."

The women exchanged a look. "We're all ears," said Pam. "Let me wrangle some chairs."

"Actually, I'm wondering if there's somewhere else we can

talk, even briefly." Becca turned from the women to take in the crowd. "It's about a pending project, and—"

"Say no more." Linda stepped forward. "Pam, you think that place across the street is still open?"

"I don't want to take you out of your way," Becca began apologizing.

"Nonsense." Leaving their boxes, the two hustled Becca out of the hall. "I'd like to think we can trust our peers," began Linda.

"But we can't," finished Pam, looking both ways as she led them across a hall and out a side door. "At any rate, if it's confidential, it's always better to be safe. The spyware that's out there now is incredible."

"Spyware?" Becca's voice squeaked as the couple walked her quickly to an open-air pavilion. At this time of day—the lunch rush hadn't started yet—its picnic tables were mostly empty, and Pam led them to the farthest from the building.

"It's mostly industrial," explained Linda as she sat facing the street, waiting while Pam slid onto the bench beside her. "But some of what we've seen this weekend is scary. Listening devices triggered by human heartbeats. Phones that can mirror others with a touch."

"Those are legal?" Becca sat facing the pair.

Linda shrugged. "A lot of them have military or police designations," said Pam. "But realistically? Anyone can get them."

"Great." Becca sighed. "But I guess that makes sense."

Linda and Pam exchanged another glance as Becca took a breath and dove in, giving the two a quick history of everything that had happened since she ran into that alley.

"So, anyway, my ex was working on some kind of universal password or something like that. Something that would allow people to break into any program, or maybe even devices, without a password."

"Wow, I can see why he was getting the big money." Pam nodded, taking it all in. "Though to go from security to the opposite, well, that's kind of going over to the dark side."

"Really?" Becca leaned forward. "I mean, Jeff was always careless, but I didn't think of him as evil."

"She doesn't mean evil," Linda chimed in. "I'm sure there are legitimate uses for such an application. But that kind of software is very controversial."

"For sure," agreed Pam. "For every person who forgets their password, or, say, a survivor who can't access their dead partner's accounts, there's going to be a troll who wants the same info."

"Or a government agency looking to uncover a whistleblower's identity," added Linda. "And that's only off the top of our heads."

"Great." Becca sighed again, her shoulders heaving. "That should be a load off, but it really just complicates matters. If it weren't for the argument, I'd think this might be what got Jeff killed."

"What argument?"

"Someone heard a man and a woman fighting right before Jeff ran into that alley. A woman who looked like me." Becca swallowed. "And then, since I found him..."

"That's not right." Pam frowned. "There's so much else going on here. For example, what about his old clients, the ones who counted on him for security? Or simply someone who knew he'd struck it rich?"

"That's another thing," said Becca. "I don't think Jeff had gotten any money yet."

"Maybe whoever attacked him didn't know that." Linda and Pam looked at each other. "Either way, I can list a dozen reasons for someone else to have come after your ex, and none of them have anything to do with you."

Thirty-Six

Becca left the women to finish their packing with promises all around to keep in touch. As Pam led the way, Becca grabbed Linda's arm, holding her back. "Don't worry," she whispered. "I haven't forgotten the globe."

Linda smiled. "Thanks, but you've got a lot on your plate. You take care of yourself, okay?"

"I'll send that link," Pam called as the two disappeared inside the building. "I bet you'll be a great teacher."

Becca certainly looked more confident, walking with a spring in her step as she headed back toward Central Square and the Cambridge police headquarters. She may have slowed a little as she climbed up to the big glass doors, but her hesitation might have been triggered by the sight of the red-haired man who had just emerged.

"Darien!" she called to the man who stood at the top of the stairs, blinking in the sun.

"Becca." He looked down at her in surprise, his whole face lighting up. "You're a sight for sore eyes."

"Were you in talking to them about Jeff?"

"Yeah. It's been...unpleasant." His Adam's apple bobbed as he swallowed. Clearly, whatever had just happened had left a bad taste in his mouth.

"I'm sorry." Her own anxiety momentarily forgotten, she reached out to touch his arm. "Do you want to talk about it?"

"No, I'm fine. Thanks." The gesture, or the warmth in her tone, must have eased him. While his eyes still looked drawn, some color had come back into his face, and he smiled down at Becca. "It's probably nothing."

Becca dropped her voice, her eyes darting around. "They weren't rude to you, were they?"

Clara knew she was thinking of her own upcoming interview, but to her surprise, Darien burst out with a surprised laugh.

"What? No. I'm not—" He wiped his eyes, his voice settling back to normal. "I'm not here as a suspect. I came in to report something."

"Did you find something out?" Becca nearly jumped in her eagerness. "A clue?"

"No. Nothing like that. I wish." He looked back up at the glass doors. "No, I came in to report a threat."

Becca's confusion knotted her brows.

"Someone called and threatened me. Said I was next."

"Because of what you were doing?" Clara knew she was thinking of what Pam and Linda had told her. "The unlocking software?"

He nodded, his mouth set in a grim line. "Seems like word has gotten out. Of course, the call was from an unknown number, so if our app was up and functioning..."

"That's so awful. I never thought that a software project..." She paused, biting her lip. "Darien, do you think your project, the one Jeff was working on, is what got him killed?"

"I'd hate for that to be true." His eyes widened as the import of her words hit home. "For me, it's always been about the puzzle aspect as much as anything. I love how software can be used to untangle a knot and how smart developers can visualize solutions to problems, even problems we didn't realize we had. Jeff had that, that almost magic touch of seeing what was right there in front of us that somehow nobody had ever seen before. He knew how to figure things out."

Darien paused and stared out at the road, blinking. For a moment, Clara thought he was going to cry.

"That's what does it for me, Becca. Even more than the money. Believe me, I never would have agreed to fund him if I thought this project would result in anyone getting hurt. No breakthrough, certainly no IPO, is worth that."

He swallowed again and forced a tentative smile. "But here I am talking about myself. What's up with you?" The reality of where they stood suddenly seemed to hit him, and he reached out anxiously. "Are you okay, Becca? They can't think you...?"

"No, I'm fine." She took his hand and squeezed it. "I got a call asking me to come in and speak with them again at my convenience, and this is my day off. I know I should get a lawyer, but I've been trying to figure out what happened myself, you know. Talking to..." she waved the thought away, "...some people. But from what you're saying, I don't know if there's anything I can contribute at all. I actually spent last night playing a silly old game Jeff installed on my laptop. That's about the extent of my exposure to his software, no matter what he might have said. But I guess I should go and tell them that. Let them check me off their list."

"I won't keep you, then." Darien smiled for real this time. "I'm so glad I ran into you. I've been meaning to call. Would you still be up for dinner?"

It only took Becca a second to readjust. "Yeah," she said. "I think that would be nice."

Sadly, the Cambridge police weren't as visionary as Darien Hughes. Forty minutes later, Becca was growing increasingly frustrated with the dull-eyed bureaucrat sitting across from her. She'd gone into the small room eagerly, almost skipping down the hall as her wary cat followed after, body low to the ground in the classic feline defensive posture. Now she slumped in her seat, one foot kicking the air in the kind of aimless pattern that was difficult for her shaded pet to ignore.

"Ms. Colwin, I understand what you're saying." Despite his reassuring words, the detective interviewing her didn't exactly ooze empathy. More worrisome, to Clara's sensitive ears, he sounded like he was growing testy. Almost, she thought, as if he was becoming as impatient as Becca. And that, the cat suspected, was not a good sign.

"No, no, you don't." Becca pulled herself forward as if she were about to diagram her points on the table between them. "I know you and your colleagues first wanted to talk to me because I used to go out with Jeff—the victim. I get that. Also, because I found him. And I know that Renee, his most recent girlfriend, was getting threatening letters. I get it that this may surprise you, but she and I have talked about them. And I understand jealousy as a motive. *Cherchez la femme*, and all that. But there's more to life than sex. And to death too."

That registered with the man facing her. He too leaned forward, as if readying himself to speak. But when Becca continued after her brief pause, he sat back again, and Clara began to fear the worst.

"I know you know there are other possibilities, right? I mean, you are probably aware that Jeff just got major funding for a software project that he'd been working on. I don't think he'd gotten the money yet." She paused, but before the detective could break in, she picked up the thread again. "No, he wouldn't have. He hadn't started hiring yet."

She paused again, but this time the man facing her seemed content to let her finish what even her cat knew was a rambling argument. "What I'm wondering is if you folks are aware of the implications of his new project. It was going to be incredibly controversial, with implications for privacy rights. I mean, it would have been a powder keg."

With that, she sat back, and her pet, who loved her dearly, could only close her eyes.

"I understand, Ms. Colwin. And, yes, we are aware of the

deceased's project, and it's, ah, national security implications." Clara could hear a piece of paper being turned over, but she doubted the man above her really needed to check his notes.

"We asked you to come in and answer some questions because there is some information that we believe you may have access to that we don't."

"Of course. Ask away."

He nodded. "Before we start, would you like to revise anything you've said in our previous conversations?"

Becca, thought Clara, did not give this question the consideration it deserved.

"No," she said. "I'm good."

"Perhaps, with everything that's been going on, you've forgotten to tell us something?"

"No." She drew the word out, her earlier ease beginning to evaporate. "Why are you asking?"

He sighed. "We're very thorough, Ms. Colwin. We may not be speedy, but we check everything. Even the little things. And when we get a report that something has gone missing from a crime scene, we do our best to figure out why. And who, as in this case, may have taken it."

At first, Clara thought her person was choking. The sharp inhalation of breath followed by a cough sounded so like the time she had swallowed a bug that her cat wanted to jump up and head butt her. To unshade herself and makes herself known. Anything to get her to breathe.

"What do you mean?" That rasp gave away too much, Clara knew, and she readied herself to attack. One small cat couldn't take on the city's entire police force, but if she jumped on this man with claws outstretched, she could buy Becca time.

"Why don't you tell me?"

"I don't—I'm sorry, I still don't know what you're talking about," said Becca as she pushed back her chair and stood. "You asked me to come in because you said I could help with the investigation, and so I did. However, if you're going to question me as if I were a person of interest, I'm going to have to insist that I have a lawyer present. Good day."

With that, and with her cat at her heels, she turned and walked out of the room, not stopping until she was once more in the open air. It wasn't until she was blocks away—the result of random race-walking that had both her and the unseen feline by her side dodging traffic to cross the street multiple times—that she came to a halt. Whether by design or habit, she was a doorway down from Charm and Cherish. Taking shelter in the recessed entrance which led to the apartments above, she stared back the way she had come and then scanned the street in the other direction, staring hard at two parked cars and a woman who had paused to fish a quarter out of her bag. Clara could tell how nervous she was by the tension in her body. If a cat had been licking her lips like that, it would mean nausea—or worse.

Finally, Becca started to breathe normally again, and her cat began to relax. Reaching into her pocket, she drew out a small, yellow piece of paper, which she cupped in the palm of her hand, her head swiveling once more as she scanned the avenue. Apparently satisfied, she tore the sticky note in half and then in half again, before looking around for some place to toss it.

Clara was sure it must have been coincidence that sent a Cambridge police cruiser down Mass Ave at just that moment. Flowing with the rest of the weekday traffic, without its lights or siren, it was most probably on a routine errand. But its appearance was enough to cause Becca to shrink back into the entranceway and shove the torn paper once again into her pocket. Not until the black-and-white had disappeared on its way toward Harvard did Becca pull away from the wall. And then, to her cat's surprise, she didn't step back out into the street. Instead, she pulled open the heavy outer door of the building's foyer and pressed one of the buzzers.

"Elizabeth, are you there? I really need to talk."

Thirty-Seven

Becca visibly relaxed as she reached the top floor and saw Elizabeth by the open door. Clara, however, eyed the older of the two sisters warily. Although a warm smile lit up her face, and the mop of gray curls and another of her flowing caftans, this one emerald with gold lace trim, made the tall, slim woman appear like some slightly goofy, if benevolent, goddess, the little cat kept her distance. She remembered all too well the sly comments that seemed to indicate that Elizabeth saw more than she should for a human, but when Becca hurried down the hall, her pet had no choice but to follow.

"Thanks, Elizabeth, I was hoping to bounce some ideas off you." Clara shimmied through the door in time to see Elizabeth usher Becca into the living room. Surely, it was only her imagination that made the tall woman's sweeping gesture, accentuated by that flowing robe, appear to envelope the shaded cat as well.

"I was just at—" Becca caught herself mid-sentence, stopped by the sight of Margaret, who glared up from one of two low sofas. With her dyed red hair and heavy lipstick, her powdered cheeks unnaturally pink, the stout little woman almost blended in with the brocade upholstery.

"If you're looking to butter up my sister, you should think

again," she growled, her scowl bringing her heavy brows down in judgment. Despite being Elizabeth's junior, she appeared older than her sister. Less colorful too, Clara thought, despite all the paint. "I'd think it should be enough that she saved your job."

"I'm grateful, really." Becca backtracked, her voice taking on a conciliatory tone. "But I actually wanted to ask Elizabeth's advice —and yours too, of course—about my investigation."

"There she goes again." Margaret raised her hands, as if presenting the self-evident.

"Why don't you have a seat, dear," Elizabeth said from behind Becca. "I was just going to make more tea."

"Don't forget the milk," her sister called after her as Becca perched on the edge of the other sofa. "She's growing absent-minded. If I left the business to her, it would be ruined."

"She cares about Charm and Cherish." Becca's defense of Elizabeth was automatic, but on seeing Margaret's reaction, she kept talking. "Of course, I think it's great that you brought in Tina."

"Frees you up to do more of your investigating." Margaret pursed her lips as if the word were sour. "At least our new girl has a real interest in the shop. The running of it, not just what she can take home."

Becca's mouth opened, but closed again. Clara tilted an ear toward the kitchen, but the kettle wasn't yet boiling.

"She's very eager to learn." Becca said at last.

Margaret snorted. "And, finally, you're teaching her."

Becca's confused silence was broken by the screech of the kettle.

"I can't tell you how often she'd drop by when I was forced to cover. Or Elizabeth," she added as an afterthought, with a nod to her sister. "She'd always ask for you, like you were her idol."

"She's a smart girl." Elizabeth appeared with a tray in her hand. "She wanted to learn about the craft."

"The craft of *selling*." Another scowl, this one directed at her older sister.

"I know she's always loved the store." Becca sounded a bit

abashed. "And that she's long been interested in Wicca. I don't think it was me particularly."

Elizabeth raised her own bushy brows, but Margaret clearly didn't find the idea amusing. "It was." The admission seemed to pain her. "Not that I know why."

Clara turned from one to another, trying to read the play of emotions. Becca, clearly, was made uncomfortable by what sounded like a case of hero worship. Margaret, meanwhile, was sounding like a neglected suitor. Elizabeth's face, however, was unreadable, the half smile playing across her face could have been for Becca, or amusement at her sister's pique, or, the calico realized with a shudder, for Clara herself.

"Well, I'm glad we've become friends for real, then, and that we're now working together," Becca said with finality.

"So, what brings you here today?" Elizabeth had settled onto the sofa beside her sister and poured the tea. "I hope you're not worried about your position with Charm and Cherish."

Her sister harrumphed, and Becca shifted uneasily. "I actually just came from talking to the Cambridge police again."

Margaret made a sound that could have been a bark, Elizabeth only nodded. "You're being a good citizen."

"That's just it. I'm trying." Becca leaned into her explanation. "But I'm worried that the police are overlooking the obvious. They're talking to me and Jeff's other friends like they think this was a personal crime. Only, there are other more compelling reasons why someone would have wanted to hurt him."

"Money?" Elizabeth took a sip.

Becca shook her head. "He wasn't robbed, and although he'd gotten backing for his project, it wasn't like he was suddenly a millionaire." She paused at that, and Clara could tell she was suddenly distracted. "Not like Darien Hughes," she said, and her cat realized she was thinking of how the financier had been threatened.

"No." She shook the thought off, returning to her theme. "I think it's something to do with his project. My ex was working on software that could break open encryption. It had the potential to be huge, and maybe in some cases life-saving. But if it fell into the wrong hands? Or if the government, any government, decided to use it against private citizens? That would be catastrophic."

Her eyes wide, she took in Elizabeth and even turned toward Margaret as well. "I think that, more than simple jealousy, is more of a motive for murder. Don't you? And yet the Cambridge police don't even seem to be considering it."

"She's a conspiracy theorist now," Margaret huffed, as she reached for the teapot. "People are going to say I have a crazy girl in my shop."

"That's not fair." Becca caught herself. "It's just an idea, but I thought it was worth talking over."

In the silence that followed, Clara scanned the faces of the three women. After a glance that could have shot daggers at Becca, Margaret was frowning down into her teacup. A slight retreat, the cat thought. Becca, however, was looking mortified, while even Elizabeth seemed troubled, breaking the moment with a sigh.

"There does seem to be a lot going on," she said, her voice gentle. "Have you shared any of this with Tina?"

"Don't go dragging her into this," Margaret snarled, looking up at Becca again. "She's turning into a good employee, and I need one of those at least."

Becca blanched, and Elizabeth reached over to place her hand on Becca's shoulder. "That's not fair, Mags, and you know it. We all have some history, and as you recall, Becca has helped us out before."

This time it was Elizabeth who was the recipient of her sister's poisonous glare.

"I think there's an important lesson here we should all remember," Elizabeth continued, apparently unfazed by her sister's venom. "Everybody deserves a second chance."

"Harrumph," her sister said.

Thirty-Eight

Becca left the sisters feeling no more resolved than she had before. Clara could tell from the way her face knotted up as soon as she was on the stairs that she was disappointed. Some of that, she figured, was because Margaret had been there. Her constant carping didn't invite confidences, and it was all the little cat could do to keep from hissing as Becca's troll-like boss made another dig at her beleaguered employee.

Some of Becca's disappointment, her cat suspected, was due to the other elderly sister. Elizabeth was usually a staunch ally, as she had shown when Margaret had nearly fired Becca. But just now, Clara thought, the older, taller woman had been strangely vague, her responses to Becca as insubstantial as the sleeves of her caftan, floating one way or the other as she swanned around the room.

"Maybe it's her age catching up with her." Becca clearly had the same thought as she descended to the street, her pet hard on her heels. And when Becca paused on the sidewalk, standing back to let the midday crowds pass by, her cat found herself wondering who else Becca could go to. At times like this, the calico dearly wished she and her sisters could converse with Becca directly. She knew her person had human friends—in addition to Maddy,

Becca's coven was a continued source of support—but none of them knew her as her pets did. And no human could draw on the instinctive knowledge of generations as Clara and her sisters could.

Maybe that was the kitten's problem, she mused. The tiny tortie had been found out on the street alone, and although she was clearly old enough to be weaned, she very likely had only survived because Becca had scooped her up. Harriet, her baby sister grudgingly admitted, was doing a good job of teaching the kitten basic cat skills, from grooming to fitting into a human household. A cat had to know more than how to survive, however. What if the kitten had become separated from her mother before she could learn of her own heritage? Harriet and Laurel both acted as if the kitten were a dumb animal, but Clara was growing increasingly confident that there was more to the infant. Possibly much more than her sisters could suspect.

Clara was so caught up in thinking about the kitten's family and her odds of reconnecting the fuzzy thing with any ancestral birthright she nearly didn't notice the familiar jingling of bells. Becca had ducked into Charm and Cherish, locking the door behind her and double checking to make sure the "Closed" sign still faced out. Only then did she retreat to the back room to hang her jacket and leave her bag, with Clara trotting behind her, curious as to what had drawn her person to the little shop on her day off.

The mystery only deepened as she ventured back into the shop's main room. As Clara watched, Becca moved almost furtively, keeping to the walls as if she were a prey animal afraid of an ambush. Or, no, it hit Clara. Afraid that a passerby would spot her and want to come in. That seemed odd to the cat. Becca usually welcomed customers and seemed to take a genuine pleasure in talking with them, at least until that blog had begun to draw a more morbid kind of interest. Clara had limited knowledge of what it meant to have a job, but this was about interaction —and with a flash of insight, Clara suddenly understood. As much as she loved her sisters, there were times when she didn't want Laurel or Harriet around. Perhaps, she thought, for Becca this was something similar.

The mystery was further explained when Becca darted from the wall to the aisle between two of the big bookshelves that filled the shop. A look as intent as Laurel's when she spotted a bug came over her, to the point that Clara followed her and scanned the shelves as well, convinced that in a moment she too would see something crawl by.

Nothing did, but before long, Becca reached up for a thick, dark book, pulling it gently so as not to damage its leather spine. Cradling it against her body, and with another glance at the front window, she retreated to the back room, settling on the sofa with the tome on her lap.

"Seeking spells. Truth, uncovering untruths..." Becca muttered as she opened the cover and ran her finger down a page. "Concealment, that should do it."

Clara could only sigh. Becca had never stopped trying spells, but she'd confined her attempts to the coven recently. And while none of the humans could command any real power, at least the company had kept Becca from growing despondent. If she was trying to work magic on her own, it wasn't going to end well, her cat feared.

Sure enough, Clara woke from a nap to a gust of air and dust as Becca slammed the book closed. But although the cat briefly hoped this meant an end to the venture, Becca soon pulled another book.

"Traces, of course!' Becca sounded so happy it nearly broke her cat's heart.

When Clara next woke, the sun had shifted, casting the colors of the rainbow window display with its vibrant zodiac signs across the floor. Becca had given up her stealth by then and stood before the front bookshelf, paging through the thickest book yet—a dark green volume decorated with gold that gave off a different scent than its predecessors, a combination of cinnamon and pepper, and seemed to offer Becca something enticing too.

"'Making the unseen visible,'" she read aloud, holding the

book open before her. "'If this web before me lies, hidden from my open eyes...'"

Clara blinked. Her own eyes were open, but for a moment she thought she'd seen something that could not be. A faint glow had seemed to emanate off the page, illuminating Becca's face as she read. Only, her back was to the window, the colorful shadows of the zodiac cutouts making patterns on her pale green blouse. It wasn't possible...

"'If this...' Bother." A gentle rapping caused Becca to turn—breaking whatever spell it was that had held Clara—as the door began to open.

"Tina." Becca closed the book as she greeted her colleague.

"Hi. I thought I saw you in here." Tina paused, taking in Becca's expression and the book in her hands. "I'm sorry. I didn't mean to disturb you. Margaret gave me a key so I could start closing, and I thought I would try it out."

"You just startled me." Becca conjured a smile, holding the book close. "No contract work today?"

"Oh, that." The petite woman gave a sigh big enough to deflate her. "My latest contract hasn't been picked up, so, for a while at least, this is it for me."

"I'm sorry."

Clara scanned her human's face, aware of the play of emotions. Becca wasn't usually territorial. Harriet was more likely to growl than their person was, especially if her favorite gold-tassled pillow was encroached upon. Still, Clara knew that her person had been disconcerted by what Margaret had told her.

Luckily, Tina seemed to take no notice of Becca's turmoil, shrugging off her expression of sympathy. "It's nothing," she said, before focusing in on the book in Becca's arms. "*Ars Compendium*?"

"Yeah." Becca looked down at the heavy volume. She didn't, her cat noticed, make a move to shelve it. "I was practicing."

"Cool!" Tina hopped up to sit on the counter. "Do you want to try something with me?"

Clara didn't know if it was Tina's move—her swinging feet

bumping back against the glass—or the accumulation of all the annoyances of the day, but Becca sputtered.

"Could you not sit there?"

As the other girl jumped down and began to apologize, the rest spilled out.

"And, no, I came here to read and be alone." She didn't wait for a response. "And by the way, Margaret told me something that disturbed me. She said that you used to come in and ask when I'd be working?"

"Well, yeah." Tina had the grace to look embarrassed, kicking at the old linoleum and staring at the floor. "I know that sounds weird, but I've always admired you. You know, I wanted to join your coven because I knew about you and your witch detective work."

"I know, I'm sorry." Becca's outburst, short as it had been, seemed to drain her pique. "And I'm happy to share what I'm working on when the coven meets. I'm just having a bad day." She looked over at her colleague, hope creasing her brow. "You haven't been able to find out anything more about that nasty blog, have you?"

"No." Tina looked crushed. "But maybe that's not a bad thing?"

Becca shook her head, confused.

"I've been reading it, and I think you might be taking it the wrong way."

Becca opened her mouth to protest, but Tina kept talking. "It isn't saying that you're involved in—in Jeff's death. Not any longer anyway. It's just going on about your power."

"Great." Becca closed her eyes.

"No, it really is. Considering the number of hits it's getting, it's great publicity for your work as a witch detective, and we know it's bringing people into Charm and Cherish."

"Not the kind of people we want."

"You can't know that." Tina was insistent. "You only know about the ones who came in to gawk at you. But you don't know how many actual customers found out about us because of that one blog."

Becca had no answer to that, but Clara could tell she wasn't happy. "I just wish it was shut down."

"Maybe we can do something about it tonight."

Becca looked at her, uncomprehending.

"When the coven meets. It's Monday, isn't it?" Tina spoke as she would to a small kitten. "I'm telling you, Becca. I believe that you have power. When all of us get together? I bet we could do anything."

Thirty-Nine

"W*here have you been?"* Harriet was puffed with annoyance when Clara whisked through the apartment door, minutes ahead of Becca. *"We expected you hours ago."*

Even Laurel was acting disturbed, pacing back and forth on top of the sofa. *"This isn't like Becca,"* she said. *"She's usually all warm and buzzy when she's been out."*

"She wasn't visiting with her friend Maddy or working." Clara didn't have time to explain. *"But she's almost here, and she's having the coven over again!"*

That provoked some furious tail lashing from Harriet, while the kitten looked on, readying to pounce. Laurel took the news as provocation to leap up to the bookcase, dislodging one of Becca's favorite figurines as she landed. The ceramic cat, which for some reason was playing a bass fiddle, didn't break, Clara was relieved to notice. And her sister had no more opportunity to wreak havoc because Becca was just then coming through the door, a white bakery box in hand.

"Hey, kitties! How have you been? Oh!" This last was addressed to the kitten, who had begun to climb Becca's leg. Dropping her bag and placing the box on top of the key bowl,

Becca carefully unhooked the tortie's claws and carried her into the kitchen, the other three cats in tow. "I know, it's early for dinner, but you won't complain, will you?"

The question was addressed to the kitten, who stretched out her paws toward Becca's face.

Laurel, by Clara's side, grunted. *"She thinks she can get away with anything just by being small and cute."*

"We're cute," Harriet objected.

"Small, then."

Clara paused, about to comment, Laurel's observation having sparked a thought. But then Becca placed the kitten down on the floor, and as her sisters began jockeying for position, she found herself standing by the tortie as Becca began opening their cans.

"You really shouldn't do things like that," Clara whispered to the little kitten. *"It might be cute in a kitten, but real cats don't use their claws on their people."*

The kitten blinked up at her, and for a moment Clara was sure she understood. Then she yawned, pink mouth opened so wide Clara could see all her new teeth, and promptly decided to chase her tail.

"Give it up, Clown. That baby's never going to be a real cat."

Clara bristled ever so slightly at Laurel's use of her nickname, but she couldn't argue, and instead focused on her dinner. While she ate, she was aware of Becca readying her apartment for the evening's gathering. Cocking her black-tipped ear, she heard her rearranging chairs and wiping down the table where the four women would gather. As she washed her face, she saw Becca pulling mugs from the cabinet and decided this would be a good opportunity to inspect the living room, when she was interrupted by a squeal: Harriet was bathing the kitten, lapping at her with an enthusiasm that suggested the tiny tortie's face had been at least briefly submerged in her food dish.

"Everything's in order." Clara turned to see Laurel saunter back into the kitchen, tail high. *"She hasn't put out any extra chairs and the table is far enough from the wall to allow even Miss Thorough here access to any leftovers."*

Clara dipped her head in acknowledgement. She'd been thinking of sniffing around for that book. But at that moment, a high-pitched ping had all the cats turning to their person.

"What is it now?" Becca didn't seem too happy about the interruption and kept filling the kettle as she looked over at her phone. "Oh, that's good," she said to herself before reaching over to press the device's surface. "Thanks, Renee. If you could drop those letters off, that would be great," she said, as her words disappeared with a whoosh.

Fifteen minutes later, the doorbell rang, catching Becca with a mouthful of peanut butter and jelly.

"Hang on." Wiping her mouth with the back of her hand, she headed to the door. "Ande!"

Her cats could have told her that the woman at the door was her coven mate, but Becca seemed surprised.

"You're early." She stepped back to let the taller woman into the apartment, gesturing with her sandwich. "Dinner."

"Sorry to interrupt." Ande looked around, her long face tight with tension. "I was hoping to catch you alone."

Becca swallowed hard and nodded for her to continue.

"I've been looking into Jeff's project, the one with Darien Hughes." Ande followed Becca back into the kitchen, her hands working nervously. "And this might not mean anything, but I didn't find any SEC filing."

Becca shook her head. "I don't understand."

"Venture capital investments have to be registered," her friend explained. "They have to report all kinds of information. It's a lot of paperwork, but it's for bank safety and to keep an eye on foreign investors who might be using domestic fronts."

Becca turned to pull a stack of plates from the cabinet. "You think Darien is a front for the Chinese?"

"No." Ande chuckled. "I mean, I doubt it. It could be a lot of things. Maybe the initial investment wasn't that big. Or maybe the paperwork simply hadn't gone through yet."

Becca frowned as she placed the plates on the table. "But you think something was hinky about the deal."

Ande exhaled as if she'd been holding her breath all day. "I don't know, Becca. It's not my area of expertise, and I'm not sure what I was even expecting to find, poking around online. If Jeff hadn't been murdered, I doubt I'd have had a second thought about any of it."

"But he was." Becca frowned, even as she opened the bakery box and began to plate the cookies within. "And money is at least as good a motive as jealousy."

"Let's not jump to conclusions." Ande followed her back into the kitchen. "I'm not a forensic accountant, but I thought it was strange. And why did you say China?"

"I've been thinking about the nature of the project and that a foreign government might want it. And then someone threatened Darien." Becca scooped up the mugs and carried them over to the table.

"Threatened Darien?" Ande followed, cookies held high.

"Yeah, I ran into him at the Cambridge police headquarters. He was there to report it." Becca took the plate from her, unaware that Harriet and Laurel were watching every move. Clara had tagged along, in part to make sure her sisters didn't cause too much havoc. But the little calico found herself gazing at the tall witch, particularly at the questioning V that had appeared between her hazel eyes. "I don't think they see the implications of Jeff's software," Becca kept on. "I mean, when I brought it up —hang on."

Ande looked about to speak, but Becca was already on the move, hurrying to let in the newest arrivals, Marcia and Tina, who held up another white box.

"More cookies." Harriet looked up from her perch on one of the chairs, golden eyes growing wide.

"Bird in the hand." Laurel didn't hesitate, leaping across the table and landing on the floor, an almond cookie in her mouth, even as Ande yelled and clapped her hands.

"Hey, that's mine!" Harriet took off after her sister, leaving Clara and the kitten, who looked up as the newcomers approached.

"What a little darling." Marcia reached for the kitten, who allowed herself to be lifted to face height with only a soft peep. "Are you going to keep her?"

"I shouldn't," Becca called from the kitchen. "My vet has found someone who wants to take her. He's going to bring her by."

"But you have first dibs, right?" Marcia held the tortie to her cheek. Even from her place on the floor, Clara could hear the purr.

"It's always about the kittens." Laurel had crept up behind her silently and was now licking crumbs from her dark chocolate muzzle.

"Not with Becca. She loves us all." Clara's defense of their person caused her to miss Becca's response.

A moment of quiet contemplation always followed that last invocation, and Clara felt her eyes beginning to close when a shift in the atmosphere caused her ears to prick up.

"This should be interesting." Laurel sat up and stared at the door, just as a sharp knock interrupted the peace of the room.

"What's that?" Ande looked up.

Tina craned around to look, as Becca got up.

"I'll get it." Accompanied by her three cats, Becca opened the door to find Renee, a manila folder in her hands.

"I'm sorry it's so late." She held out the folder. "I wanted to copy these before I gave them to you."

"Please don't apologize." Becca held the door open. "Would you like to come in?"

Renee peered in. "I don't want to interrupt."

"Nonsense, we're just finishing up." Becca turned back toward the group. "Everyone, this is Renee."

Marcia raised her eyebrows to her colleagues, but Ande stood and extended her hand. "Good to meet you."

"You too. Sorry to interrupt. Is this your witch group?"

"We call it a coven," Ande explained. Under the table, Clara watched as she kicked Marcia. "It's all very good-natured," she continued. "No curses or anything like that."

"I didn't think you would." Renee blushed.

"She knows they've talked about her." Laurel murmured in Clara's orange ear. While this wasn't news to the calico—the awkwardness around the table had made that clear—she lashed her tail once in acknowledgement.

"Anyway, I'm Marcia." Clara didn't know if she'd missed a second kick, but clearly the short witch had remembered her manners. "And this is Tina."

"Hi." The newest member of the coven reached for the plate in the center of the table. "Excuse me." She rose to take the empty dish into the kitchen.

"We've met, I think," Renee called after her. "Did we work together at some point?"

The sound of running water drowned out Tina's response.

"You two know each other?" Marcia gathered up two of the mugs, while Becca grabbed the rest.

"I don't think so," Tina had filled the sink with suds and was sponging down the plate.

"I'll do that." Becca reached for the tap. "You brought cookies."

"But you always host." Tina shook off the proffered dish towel, instead turning the tap back on.

"CodePhool." Renee, standing in the kitchen doorway, nodded. "You were at CodePhool with my late boyfriend, Jeff."

"Yeah, briefly." Tina turned back to the dishes.

"Tina's a contract worker," said Becca, leading Renee out of the kitchen. "She's worked all over this town."

"What was that about?" Laurel, with her appetite for intrigue, brushed against the doorway.

"Death makes humans uncomfortable." Clara gave the feline equivalent of a shrug, but she knew it was more.

So did Laurel. *"You're a terrible liar, Clown. I can smell something. Fear? Discomfort?"*

"She was gossiping about the blonde," Clara admitted. *"Tina was telling Becca that everyone knew Jeff was cheating on her."*

"Interesting." Laurel gazed up at the petite woman. *"Yes, I'm getting discomfort."*

"Oh, how adorable!" The two adult cats looked at each other. Renee's exclamation could only mean one thing.

"You missed it." Harriet waddled in, licking her chops. *"There were crumbs."*

"Are you going to hang?" Marcia stuck her head in.

"Just finishing up." Giving the last of the mugs a cursory wipe-down, Tina hung the dishcloth. "I've got an early day tomorrow."

"Thanks for doing the cleanup." Becca followed Marcia and Tina through the living room, to where Ande was already waiting by the door. "I'm glad you've gotten another gig," she added softly as Tina pulled on her jacket.

"It's just an interview, but thanks." Tina shrugged. "Good to see you all."

"Blessed be." Ande peeked over to the living room, where Renee was on her hands and knees, speaking to the kitten in a high-pitched voice. "We'll talk." She mouthed the words over Marcia's head and then reached out to encompass both her and Becca in a quick group hug.

"Blessed be."

Forty

Once the others had left, Becca returned to the living room, where Renee was still on all fours, playing with the kitten.

"Thanks for these." Becca lifted the folder and stood, watching the other woman.

Clara, from her vantage point on the table, didn't need Laurel's particular sensitivity to know that her person wanted the other woman to leave. What she couldn't understand was why Renee remained.

"It's not that that kitten is so cute." Laurel, jumping silently to sit beside her, read her mind. *"Something else is going on. She's embarrassed."*

"As well she should be." Harriet landed somewhat less gracefully beside them. *"Down there on the rug with that infant."*

Clara didn't want to hush her sisters. In fact, she quickly banished the thought before Laurel could take offense. However, she did turn her ears forward, the better to pick up what Becca would say next.

"So, you've shown these to the police, right?" Becca appeared loathe to disturb Renee. The kitten, however, decided the issue by suddenly darting off.

"Well, that's the thing." Renee sat back on her heels. "I meant to, you see..."

Becca sat on the sofa. "Tell."

"I feel bad about this, but, well, you remember. When the police first spoke to me, they made the worst kind of assumptions, and, well, I sort of felt attacked."

Becca waited, and Clara could feel her person's growing skepticism. Beside her, Laurel started to growl softly, the sound emanating from deep inside her tawny chest.

"So you lied?" She spoke softly, but the word still had enough of a sting that Renee winced.

"I was in denial, I guess." Renee looked down at her hands that, now that they weren't holding the kitten, were clenched together. "Not just about Jeff's death, but about how we left things."

Becca waited, but from the way she was chewing her lip, Clara could tell she was working very hard at keeping her silence.

"I know this is awkward." Renee addressed her hands. "But I figured you were the one person who would understand how Jeff could be."

All three cats were frozen in place, but Clara could feel that low growl beginning to rise in pitch as Harriet joined in. They might squabble among themselves, but all of them were committed to Becca. Something was going to happen. But just as the calico began to tense, her claws digging into the placemat in preparation for a lunge, Becca broke the silence.

"He was cheating on you. Wasn't he?" Becca's tone, as much as her question, startled the cat. Was Becca sympathizing with this woman who had been the cause of so much heartache?

Renee broke into tears, hiding her face in her hands, and for a moment, Clara flashed back to those bad days, when Becca would cry so. Fighting the feline urge to comfort the weeping woman, she looked up at her person.

"Tell her off!" Laurel practically hissed.

"Good! What goes around comes around," Harriet gloated,

settling in to watch what she clearly anticipated would be an enjoyable exchange.

Clara wasn't sure what to expect. Certainly, this blonde person deserved her heartbreak. From everything Becca had shared with her cats, Renee hadn't hesitated in getting involved with Jeff back when he'd been seeing Becca. Even if she hadn't been aware at the very beginning, she certainly was now, and Clara was pretty sure she'd not missed anything like a belated apology for what was surely unsisterly behavior.

But although her own sisters waited for Becca to unsheathe her metaphorical claws, or at least explain the Wiccan rule of three, Clara wondered if something else was going on. Sure enough, Becca's expression remained unreadable, but her eyes began to glitter with what could only be tears.

"He could be a real jerk, couldn't he?" she said. And as Renee looked up, she opened her arms, gathering up the crying woman as if she were some bedraggled kitten who had come in out of the rain.

"Well, that's disappointing." Harriet rose and began snuffling along the tabletop, searching for stray crumbs.

"I did what I could." Laurel began to wash. *"Did you see the fury in her eyes? But ultimately, I decided this would be better."*

"How so?" Clara wasn't convinced her sister was telling the truth. She was, however, interested in her logic.

"Well, now she'll tell her everything she knows. Won't she?" said Laurel in that self-satisfied tone Siamese use so well.

Much to Clara's surprise, Laurel turned out to be correct, and within minutes Becca was fetching more tea as Renee recounted her weeks of growing suspicion.

"I knew he was working late on his new project, so at first I didn't think anything of it," she said, taking a mug from Becca. "And I'm sure a lot of it was about the project. Jeff had to meet with Darien and had to get a business team together. He even hired an accountant, because of tax liability. In fact, the day he died, he spent the day in meetings. He had an appointment with the bank and the accountant too.

"He hated all that stuff." Renee sniffed, and Becca passed her a box of tissues. "Darien told me after that he did too. That one of the advantages of having money is that he didn't have to deal with it directly anymore. But I don't know if Jeff would ever have been like that. He really cared about the details."

"I assume the police know about those meetings?"

"Oh yeah." Renee nodded. "They took his calendar and his phone, and I told them. I mean, what I could. I mean, because the deal is still in place, some of the money stuff is confidential, but everyone he was meeting with had an alibi."

"So did I," said Becca under her breath.

"They questioned me too." Renee must have heard her. "I guess that's why I pretended... By the time I realized I should have said something, I knew it was going to look bad. So I said he and I both had been getting threats."

"But that wasn't true, was it?" Becca was being awfully calm, but Clara could hear the tension in her voice.

"No," Renee whispered. "I'd been getting the letters for weeks by then, and I started to realize that not all of Jeff's late-night meetings were with Darien. They certainly weren't with the lawyers."

"And he wasn't meeting with Carl?" Becca's question seemed to take the blonde by surprise.

"What? No." She shook the idea off, prompting Becca to lower her voice.

"Do you know who he was seeing?"

Renee pursed her lips and shook her head. "I thought I saw him one night when he told me he was going over contracts. I was walking into Harvard Square, and I was sure it was him. I called out, but he either didn't hear me or he didn't want to." Her voice had dropped so low as to be barely audible.

Clara tilted her ears forward as Becca leaned in. "He was standing really close to a woman when I saw him. He was—" She paused and swallowed. "He was kind of stroking her hair. She had these glossy curls. Anyway, when I called over to him, he moved away from her. Like he wasn't with her. Like she didn't exist. And I remembered..."

Renee stopped and hung her head. "I remember him doing that with me, back when he was still seeing you, and I realized how much it hurt.

"Becca, I guess I just wanted to say I'm sorry."

Forty-One

"T*ime to bring the pain!"* Harriet stretched to her full length made quite an impressive sight as she demonstrated digging her front claws into the rug. But, to the large marmalade's dismay, neither Becca nor the woman seated beside her, head hanging down, appeared to notice.

"No need," Laurel, still perched on the sofa's back, chimed in. *"That girl feels awful."*

"As well she should." Harriet sat up and began grooming. She was, her youngest sister thought, a bit embarrassed at having been caught with her claws out needlessly. *"Hurting our Becca."*

"Technically, it was Jeff who betrayed her." Despite her loyalty to Becca, Clara couldn't help but feel some sympathy for the blonde girl, who was still sniffling as she rose to leave. Becca, apparently felt the same way, for she was now awkwardly patting the other girl's back as the three cats followed the pair the door.

"At the very least, it wasn't very sisterly." The door had only just closed when a small voice made them all jump.

"What was that?"

Six eyes, ranging from blue to gold, took in the tortoiseshell kitten. Oblivious to the world, it seemed, she tossed one of Clara's favorite catnip mice in the air, pounced, and then tossed it again.

. . .

Becca's sleep that night was as restless as that toy's. While Laurel was abuzz with questions, their person tossed and turned, and more than once Clara heard her mention the rule of three.

Laurel, meanwhile, kept Harriet and Clara awake, interrogating her sisters about what they had noticed about the kitten and when. She knew enough to keep the conversation silent, as much out of respect for their person as for her newly awakened privacy concerns. Even as they continued to second-guess what they each had heard, they assumed their places on Becca's bed in relative calm.

"We've got to let her sleep." Clara had been firm. *"This has been a difficult day for her, and she's working tomorrow."*

"We need a plan." Laurel's sharp green gaze flipped from one sister to the other.

"For Blondie? She's gone." Harriet yawned.

"No, silly. For that one." A flick of the tail indicated the kitten, who lay snoring on Becca's pillow.

"So she's learning to talk. So what?" Harriet walked in a tight circle, tamping down the comforter to her liking.

"I think it's more than that." Clara didn't want to cross Harriet. She also wasn't comfortable with Laurel's distrustful take. *"It's possible that we've been underestimating the kitten."*

"Doesn't matter." Harriet settled. *"It'll be gone soon enough."*

Harriet liked to have the last word on any subject, and so Clara kept her thoughts to herself, or at least tried to, focusing instead on a loose thread handing from Becca's pillowcase. Laurel, meanwhile, was staring at the kitten, but despite the Siamese's vaunted ability to suggest emotional states, the tiny tortie slept on peacefully, even as Becca muttered, lost in a dream.

Becca was dragging the next morning, and Clara was pretty sure that more than her interrupted sleep was to blame. Abnormally quiet as she'd gone through her morning routine, she hadn't chuckled once at the kitten's antics, and even Harriet's best big-eyed beg, which had the stout marmalade up on her haunches as her can was opened, didn't elicit the usual cooing.

Instead, their person seemed much more interested in the file of letters and the typed notes she had made before her futile attempt at sleep. It didn't take Laurel's sensitivity to suss out that Becca wanted to go back to those letters now. But once the cats were fed and she caught sight of the time, she simply grabbed her laptop and shoved it into her bag. Out on the street, her feet dragged to the point that Clara began to worry that her person was getting sick. But once they neared Charm and Cherish, Becca's pace as well as her mood began to pick up. A glance up at her person's face hinted at a certain preoccupied thoughtfulness that her cat believed she understood.

"Good morning." Becca had just brought out the tray of stones when Elizabeth entered through the front, the cascading bells announcing her arrival.

"Good morning, dear." Lighting up with a smile that turned her wrinkles into dimples, she extended a cardboard tray with two takeout coffees on it. Balanced between was a white paper bag that smelled deliciously of something freshly baked. "I thought you might need this this morning."

"Thanks." Becca reached for a cup as Elizabeth placed the tray beside the pretty gemstones. She no longer questioned the wiry-haired woman's prescience, her cat noted. But she did pause before sipping her cappuccino.

"Elizabeth, may I ask you about something?"

"Of course." Her warm smile was a marked contrast to her sister's habitual scowl.

"Had you met Tina before Margaret hired her?"

One eyebrow arched. "You know I see quite a few people."

"Yes, but..."

"I think maybe you two need to have a talk." She headed back toward the door.

"Don't you want the other coffee?"

"That's not for me," she called over her shoulder. "Enjoy the beignets!"

Becca had only just reached into the bag when the bells rang again, and she looked up to see Tina coming in.

"Tina!" Becca eyed her. "I didn't expect you. Though maybe I should have." She eyed the tray. "How did the interview go?"

"It was informational." The other woman waved it off. "Are those beignets?"

"Elizabeth brought you a coffee too." Becca gestured toward the tray. "She and Margaret must have put you on the schedule."

"Well, I've asked for as many hours as they can give me." Taking the mug in one hand, she reached into the bag with the other before pausing. "Is that okay? I don't want to mess with your schedule."

"It's fine. Margaret wants two people working, and it's not fair to Elizabeth to expect her to cover. Besides," Becca paused, "I wanted a chance to talk with you."

"Oh? Did you learn anything from what's-her-name? Renee?" Tina took a big bite of the sugar-coated morsel, blocking any further response. That seemed to be fine with Becca, who was clearly wrestling with what to say.

"No, this is something different. I gather you used to come into the shop before we officially met."

Tina nodded enthusiastically, her mouth full.

"And you would ask for me?"

Tina managed to swallow. "I'd seen your notices about being a witch detective, and I thought that was so cool. Well, you know. That's why I wanted to join the coven."

Becca nodded slowly, as if weighing something. "Did you cut your hair to look like mine?"

Tina coughed. "Sorry," she said. "The sugar." She paused. "I was due for a change. I'd let my hair grow out after a bad breakup a while ago, and I wanted something new. Something neat, and I thought your hairstyle was perfect. Especially for working in retail."

"And you knew you wanted to work here."

Tina shrugged as she reached for another beignet.

"So you wanted to be like me." Becca spoke softly, her eyes on the other woman.

Tina looked down at the sugared donut in her hand. "I admire you." She could have been speaking to the beignet. "You know that."

Becca licked her lips, but Clara didn't think she was tasting the powdered sugar that lingered there.

"Tina," she said after a moment's pause. "Were you seeing Jeff?"

FORTY-TWO

It was a good thing business was slow, Clara thought. Because Becca soon had her hands full. For the second time in twelve hours, her person was comforting a crying woman—and wishing that she was elsewhere.

"I know, believe me, I know," Becca repeated herself for the umpteenth time. "He's—he was—very charming."

Tina hadn't confessed to anything, exactly. But even without her pets' feline sensitivities, Becca had picked up on the dark-haired woman's increasing discomfort with her questions. And her total collapse at the last one—a blubbering outpouring of grief and relief—seemed to confirm things for Becca. Not, Clara thought, that any of this would stand up in court.

"He really loved you, you know." Tina's tears had given way to sniffles, but her reddened eyes didn't seem to take in Becca's discomfort with the subject. As her human let her bleary-eyed colleague ramble on, emptying most of a box of tissues along the way, Clara realized that Becca wasn't simply humoring her. She was listening with patience that would do Laurel proud. "He knew he made a mistake leaving you for Renee."

At that, Becca made a noise—half grunt, half denial—but Tina was too involved in her tale to take notice. "That's when I realized how much I loved him. He wasn't going to stay with some ditzy blonde forever." She made a fist, clenching the most recent Kleenex tight. "He wanted a woman of power."

"So that's when you decided to join the coven?" Becca was trying to be sympathetic. Clara could hear it in her voice, even if the edge broke through.

Tina might have caught the sympathy, but she clearly missed the anger Becca was holding back. "I'd already checked you out, of course. I knew you had been together for a few years, and that Renee, well, Renee was a flash in the pan. And when I started hearing about what you'd done, setting yourself up as a witch detective and solving crimes, I knew I wanted to be like you."

"Did you ever think I might want Jeff back?"

That stopped her and took Clara by surprise too. As Tina blinked, mouth open, Clara looked up at her person inquisitively. Yes, Becca had mourned the end of the relationship, but she'd had the sense to reject Jeff's half-hearted attempts to reconcile. Surely, she didn't regret that now. And if she did, was this messy newcomer really an appropriate confidante?

"No, I-I didn't." Tina stammered out a response.

Becca sighed. Whether she'd simply been speaking out of pique or truly wanted to know, she apparently believed the woman sitting by her side.

"You're so strong and together, and...and ..."

"And he had you." Becca smiled, a sad, close-mouthed smile.

Tina swallowed but as the seconds dragged on, she nodded.

"I thought of you as my role model." She stared into Becca's soft brown eyes as if transfixed, and as she did, all the studied similarities between the two—the short curls, a certain style of dressing—faded away and any resemblance disappeared.

Drawing a deep breath, Becca took both of Tina's hands, thinner, their nails bitten to the quick, in her own. "Did you write those letters to Renee?"

Tina nodded, looking for all the world like she was about to start crying again. "But I never threatened anyone," she said. "I just—I just ..."

"Not directly." Becca spoke carefully. "I read them last night, after Renee dropped them off, Tina. You called her a faker and a poser, and in one you said she was a brainless ditz."

"She is a ditz. And a homewrecker." Tina spoke so quietly, Clara had to flip her ears to hear her.

Becca shot her a look.

"I mean, she broke you two up." Tina must have gotten over her initial shock, because she seemed to be rallying to her theme.

"Jeff broke us up." Becca kept speaking. "And you got involved with him knowing he had another girlfriend."

"Don't tell me you're taking her side."

Becca sat up then and stared at the woman beside her, as if taking her measure. "Did you fight with Jeff about Renee?"

"What? No. You can't think..." Tina reached for Becca, but she stepped back.

"Where were you the night Jeff was killed?"

"I was working! I mean, at home, but I was online by seven. You can see my web log, if you want."

"I'm not going to be the one looking at it, Tina. I'm going to go to the police." She paused, taking in the wide-eyed woman before her. "It might be a good idea if you come in with me."

Becca began gathering her things, and Tina clutched at her. "Are you going there now?"

"Not yet." Becca shook her off with a stern look. "I have my notes, but I'm going to get the letters themselves. That will give you time to decide if you should come with me and explain why you were arguing with Jeff. In the meantime..." She pulled out her phone.

"Elizabeth? Would you be able to cover the shop with Tina for about an hour? I have to run out."

Tina hunched miserably, hands in her pockets, as Becca returned to the front of the shop to wait for the older woman. When Elizabeth breezed in, her usual jolly mien drawn with concern, it was clear she had quickly picked up on the body language of the two employees—either that or some sensitivity of her own had alerted her.

"I can cover for either or both of you," she said, looking from one to the other. "But I do hope you remember what I was saying about second chances, Becca. And, Tina? I believe there's something you need to do."

With that, Tina nodded, slowly extending her hand, which was closed in a fist. "I'm sorry, Becca. Truly, I am," she said as she turned her fist palm up and opened her fingers to reveal a lopsided stone: Becca's tiger eye.

Forty-Three

"Maddy, you wouldn't believe it." Becca was on her phone as soon as the door shut, jingling behind her. "Tina, our newest witch, was seeing Jeff. Yeah, he was cheating on Renee too."

A grim smile lit her face as she listened to her friend. "I know." She nodded as she spoke, one eye on the threatening sky. "Turnabout is fair play and all that. But, listen, this was really weird. Tina is kind of fixated on me. Like, she decided that I was Jeff's ideal and so she tried to turn herself into a version of me. My boss had told me that she used to come by and ask for me when I wasn't there, and I figured out that she cut her hair to look like me. It's just too—"

Another question from Maddy interrupted her flow.

"That's just it, Mads. I don't know. I was sure it was something with Carl, only this is too weird. And, no, I don't see any way they were working together. Though Carl was looking for something in Jeff's apartment."

She stopped short on the pavement, oblivious to the raindrops that had started to fall. "The key," she said. "That's what he was looking for."

An inquisitive squawk came through the line.

"My key, the one I gave to Jeff. Tina said she found it in the alley, but I didn't see it out there, and the cops didn't either."

Maddy's complaint, that Tina had had a key to Becca's apartment, could have been heard by a creature with even less sensitive hearing than Clara's. But Becca barely acknowledged her friend's distress, instead musing on the possible coincidence.

"I bet she found it in Jeff's apartment, and if she was in there after he was killed, then—I know, I know, Maddy, but we know I wasn't involved. Hang on, I have to get my own key out."

Phone nestled under her chin, she reached into her bag. "No, I'm at my apartment. Elizabeth is staying with Tina. She was talking about second chances and everything, but not if she's a murderer, right? Anyway, I came home to get the letters, the ones Tina sent Renee. I'm going to hand them over to the police."

She nodded at Maddy's response as she climbed the stairs. "You're right, Maddy. You were from the start. But at least now I have something to give the cops."

The sound of her friend's delighted response faded as Becca dropped the phone.

"Maddy?" She scrambled to pick it up, dropping her bag in the process. "I've got to go. My door is open. Someone's broken into my apartment."

Forty-Four

Leaving Becca on the landing, Clara hurried into the apartment. She wasn't feeling particularly brave: her acute hearing had already assured her nobody was inside besides her sisters and the kitten. However, she hadn't foreseen this particular complication, and she was determined to find out what had happened and, if possible, why.

"Hello?" For once, the little calico hadn't had to pass through a closed door, and so her leap carried her nearly into the living room. She could see the mess the intruder had wrought. The big armchair had been turned over, and papers were everywhere. What the little cat didn't see were her sisters. *"Harriet? Laurel?"*

"We're in here," a muffled voice called from the bedroom, summoning Clara. Only, just then, she heard another sound, a soft mew, from beneath the overturned chair, and Clara turned to see the tortie kitten's face appear.

"Kitten, are you okay?" Clara rushed over to touch noses and was rewarded with a deep purr. *"Oh, thank Bast!"*

With one sheathed paw, she reached out to the kitten, hoping to urge her into the bedroom. It would be easier to find out what happened if everyone was in one place. Only just then the sound of heavy treads on the stairs spooked them both. Without thinking, Clara grabbed the kitten by the scruff and dashed into the bedroom.

"We're under here!" Laurel's drawl emerged from under the bed, and so Clara, kitten in her mouth, dove to join them.

"Step back, miss." A male voice, loud and authoritative, boomed in. Clara, having released the kitten, peeked out to spy the speaker—a large man in a blue uniform—standing in the doorway. "Let us ascertain if the intruder is gone."

"Of course there's nobody here." Behind her, Harriet shifted. Clara didn't know how long her sisters had been hiding, but clearly it had been long enough for the big marmalade to grow uncomfortable with the tight space.

"We weren't hiding," Laurel whined. *"Strategically, this was the smart move."*

"Why?" Clara was watching as the big man and his thinner companion moved into the apartment. She heard the chair being righted as the heavy footsteps progressed into the apartment. *"What happened?"*

"A person broke in. What do you think?" Laurel had either picked up on Harriet's pique or she was equally uncomfortable. *"We heard the crash and did the sensible thing."*

"The crash?"

More moving of furniture. Clara could make out the pantry door being opened and, soon after closed.

"Yes, the crash!" Even in the dark, Clara could see Laurel's green eyes flash. *"Didn't you see the door?"*

In truth, Clara hadn't paused to look. But they could all hear the police now.

"It's safe to come in, miss." The big guy took the lead, talking even as Becca pushed past him and ran into the kitchen. Searching, Clara realized, for her and her sisters.

"The apartment is empty. We'll need some information before we file our report, but you might want to look around and make a list of what's missing," the cop was saying. Becca had gone to the pantry first, and even from the bedroom, Clara could hear her ragged, panicked breathing.

"We can also give you some names of emergency repair services. You'll want to get that door taken care of. Until then, do you have somewhere you can stay?"

"Where are my cats?"

The cop shut up, and from her vantage point, Clara could see him turn toward his companion. Before they could respond, however, they heard a skid and a welcome thud. Becca had landed on the bedroom floor and was peering in at them.

"There you are!" Wiggling under the bed, she would have reached for Clara first, but the little calico had already emerged and was rubbing against her. "Harriet? Laurel?"

Laurel gave an obligatory hiss. *"She should know we were inconvenienced,"* she told her sisters, while Harriet allowed herself to be dragged out and cradled, limp as a pillow, in their person's arms. Clara held her tongue, but she did make sure to nudge the kitten to follow as Becca headed toward the kitchen.

"Miss?" The big cop followed her. "Do you want to pack a bag? We can drop you anywhere in the city."

"That won't be necessary, Officer." Becca called over her shoulder as she reached into the cabinet for four familiar cans. "I'll call one of those services to fix my door, but I'm not leaving my cats."

"Please tell me everything." Once the four had eaten, Clara corralled her sisters under the bed once more. The loud hammering as the door was repaired had Laurel's ears back. But Harriet seemed calm enough now that she had eaten.

"There isn't much to tell," said Harriet, sounding nonchalant, though that could have been the result of the fur in her mouth. It had to be difficult for the marmalade to maneuver in the tight space, but she was doing her best to wash her left hind paw.

"Was it a man or a woman?" Clara pictured Renee in her mind, trying to imagine her angry rather than sobbing and sympathetic. When that image didn't evoke a response, she tried

summoning Carl's round face, putting a frown on it for good measure.

"You're asking the wrong question." Laurel examined her own chocolate paws, fully aware that she was showing her own flexibility to advantage. *"You should be asking what we felt."*

Clara waited, knowing Laurel loved the drama.

"A wave of anger," she said at last. *"But more than that, fear, as if whoever it was was starving. Even before the door opened, we felt that hunger. You've never seen Harriet move so fast."* This was accompanied by an image of a marauding wolf, fangs bared as it leaped—Laurel's best imagining of the terror she had sensed.

And you left the kitten out there alone? The thought sprang unbidden to Clara's mind, and she ducked her head, anxious that either of her sisters would take offense at her unintended rebuke. Fear rarely brought out the best in anyone.

"Why don't you question it, then?" Harriet sniffed.

Before Clara could respond, a familiar voice broke in—"Becca! What happened?"—and she peered out from under the bed to see her person fall into Maddy's arms.

Forty-Five

Maddy, Clara thought, had many cat-like qualities. For starters, as soon as she was able to disengage from Becca, she began to clean. That took a while, though. Becca had managed a stoic front for the two officers, but when her friend had appeared, she had collapsed in heaving sobs.

"I'm okay," she kept saying, despite evidence to the contrary. "I'm just shaken up."

"I know, dear." Maddy continued patting her on the back as yet another wave of tears arrived, but Clara could see her looking around, planning her line of attack. "It's unsettling. I bet if we could just make your place look like itself again, you'd feel better. Would you like to help me pick up?"

With a few sniffles, Becca agreed.

"There you go." Maddy hugged her close once again, before sending her off to the bathroom to blow her nose and wash her face. While Harriet and Laurel trotted after Becca, Clara hung back, curious as to what the other woman had in mind.

The police had already righted the chair that had been tossed, and so Maddy began gathering papers.

"Have you already checked your bedroom?" she called over to her friend.

Becca emerged, red-eyed but calm. “Yeah. It looks like they went through my jewelry box. My hoop earrings were on the floor. But nothing’s missing.” She made a face. “Maybe there wasn’t anything good enough for them.”

“Well, the building has gone upscale.” Maddy tapped a bundle of papers on the tabletop, neatening them.

Becca shook her head. “This wasn’t a burglary. It’s related to the case.”

“The case?” Maddy snorted. “Your ex was murdered, Becca. This isn’t a case, and you shouldn’t be involved. You know that, you were telling me that not an hour ago.”

“That was before all this.” Her arm swept the room, which actually didn’t look so bad anymore. “Not to mention that I think whoever broke in took Renee’s letters, which are what I came home for in the first place.”

“You’re thinking that this Tina was behind it?”

Becca nodded, her face growing thoughtful. “She kept saying, ‘I didn’t threaten anyone.’ But those letters were kind of unhinged, and she doesn’t have an alibi. But, Maddy, she was with me this morning. Unless…”

Becca chewed her lower lip, a sure sign she was quizzing over a problem.

“What?” Maddy wiped her own curls back from her brow.

“Maybe she broke in after I left, and then hurried over to Charm and Cherish to give herself an alibi. I mean, I’m sure she was the woman arguing with Jeff before he was killed, even if she ran home after and went online.”

Maddy collapsed on the sofa with a thud. “You’ve got to tell the police all this. Like, now.”

“Yeah.” Becca looked around. “I wonder if I can get another copy of those letters from Renee, though. She didn’t want to give them to the cops at first, but at this point I think she has to.”

“Just tell the cops about the letters and let them convince her.” Maddy’s patience was wearing thin. “That’s their job.”

“But it doesn’t seem like they’re really investigating. Not like they should, and besides.” Becca turned back to her friend with what looked like chagrin. "I don't know if I have any credibility with the Cambridge police anymore."

"Excuse me," a voice called from the doorway. "I think I'm done here."

"Great." While Becca went to deal, Maddy started leafing through the papers she'd collected. As Clara watched, she grew increasingly intent.

"Becca?"

"Hang on." Becca ran to get her wallet and back to the front door. Laurel, meanwhile, had emerged to sniff at the carpenter's shoes.

"Forget it." She sashayed into the living room.

"Not fancy enough?" Clara had her own feelings about her sister's priorities and had come up with this phrasing as one her sister might not bridle at.

"Worse than that." She shook herself, making her satin coat ripple. *"He has a dog."*

"Well, here's hoping I don't lose my job soon." Becca returned, flopping onto the sofa beside her friend.

"At least the door's fixed." Maddy's eyes were still glued to the page in front of her. "But, Becca?"

"The lock still works too. I was worried. Oh!" She jumped up as if something in the sofa had bitten her. Laurel and Clara exchanged a look, and Clara trotted after Becca as she ran into the bedroom.

"Becca, I think you should see this," Maddy called again, oblivious to her friend's sudden shift.

"Hang on." Becca's voice carried over the sound of drawers being opened, their contents rustling as she pawed through them.

"Listen, then." Maddy appeared in the doorway, the pages in her hand. "I think I found the letters, Becs."

"That's great." Becca was beneath her desk now, hands sweeping the floor as her three cats looked on.

"Did you read this?" Maddy didn't wait for an answer. "'Everyone knows the truth,'" she read aloud. "'Jeff's closest friend has been telling anyone who will listen that your days are numbered. That Jeff is out the door.'"

"You found them." Becca sat up, banging her head on the underside of the desk. "Ow!"

"Yeah, they were scattered on the floor." Maddy didn't seem to notice her friend rubbing her pate as she crawled out. "They were mixed in with printouts about the solstice. But there's more: 'You may as well prepare yourself, if even his best friend says he's gone.'"

"That's not a threat exactly." Becca, who had flipped on her belly, was peering under the bed.

"Not from Tina. But what if she misinterpreted? What if Carl wasn't talking about Jeff and Renee, but about Jeff himself. I mean, 'he's gone'?"

Becca emerged, a dust bunny clinging to her curls. "I hadn't thought of that. But, Maddy, I might have a bigger problem."

Her friend looked at her, the question puckering her brow.

"My key, Maddy. The one that I gave Jeff. It's gone. I think that's the one thing they took."

Forty-Six

It didn't help Becca's mood that the skies had opened up while they waited. The emergency locksmith explained that bad weather always brought a slew of calls. "Nobody wants to be waiting outside in a thunderstorm." And then the Chinese food Maddy ordered—"my treat"—was delayed for the same reason.

"I can't believe I'm stuck here." Becca stared out the window as raindrops pelted down. "That *we're* stuck here. No offense."

"None taken." Maddy had found the kitten and was watching, entranced, as the little beast batted at the catnip mouse she held by its tail. "But I'm glad you're getting the lock switched—I don't like the idea that a copy of your key could be out there. And I'm sorry I even brought up that letter."

"I had a feeling something was up with Carl, even before then." Becca frowned. "But I still want to talk to Tina again. I mean, she could have made that up, Maddy. She wanted to hurt Renee."

"And you'd believe whatever she told you?" Maddy looked up, and the kitten successfully swatted the toy to the floor.

"No." Becca frowned. "She's been lying since day one, but I don't know exactly about what. I don't think she's big enough to have broken the door down. Besides, she wouldn't have had to. As you said, she could have had my key copied. Still, there's something going on with her. Anyway, I told her that I'd give her a chance to come in with me."

"You're still going to trust her after...?" Maddy gestured, her voice trailing off as she searched for the right word.

Maddy was saved from having to respond by the arrival of the locksmith and, right after, their dinner.

"Is that for me?" The locksmith, a gray-haired imp of a man, stood back as Maddy paid the delivery woman. "You just go ahead," he nodded to the bag, "this won't take more than a few minutes."

True enough, by the time Becca had fetched her rice bowls, he was done, and she settled up as the three cats circled the fragrant bag.

"You don't even like dan dan noodles." Laurel tried to edge Harriet out of the way.

"There might be chicken in there." Her sister refused to budge.

"Perfect timing." Ignoring the curious felines, Maddy reached in, pulling out the first container of fragrant food as Becca returned with the dishes. "Your cats don't eat dumplings, do they?"

"I'm sure they'd like to try. But hang on..."

While Maddy continued to unpack, Becca returned to the kitchen. "Dinner," she called.

"I knew trying to get into the bag would remind her." Laurel mewed an aside to Harriet, whose eyes were riveted on their person. Lagging behind, Clara scanned the room for the kitten. She'd run off with that catnip mouse, dragging it by its tail. Surely, the kitten had worked up an appetite, but had she gotten herself into trouble with the oversize toy? Maybe when the locksmith had left, she'd slipped out into the storm.

"It's dinnertime, Clown!" Laurel's yowl reached her in the bedroom. No kitten.

"Coming!" Increasingly desperate, Clara darted to the front of the apartment—and sighed with relief. Somehow the kitten had

managed to climb up to the windowsill, high above where her elders had thought she could leap. And there she sat, licking the window, as if she could taste the raindrops that rolled down on the other side.

While a relieved Clara joined her sisters in the kitchen, the two humans remained oblivious to the kitten's antics. While the little tortie kept glancing over, as if eager to attract their attention, Maddy and Becca were doing what they would call strategizing, laying out the facts as they knew them for and against each of the suspects in both Jeff's murder and the break-in.

"I think we have to strike Tina off the list," Becca said as she reached for more of the noodles. "Even if she had broken in and then run over to the shop, she wouldn't have had to force the door. Unless..." She chewed thoughtfully.

"She realized that *you've* realized that she lied about where she found it." Maddy frowned at her dumpling. "And she could have used a crowbar to deflect suspicion. No, she stays on the list. As does Renee."

"You're just down on her because Jeff cheated on me with her." Becca paused. "And, yeah, I was too. But if you'd seen her, Maddy. She really did feel awful."

"Crocodile tears," Maddy replied.

"What does that mean?" Laurel, who had finished her meal, glared, eyes wide. *"Is there a lizard in the house?"*

"We'd know." Harriet, sated and content, settled on the sofa, leaving it to Clara to explain the ins and outs of human colloquialisms.

"She wasn't faking," Laurel cut her off. *"I would know."*

Clara bowed her head, acknowledging her sister's skill. Besides, Becca had just made the same point to Maddy.

"She was really crying, Maddy. And part of what was eating at her was guilt, so I believe her."

"Well, good." Maddy speared another dumpling. "She should feel bad."

As loyal as she was, Clara found herself siding with Maddy on this one. Not that Becca's instincts were wrong. As much as she sometimes doubted the scope of human intelligence—she truly wished her person would give up her pursuit of powers beyond her reach—Clara trusted her person's heart. That didn't mean that someone who had hurt her person, inadvertently or not, should escape. If that blonde woman was hurting now, well, that was only fair.

"And that, Clown, is what they call being catty." Laurel's voice, deep in her head, made Clara jump. Perhaps because she'd only recently learned about her sisters' ability to read her thoughts, it still had the power to startle her.

"It does mean we can pool our powers, though." Harriet, half asleep, nodded at her sagely from her pillow.

"But how?" The little calico was at her wit's end. As Becca and her friend kept talking, all she could do was curl up next to her person and offer the quiet consolation of a purr.

By the time the food was finished and the dishes squared away, the two friends had reached something of an accord.

"You'll bring those letters to the police tomorrow." Maddy, shrugging into her coat, looked concerned. "First thing."

"I already said I would." Becca softened her words with a smile. "That's what I was planning on doing before I came home to...all this." Her gesture took in the sofa where all three adult cats now lounged, as well as the windowsill, where the kitten slept, belly and paws up.

"That was also before you read them carefully." Despite having zipped up her rain jacket, Maddy didn't reach for the door.

"I do want to speak to Carl again," Becca admitted. "I just don't know what to ask him. I mean, besides why he's been hitting on me and Renee both." She stopped her friend's protest with a raised hand. "I know, Maddy. That's not criminal. But it is odd. But, I promise, I'll bring those letters to the cops first thing. Now, are you okay getting home in this or do you want me to call you a Lyft?"

"I'll be fine, dear." Maddy reached out for a hug. "You're the one who keeps running into trouble."

FORTY-SEVEN

It must have been the rain, Clara thought, with its purr-like rhythmic lull, but everyone in the household slept well that night, from Becca, who crawled into bed not long after her friend left, to the three sisters, to the tiny kitten, who apparently had exhausted herself trying to lick up all those drops.

Becca was humming to herself the next morning as she prepared breakfast for the cats and then herself. (*"As is proper,"* Harriet observed.) But it wasn't simply a good night's sleep that had cheered her person so, Clara realized. Becca had clicked on her phone as she made coffee to find a voicemail waiting.

"Hey, Becca." The voice emanating from the device was tinny and small, and Becca had paused her morning ritual before identifying it as Darien Hughes. "I'm sorry to call so late. Dropped by Charm and Cherish hoping to run into you, but it seems I missed you. I know I asked you about next weekend, but I was wondering if I could see you sooner. What would you say to dinner tonight? I'll try you later. Please say yes!"

"Yes," Becca said as she poured the water over the beans. "Yes, dinner would be nice," she said again as she reached for the yogurt.

"She's talking to a machine." Harriet looked up from her empty dish.

"She's happy." Laurel had already begun to bathe.

Clara, meanwhile, kept silent. As much as she wanted her person to be happy—and as much as she thought her the most wonderful, most desirable human possible—there was something about the handsome financier's pursuit that bothered her.

"He asked Renee out too," she murmured, almost as if talking to herself.

Laurel looked at her over one dark paw, the implication in her blue eyes clear: *"You're acting like a kitten again, as if you're unaware how real-life romance works."*

"I know Becca is prettier," Clara countered her sister's silent rejoinder. *"I just want her to be with someone who isn't even interested in anyone else."*

A dismissive snort, accompanied by a flick of the tail, revealed her Siamese sister's take on that. And by then, Becca was getting ready to leave.

Befitting her mood, the morning was as bright as the day before had been grim. Becca's earlier elation had grown muted, however. In part, her cat suspected, because of the folder of letters she had tucked into her bag. In part, because despite her promises to her friend the night before, Becca was still weighing a course of action that differed from a quick and clean delivery of the letters —and her own dropping of what she had come to call her case.

When Becca reached into her bag, while waiting for a light, Clara's fears began to take on flesh. But when her hand emerged holding her phone, the little cat relaxed. Until, that is, she heard her person speak.

"Hi, Carl. It's Becca," she began, in that particular measured way that humans have when they're talking to another person's device. "I believe I have something you might want to see. Call me?"

Neither Becca's mood nor her steps grew any heavier after she disconnected, but her pet eyed her person with concern, even as she trotted along to keep up. That worry grew when Becca stopped on a corner and made an abrupt about face. Becca wasn't going to the cops, Clara realized. She was going directly to Charm and Cherish.

Her cheery mood crumbled quickly, however, on finding the front door of the little shop unlocked.

"Hello?" Sticking her head in, she called, "Elizabeth?"

"Becca, you're here!" Tina rushed out from the back room. Dressed in a flowered blouse that resembled one of Becca's favorites, the shorter girl looked lost, too thin and pale to carry all that color. "Elizabeth told me what happened."

"Is she here?" Becca disengaged herself from Tina and looked past her.

"She was. You just missed her." Tina followed Becca's gaze with shadowed eyes. "I was just going to open."

"She called you in?" Becca's voice had an edge her cat didn't understand. She knew her person had phoned her boss after the police had left to explain why she wasn't going to return that day. It wasn't that farfetched, therefore, to assume that Becca might be out until further notice. Maybe it was just as well, Clara thought, as she studied Becca. Her person was focusing on the shorter girl like Laurel would on a spider.

"Yes, she asked if I could fill in." Her reply, directed down at the shaded cat, must have been barely audible to Becca. "I didn't know if you were coming in, but I was hoping." Before Becca could respond, she kept talking. "And before you ask, I will go to the police after my shift today. Honest, but I wanted to talk to you again first." Her voice dropped to a whisper. "I know what I did was wrong, but I really do admire you and I thought if I could explain—"

"So there's more you'd like to tell me?" The edge, Clara thought, might be softening, but Becca was still staring at the other girl as if she could pin her in place.

Tina shrugged, her shoulders all bone beneath the blouse. "It was a feeling, more than anything. I mean, I could tell that Jeff wasn't happy. He didn't belong with Renee."

"Never mind about Jeff," Becca interrupted. "Tell me more

about what you did, Tina. That's what I want to hear about."

"What do you mean?" She looked up, blinking, her voice suddenly tight.

"I don't think you found my key in that alley."

Tina's mouth opened and closed. A goldfish, then, not a spider.

"I know you went into the alley because you were seen. But I think you found my key in Jeff's apartment. After he was killed," said Becca, as the other woman turned deathly pale. "You wanted to get involved, to bring me something. But it rained the night after Jeff's murder, before you say you found it, and when you gave it to me, its yarn tag was clean and dry. Even if you'd wiped down the key itself, that yarn would've been muddy."

"But..."

Becca wasn't finished. "You knew Jeff kept his extra key above the door. I bet you brought that bucket to stand on too."

Tina didn't deny it.

"I'd seen him looking at your key. He even said something once, about how he ought to return it. I thought that showed how he still felt—and how wrong he and Renee were."

Becca's only response was to raise her brows.

"I shouldn't have been in there. But, yeah, I knew about his spare key—once, he'd had to use it. We were drunk and...anyway, I knew it was there." The frail girl spoke in a monotone. "And I was having a hard time. I mean, everyone was slathering Renee with sympathy, and I knew you had friends who would ask after you. I wanted to feel close to him."

"You really hate Renee, don't you?"

"She's a sleaze."

Clara could see Becca wrestling with what to say next. She could point out that what Tina had done was no better, for example. Instead, she seemed ready to try a different tack.

"Do you believe she was involved in Jeff's death?"

"What? No." Tina's surprise brought some animation to her voice. "At least, I don't think so."

"So you wouldn't plant evidence to incriminate her? You

know, to make sure she was brought to justice?" Becca was working hard to keep her voice steady.

"No, no, I just..." Tina fell back into silence.

"What?"

"I went to his place because I wanted the letters back. I thought maybe she'd brought them over to Jeff, and I knew they made it sound like I was really angry, and, well..."

Her voice trailed off, and Clara thought Becca would pounce. After all, Tina had been more than angry. By any measure of cats or human, she hadn't been acting rationally. Still, Becca's next question was not one her pet had expected.

"Tell me more about Carl," she demanded.

"Carl?" Tina parroted the name back.

"In one of your letters, you quoted something he said." Becca, tipping her head, regarded the other woman quizzically. "Do you remember what you said? Something about how Carl had said that Jeff's days were numbered."

Tina gasped. "I do. He said that. He really did. But..."

"What?" Becca was beginning to sound impatient.

"In truth, I think he was talking about the company. Because he was leaving, right? But I wanted Renee to think he was talking about her, especially when he went on about how something was missing."

"He said something was missing?" Becca went so quiet even her cat couldn't read her.

Tina nodded vigorously. "He did. He and I were out for drinks, and he got really angry about it. He said Jeff was getting cold feet just because something wasn't exactly right. Carl said that was proof Jeff needed him. Then after..."

Tina fell silent, her face going suddenly bloodless as she gasped.

"Tina, what is it?"

"After Jeff died, I heard Carl talking about it again. He was saying that he knew what was missing. That he could find it, and that Darien would have to take him on now. That he—Carl—was the one who made things happen."

Forty-Eight

From the set of her mouth and the furrow between her eyes, Becca was thinking hard about something as she left the shop, having made Tina promise once again that she would go to the police as soon as her shift ended. Whether Becca trusted her or not, her preoccupation was obvious to Clara, even as she gave up her close examination of her person to better dodge the foot traffic on the sidewalk. Becca could afford to be oblivious as she strode quickly through the rush-hour crowd. Although Clara's person wasn't tall, she was visible, which gave her an edge her shaded cat lacked, and as she pushed ahead, it was all her pet could do to keep up.

As Becca turned toward the police station, Clara tried to relax. Becca had promised Maddy that she'd turn those letters over to the detective in charge, but the little cat didn't need her sister's sensitivity to know that Becca regretted that promise. When she stopped at the base of the stairs to leaf through the folder, her cat feared the worst. Concentrating all her might, she stared at her person, and only as Becca began to climb up those stairs did the calico realize she'd been holding her breath.

"Detective Newsom, please." Becca spoke in her no-nonsense voice, the one that made the cats jump off the table even before she reached for them. The man behind the counter didn't seem to notice. In fact, he barely looked up from the typed form he held as she stood there, waiting for his reply.

"Not here." He must have caught how her lips pursed and her brow knit, though, because as he replaced the form only to pick up another, he turned toward her again. "You here to file a lost property report? A complaint?"

"No." A slight quaver in her voice betrayed her indecision. "I have something to share with him."

"Sounds interesting," he said without looking up again. "If it's something material, you can leave it here with me. I'll make sure he gets it."

For a moment, Becca hesitated, looking down at the folder in her hand and over at the clerk's desk, with its overflowing inbox. Then she shook her head, her mouth taking on a familiar set. "No, thanks," she said. "I'll come back."

Without the closure a meeting with that detective would have provided and sensing that her person hadn't been satisfied by Tina's answers, Clara feared the worst. Becca was going to investigate, and without her sisters to back her up, the calico worried about keeping her safe. But when Becca turned toward home, her pet began to relax. Although Becca didn't look particularly excited, she must be thinking of her plans with Darien. Becca, Clara recalled, sometimes looked distracted when she considered what to wear before a night out, a concept that, to a cat, was hard to grasp.

"Well, of course." Laurel greeted her sister with one brow raised as the calico raced through the door moments ahead of their person. *"She takes grooming seriously."*

"Perhaps I should summon something special for her," Harriet deigned to offer.

"Or we could trust her to figure this out." Clara made her voice as gentle as possible. Still, her sisters stared at her as if she had suddenly sprouted two heads, before both suddenly decided to groom.

. . .

Becca tried the detective twice again that afternoon without any luck, only leaving a message after the second call, and spent the rest of the day reading and re-reading the letters and jotting notes on her laptop while her cats looked on. She tucked the papers away, finally, to feed the cats—the combined efforts of Laurel and Harriet prompting her to give them an early dinner—and while they were eating, she began to dress. Without Laurel to nudge her toward the more daring extremes of her wardrobe, Becca wavered, pulling out a silk blouse that shimmered like sunlight on fur and a soft cotton sweater that Clara enjoyed sleeping on. Holding first one and then the other up in front of the mirror, she opted for both, donning the sweater like a jacket over the sleek silk, a look Clara approved of from her post at the bedroom doorway.

"Not too bad." Laurel joined her, licking her chops.

"She's not sure about this man." Clara, grateful for the truce with her sisters, knew she didn't have to explain Becca's emotions, but she did want to counter Laurel's default setting—that their person should be as seductive as possible.

"It's about power, Clown. I want her to be in control."

"She's still human." Harriet had joined them, as had the kitten, who was playing at pouncing on Harriet's big fluff of a tail. *"And if you do that again, thing..."*

Clara turned her attention to the tortie. *"Come on,"* she said. *"We can find something else to play with."*

She was batting one of her catnip mice for the kitten to chase when she sensed an impending arrival.

"Maybe he'll give us treats." Harriet was already trotting toward the door, while Laurel, her tail raised in a perfect curl, slunk behind.

Clara, however, hesitated. The vibration was familiar, and yet...

"Carl." Becca sounded as surprised as Clara, but she recovered quickly. "You got my message."

"I did. You wanted to show me something?" The fleshy man reached for the door, as if he would push it open. Becca, however, stood firm, blocking his path.

"I can just tell you," she said. "Apparently you were telling people that Jeff's days were numbered. That sounds like a threat to me, and it will to the police as well."

"I'm sorry." He exhaled, shaking his head, as if he wanted to shed an outdated notion. "It's not what you think. Really, it's not. I was talking about his time at CodePhool. That's all."

Becca took this in, as Clara remembered what Tina had said.

"Look," Carl kept talking. "I know you still have questions. I guess I should have explained my situation better."

"Well, now you're here." She didn't show any signs of moving, and for one tense moment, the two faced off. "I've got plans this evening, Carl," she offered by way of explanation. "I really don't have time, but if you want to tell me anything, I'm listening."

"Really?" He craned his head, as if he were trying to see into the apartment. "Let me guess, is Renee here?"

"No, and I'm about to head out." Clara couldn't read what passed between the two, and Laurel's ears only twitched as Becca relented, stepping back from the door. "Two minutes."

"Thanks." Carl strode into the living room, taking in everything from the table where the coven gathered to the laptop that lay open on the sofa. "Wow, are you still on the 2.0 operating system?" He reached for the laptop. "You really ought to update, you know."

"It works fine." Becca reached for the computer, pulling it from his grasp.

"Sorry!" He laughed, a high, nervous sound. "Just trying to be helpful."

"If you want to be helpful, you can answer a question: what did you mean when you said that Jeff was missing something, that the project was missing something?"

"Didn't Jeff ever tell you? I think he didn't quite trust Darien, and now that he's gone..." He shrugged as he ran his hand along the back of the sofa, disturbing Laurel, who jumped down to join Clara on the floor. "Well, Darien needs someone who can finish the work. Someone who knows how Jeff thought."

"So the software doesn't work?" Becca followed behind as Harriet joined her sisters.

"The concept is great. But you should know how these things go, Becca." He turned to give her a knowing glance. "They're not just plug-and-play. And Jeff was being careful. Too careful, I think. He withheld a component, something crucial, until all the T's were crossed the I's were dotted."

"So that's why you think Darien has to hire you." Becca turned thoughtful as she hugged the laptop to her. Carl shrugged, a self-satisfied smile spreading across his face. "Funny, he hasn't said anything about it."

"He wouldn't, would he?" Carl warmed to his topic, even as he strolled further into the apartment. "He's got his own backers to answer to, and if they knew he didn't have the goods..."

Stopping by the bookshelf, he picked up a Bast statuette and examined it, turning it upside down as if checking for some mark.

"Please don't do that." Becca darted in front of him, still holding the laptop close. "I have my things carefully placed so the cats can't knock them off."

"Oh yeah, your fabled cats." He glanced down to find three pairs of eyes—blue and gold and green—staring up at him. "Jeff said you were always on about your cats. I think he was jealous of them."

That crossed a line for Becca. "And you were jealous of Jeff, weren't you?" Clara lashed her tail as Becca spat out the words. "That's why you tried to break us up, and now you're pursuing both me and Renee."

"Hey, that was a misunderstanding." Hands up, he backed away—and into the bookshelf. "I just want to be friends," he said, turning to poke at another cat figurine, this one with wings. "I still want to be friends."

"You should go, Carl." Becca sounded tired. "I really was just about to run out."

"Of course, I get it." He sauntered in the general direction of the door but stopped to look at the table that held Becca's key bowl. "You do backup your files, don't you, Becca?"

"What? Yes, of course." She watched as he ran a finger through the bowl, clasping the laptop to her as if it were a shield.

"She's scared." Laurel's voice sounded in Clara's mind. *"And he's...hunting? No, desperate."*

"He's looking for the key." The realization shocked Clara's ears upright. *"He's not going to leave without it."*

"I'll summon one," Harriet announced. *"Then we can get rid of him."*

"Remember to put the red dot on it," Clara added. *"We want him to recognize it."*

Scrunching up her already pert nose, Harriet closed her eyes and wiggled her butt, looking for all the world like she was about to pounce. But before she could pull the forces that would change dust and wishes into something apparently solid, Becca acted. Still holding the laptop, she pulled open the door with her free hand and pushed the bearish man toward it.

"You've got to leave, Carl."

"Don't be silly." He twisted around, grabbing hold of the laptop even as he stepped into the doorway. For a split second the two wrestled with the device, but it wasn't much of a fight, and Carl wrenched it out of Becca's hands with a force that sent her flailing back against the door jamb with a thud.

"What's going on up there?" a voice called out from the floor below. Deb Miles, Becca's neighbor, was frowning up the stairs. Both Becca and Carl turned.

"The kitten!" Becca gasped. Sure enough, in all the tumult, the tortie had slipped out and now stood, teetering, on the top step.

"Got her!" Shoving the computer at Becca, Carl lunged for the kitten, scooping her up even as she fell. "Here you go."

"Thank you." Laptop firmly tucked under her arm, Becca took the kitten into her hands, stepped back into her apartment, and slammed the door shut, making sure to lock it tight before collapsing against it in exhaustion.

"Well, that was lucky." Laurel looked up at the kitten, who was now squirming to be let down.

"I had everything under control," huffed Harriet.

Clara, for her part, wasn't so sure. For now, though, her only concern was Becca, and she was relieved when, after a few deep breaths, her person roused. Releasing the kitten, she took the laptop into her bedroom, where, after a quick survey, she slid it under the mattress.

"She should put that under the litterbox, for all the trouble it's causing."

Clara turned to see Harriet, whiskers drooping.

"You would have saved us all," she said. *"That was so smart, to think of summoning a key."*

"Harrumph." Harriet dismissed her baby sister, but from the way she held her plume of a tail as she walked away, Clara knew she'd said the right thing.

Forty-Nine

Clara might have thought their person would stay in after that, but Laurel had other ideas. *"She has to groom a bit, that's all,"* the Siamese said. *"Nothing makes a girl feel better than getting her fur back in place."*

Sure enough, five minutes later, Becca had applied a bit of lipstick and was heading to the door, when a buzzer made her jump.

"That's my date," she told the assembled cats. "At least someone has the courtesy to ring the bell."

The excitement had given her a rosy glow, and all three of the sisters lined up to see her off. Laurel, of course, was purring in anticipation. Clara was a little more anxious, although all three could read the vibrations: Carl had left the building.

Becca hadn't forgotten the encounter, though. She peered through the apartment's peephole before opening the door, which she pulled shut behind her and quickly locked.

"Go," Harriet commanded with a wave of her tail.

"But don't interfere," added Laurel. *"Not tonight."*

Clara didn't argue, knowing that would be pointless anyway, and so with a dip of her head, she shimmied through the door and down the stairs in time to see the redheaded financier's dark eyes light up as she appeared.

"Becca." His gaze took in the stairwell. "So this is where you live. Didn't this building recently go condo?"

"Yeah, I've been lucky." She let the interior door shut behind her. "I helped out some of my neighbors, so they're giving me a really great residents' rate. My neighbor is even helping me finalize a mortgage."

"It looks like a great old building. If you ever feel like giving me a tour..." He turned that hundred-watt smile on Becca, but he must have noticed her hesitation. "Maybe later."

"It's not much," was all she said.

"Has Maddy's comment about all of us felines made her self-conscious?" Clara did her best to visualize her sisters. Surely one of them would be able to explain their person's reticence. But then Darien was holding the door, and Becca leaped to follow them out.

"I hope you don't mind, I thought we'd walk." He turned to gauge her reaction as he guided her toward the Square. "My car's in the shop again, and, well, it's such a nice night."

"It is," Becca agreed. "It's funny, I rarely even think about driving anywhere in the city. Though I do use ride shares."

"One of the privileges of my position." He flashed a smile. "I splurged on one of the new electrics. It's got everything, but..." He laughed. "That's what I get for being an early adopter. Anyway, I thought we'd go back to Salt and Pepper."

"That would be great." Becca relaxed into a smile, and Clara did her best to put her own concerns aside as Darien reached to take her hand.

By the time they reached the bistro, about fifteen minutes later, all of Becca's concerns seemed to have been dispersed. Darien had proved an attentive date, asking her not only about the day-to-day of her work but about her dreams and the history they shared, if only tangentially.

"I'd love to learn more about the occult," he said at one point, only to catch himself. "About Wicca, I should say. It's a nature-based religion?"

"It's more a belief system," Becca hedged. "We believe in balance and in being part of the natural world. And, yeah, that there are forces that are part of nature. So you could call it magic."

"I'm impressed." His dark eyes twinkled. "And I can relate. When we write code, sometimes it feels like we're pulling natural forces together to do our bidding."

"I don't think Jeff ever saw the similarity."

"Oh, come on," he teased. The two were waiting in the bar area by that point, sipping the sparkling wine Darien had insisted on ordering. "You must have pointed out the connection, though, right? I mean, when Jeff would show you something he'd come up with?"

"No, he didn't really do that." Becca stared into space, as if she could see her late ex out there. "He knew I didn't understand what he did," she admitted, turning back to her companion.

"Every industry has its own lingo." Darien nodded sympathetically. "But I bet you understood the gist of what he was doing. All the time you two were together? He must have helped you set up your computer system, at least."

"Yeah, he did." Becca chuckled. "He'd put games on my computer. There's one in particular. It's not even a game, really. More like a screen saver. There's this kitten—"

"Excuse me?" the bartender interrupted, holding out Darien's black credit card, a look of concern furrowing his well-manicured brow.

"You can keep the tab open. We're having dinner." Darien waved him away and turned back to Becca.

"May I have a minute?" The chic bartender wasn't going away, and so Darien excused himself.

"Sorry. It's got to be something with our reservation."

"That's fine." Becca watched him follow the bartender to the reception area, where the hostess waited.

"It's so funny about Carl, running after the kitten." Becca

might have been talking to herself, but Clara felt sure that her person sensed her presence.

She too had been surprised by the chubby man's fast-acting save. Not that the tortie would have come to much harm, the calico knew. Kittens have long taken spills without lasting damage. But Becca had been so alarmed that Clara was grateful for the big man's help. The fact that he had let go of the laptop to do so only made the move more generous—and more unexpected, a fact Becca seemed to be mulling over.

"Darien, the strangest thing happened to me today." She started talking to her date as he returned, before noticing the frown that had transformed his features. "Is everything okay?"

"This place. I've been a regular for years." He shook his head. "They lost our reservation, and they're not doing anything to make it right."

He shrugged into his jacket and held hers up, even as she turned a questioning face up to his. "So they can't seat us?"

"Can't or won't." He scowled. "Anyway, I don't think we should give them our business." With one hand on her back, he propelled her out so quickly that Clara didn't know whether Becca saw the looks Darien exchanged with the hostess and the bartender, who still stood by the door.

"Where to?" Out on the sidewalk, Becca looked up expectantly.

"All the good places are probably booked up." He scanned the street like he was looking for a cab, before turning back to Becca. "And I'm wiped. I'm sorry, but would it be okay if we just ordered in? That way I'd get to meet your famous cats."

"Sure." Becca seemed taken aback, and Clara wondered if she was thinking of Carl—or of the laptop she had slipped beneath her mattress.

"That would be such a relief." The clouds cleared from his handsome face as they started to walk back the way they'd come.

"I was thinking about what you said, about Jeff putting programs on my computer." Becca sounded a little breathless. Darien was walking quickly. "I had a visit from Carl today."

"Oh?" His brows went up, but at the same time he summoned a chuckle. "Poor guy. He really wants to take Jeff's place, but he's just not in the same league."

Becca fell silent, though that could have been because of the pace. When she finally spoke again, there was a question in her voice. "He was telling me that Jeff's program wasn't complete," she said, looking up at her date.

"Well, it isn't ready for the market," he responded, emphasizing the last word and leaning in with a smile. "That's why we do beta testing."

"Yeah, but he was saying that without Jeff, you don't have a workable model."

Darien huffed out a laugh. "Let me guess. He said that he was the only one who could finish it, right? That's low, trying to use you to get to me."

"No." Becca slowed down, her voice growing thoughtful. "He wants to be the one to finish it, but he said there was something missing, that Jeff had withheld a component."

"Did he say what this supposedly missing component was? Or where he thought he alone could find it?" Darien's voice grew sharp.

"I think he thought I had it." Becca kept walking, even as Darien speeded up again, but she might as well have been talking to herself. "He actually tried to grab my laptop, but then he let go."

"Smart man. You could have pressed charges."

"It wasn't that. It was that he rushed to rescue my kitten, and I don't think..."

"You don't think, what?" They'd reached Becca's building. She hesitated, and Clara focused on her, all the while silently reaching out to her sisters.

"It's nothing." Shaking off the idea, she pulled her keys from her bag, letting them both in. "What should we order?"

"What are you in the mood for?" He turned playful. "But while we decide, why don't you show me that screen saver Jeff put on your computer."

"It's silly, really. I mean, he only made it for me because he knew I was a cat person." She went off into the bedroom. "It's so funny about Carl."

She came back with the laptop, and Darien jumped up from the sofa. "Sorry! I made myself at home."

"That's fine." She sat next to him and waited for the computer to boot up. "There's something I still don't get."

He turned toward her quizzically, one arm stretched along the back of the couch.

"Why would Jeff make a public announcement about his project if he wasn't completing it? It almost sounds like he was pulling out. It reminds me of something Ande said."

"Ande?" His hand reached down to rest on her shoulder.

Becca pulled away absentmindedly. "She's one of my coven," she said, her face growing thoughtful as the screen lit up with photos. Clara, Laurel, Harriet—and, yes, the kitten. "Only, she's a better accountant than a witch."

"Accountants," he chuckled. "That is a form of witchcraft."

He might as well have not spoken. "She said she couldn't find the paperwork for your filing. Excuse me for asking, but did you put our drinks on your card?"

"I told them we'd pay cash." Big smile. "They usually prefer that. And, hey, is that the kitten app?"

"Especially if your credit isn't good." She closed the laptop, even as he was reaching for it. "The empty office, your car, the restaurant... Ande was right, you're in trouble. Carl was wrong about Jeff. It wasn't the program, it was you. Your financing. That's what was missing."

Darien choked out a laugh, his handsome face contorting into a humorless grimace. "I may be a bit overleveraged, sure."

"Call it what you will." Becca shifted to face him. "Jeff was going to announce that he was pulling out because you're broke. But if he made that public, then you'd lose everything."

"Not if I had his app. The kitten app—with its hidden code." Darien grabbed at the computer, pulling it from Becca before she could react.

"Darien, no!" She was on her feet, but so was he, and as Clara looked on in horror, he raised the laptop and swung it at her.

"No!" A coffee-colored flash and the computer went flying as Laurel's claws raked the financier's face.

"Never!" He stumbled and fell as Harriet's fangs sank into his ankle.

"Becca, are you okay?" Clara ran to her person, who had fallen backward in shock. *"I'll get help."*

"No need." She looked over to see the kitten sitting on top of the laptop. *"The police are on their way."*

Becca couldn't know that. She couldn't have heard the tiny but clear voice that made her three other cats turn. Couldn't have known the powers that now aligned with her as she scrambled to her feet and stared down at the man on the floor. And yet...

"It was you who killed Jeff," said Becca, towering over him like a queen. Like a goddess. "You followed Jeff, hoping to change his mind, and when you found him fighting with Tina, you saw your chance. She stormed off, and you moved in. You killed Jeff over money. Over your reputation. Over nothing."

FIFTY

The evidence was overwhelming. Alerted by Becca's message, Detective Newsom had already been on his way to pick up the letters. He detained Darien, and when the uniformed officers he summoned took the failed financier into custody, he stayed to listen as Becca laid out what she had learned.

"I knew it couldn't be Carl. He dropped the laptop, which had the app he wanted on it, to rescue my kitten. What kind of murderer would do that? And it was pretty obvious that Jeff and Tina were fighting, but she seemed truly repentant—and also like she really might have thought I had done it. Then I thought that maybe Renee had followed them. But when I realized that Darien was broke and Jeff was going to expose him, it all fell into place. He broke into my apartment, looking for the laptop. And when he didn't find it, he thought he could charm it out of me. Maddy was right. Men!"

Once he had the full story, however awkwardly delivered, Newsome didn't even need Jeff's software to go further. Ready to cooperate, Renee gave up Jeff's passwords, making it easy to find his draft of the announcement, and their forensic accountant soon outlined the increasing levels of fraud Darien had accumulated to keep his business going.

"I will never say another word against your cats," Maddy announced as she walked her friend into her building. She'd tried to convince Becca to take time off work, but Becca had been adamant about going in, especially since Tina had quit, and Maddy had acquiesced, on the condition that she wait for her at the end of the day.

"They recognized that I was in danger." Becca smiled over at her friend as they climbed the stairs to her apartment. "It's only a pity that they're not as good judges of men."

"That would be you, silly." Inside the door, Harriet glared at Laurel, whose only response was to lash her tail.

"We all misjudged Darien." Clara felt she could be generous. After all, Laurel did only want the best for Becca.

"I didn't," the tortie piped up.

"You didn't trust any of us." Harriet batted the kitten, knocking her over with her big snowy mitten. But since her claws were sheathed, and the purr underlying Harriet's retort was audible to all four felines, Clara didn't worry. At least not about that.

"I'm just glad that blog is down," Becca was saying as she unlocked the door. "Charm and Cherish does not need that kind of attention."

"Nor do you." Maddy stepped in behind her and paused, allowing the cats to sniff her familiar but not-Becca scents. "That girl was crazy."

"Tina is...troubled." Becca dropped her keys in the key bowl and headed toward the kitchen. "Let me feed these guys before —watch it!"

Maddy started, but it was only to laugh as she watched the cats racing ahead, nearly tripping Becca in their eagerness. "You'd think these four were starving to death."

"I know." The sounds of cans being opened. "I'm going to miss the sound of them all together."

"Now, now..." Maddy joined her friend in the kitchen, just as the doorbell rang. "I'll get it."

"Thanks." Becca sighed with a sadness that made Clara look up in concern.

"Hi, Dr. Keller." Maddy's voice announced the visitor. "And you must be Leila?"

"Lovely to meet you."

Becca wiped her hands and headed out to meet her visitors, while Clara tagged along.

"If you're not back by the time I finish mine..." Harriet warned, but Clara was too curious to mind.

"Becca Colwin." Her person was taking the hand of a white-haired woman in a tailored suit. Beaming at the vet with a face gone suddenly pink, Becca ushered them into the apartment. "I've been fostering the kitten."

"How generous of you." The older woman returned her smile. "Jerry was telling me about you. His mother and I are close friends."

"That's wonderful." Becca appeared to be walking on air as she led Leila and the vet into the kitchen. "I've just fed them. As you can see, the kitten is a good eater."

"And they're all getting along," the kind-faced vet noted. "Leila, you see how well socialized the kitten is?"

"I do," said the older woman, and for a few moments the four humans stood in silence, watching as the cats dug into their meal. Clara, standing beside Becca, waited for Harriet to finish hers, but to her surprise, the big marmalade interrupted her meal to pull the tortie toward her and began to groom her.

"Cut it out!" With a peep, the kitten began to squirm, but Laurel blocked her escape, leaning in to hold her still for the remainder of the tongue bath.

"Very well socialized," the vet repeated softly.

"I see," said Leila. "And what I see is a bonded family."

Becca looked up with a soft gasp.

"Am I right?"

"They do get along," Clara's person acknowledged. "And I do love having her here."

"Well, that settles it." She turned to the vet. "Jerry, I know you want me to adopt another cat, but I'd say this kitten has already found her home. Shall we get some dinner?"

"Becca?" He turned to her, his open face a question.

"I'm happy to keep her," she replied, a grin spreading across her face. "And you two go ahead. I think I need a quiet night, and Maddy and I are going to order in. But, Jerry?"

Maddy turned toward her friend, eyes wide. Even Harriet stopped herself mid-lick. Becca so rarely used the vet's first name.

"Would you want to come over for dinner soon?"

"I'd love that," he said, his plain face breaking into a broad grin.

Later that night, Becca and Maddy were ensconced on the sofa, half watching an old movie, the windows open to let in the soft spring breeze, when Clara finally broached the subject.

"What was that about?" She addressed Harriet, as the eldest, but the question could have been for either of the two older felines who were reclining over various parts of the furniture. She kept her voice low, sensing the kitten's presence nearby. *"I mean, I thought we were family."*

"We are," Harriet mumbled, half asleep on her cushion.

"All four of us," purred Laurel as she stretched along the sofa back. *"And that means the little raindrop licker here too."*

"I'm not a raindrop licker." The feisty tortie suddenly appeared at the end of the sofa and, launching herself at Laurel, landed on Maddy's thigh. *"That was a clue!"*

"Look at this little thing. How could you give her up?" Becca's friend laughed as she let the kitten wrestle with her finger.

"I couldn't," admitted Becca as she stroked Clara, who settled into her lap, utterly content.

Acknowledgments

So many people have helped this book come into existence—and helped me through this period—I barely know where to start. In addition to my agent Anne-Lise Spitzer and editor Jason Pinter, I also have a crazy wonderful support team—Caroline Leavitt, Vicki Constantine Croke, Brett Milano, Karen Schlosberg, Lisa Susser, Laurie Hoffma, Ted Drozdowski, Alan Brickman, Naomi Yang, Damon Krukowski, Erin Mitchell, Jennifer Ellwood, Stephen Cooper, Ann Porter, Kris Fell, Betsy Pollock, Frank Garelick, and Lisa Jones—who make all things seem possible. And always, always, always, Jon S. Garelick: my first and best reader, my first and best everything. Always.

About the Author

Before turning to a life of crime (fiction), Clea Simon was a journalist. Starting as a rock critic, she ended up writing about books and other arts. A native of New York, she came to Massachusetts to attend Harvard University, from which she graduated with high honors, and never left. The author of three nonfiction books and thirty mysteries, she lives with her husband, the writer Jon S. Garelick, and their cat, Thisbe in Somerville, MA. She is the author of three previous Witch Cats of Cambridge mysteries: *A Spell of Murder*, *An Incantation of Cats*, and *A Cat on the Case*, as well as the standalone suspense novel *Hold Me Down*.